Th

A Novel

By Susan Thatcher

Dedicated
To the memory
Of
Nancy Snow Kurrelmeyer
(Aug. 31, 1962 – Feb. 1, 2003)
Best friend
Soul sister
and owner of the foot up my tush that kept me writing
Miss you every day, Kurly

My deepest thanks to
Diane M. Chubb, Esq. Everybody needs such an Aries in her corner.
Susan R. Drover. Editor. Couldn't have asked for a better "second pair of eyes."
Nicole Baker Smith, MBA. This wouldn't have gotten finished without your help (Mario).

Gentle Reader,

This story was completed in 2001. Please read it with the understanding that the intended time frame is the mid to late 1990s.

Prologue

It was chilly in the hospital room. The walls were a depressing sort of green. Someone must have believed that this color was soothing and calming. However, since it had now become the standard background for hospital rooms, the shade had been carrying with it an inseparable link to sickness and pain for years. And it now surrounded her.

Elizabeth hugged herself, unable to take her eyes from the bed. Monitors and other machinery surrounded the head of the bed, their noises adding to the uncomfortable ambiance of the room. A man lay on the bed, eyes closed, his breathing assisted by at least one of the machines around him through a tube inserted in his mouth and securely taped in place. The other machines had their slender tentacles attached to him through electrodes. They fed on his heartbeat and brain waves, digesting this input and turning it into wavy lines on either a screen or a piece of paper. A clear plastic bag on a stand slowly dispensed some kind of medicated fluid into his arm. This man, usually so strong, was utterly helpless. And Elizabeth was powerless to help him. The sight of him like this was almost enough to make her faint.

No, this wasn't happening. It couldn't be. For Christ's sake, he'd been fine this morning, giving her the usual coffee-flavored kiss as he left, murmuring "I miss you so much already. I'll call and I'll be back before you know it, I swear." He had hugged and kissed their children, picked up his briefcase and garment bag, winked at her and left. She had noticed that his face looked a little more drawn this morning. When she'd asked him about it, he'd said, "It's just a headache. I took something. I'll be fine. Stop worrying." Elizabeth looked at the bed. He'd been wrong. It didn't happen very often, but when he was wrong, it was spectacular. Like right now.

There had been talk from the medical staff about "will to live" and its power to heal. She had tried to listen, tried to focus, but she could still see the bed and its occupant over their shoulders and that had commanded her attention. There had been gentle attempts to shoo her out of the room, but Elizabeth would not be moved.

Finally, the nurses had given up, one or two secretly hoping that if she lay in a coma, someone would care enough to stay with her like this.

Elizabeth heard a knock on the door. She turned and saw one of his associates peering through the small window. She beckoned the man in.

"Gee, Liz, I'm so sorry to intrude. How is he?" The man was in his mid-thirties, nicely dressed in an expensive suit and carrying an equally expensive, new briefcase. Liz steeled herself to sound casual, not to give in to the choking fear that she felt.

"It's hard to say, Fred. The term they're using is 'unresponsive.' I guess it doesn't sound as frightening as comatose. They tell me it'll be 12 hours before they know," Liz looked at the bed, an ironic smile on her face. "We were discussing retirement last night. I think this clinches my argument. If he survives, I promise I won't be telling him 'I told you so.'" It took all her strength not to sob on the words.

Fred cleared his throat. "If anyone can make it, he can. That man hates to lose." Fred's voice became almost apologetic. "Look, Liz, I really hate to ask this, but I need his files."

She could tell by the tone of his voice that he didn't really hate to make the request. In fact, one man's crisis can be another man's opportunity, particularly if the second man is looking to get a leg up on the competition for a partnership in a prestigious law firm.

Liz crossed her arms, nails digging into the palms of her hands. "Under the circumstances, maybe a continuance would be granted, don't you think? Clearly, the attorney of record is unavailable to be in court." You insensitive pig, she added mentally.

Fred gave her an annoyed shrug, "Look, I'm just doing what I was told. Come, get the file, get on the plane, which I'll miss if I'm not out of here in 5 minutes. I just got married 2 weeks ago. Dontcha think I'd rather be at home?"

Probably not, thought Liz. This was one shot at the brass ring that was too good to pass up. And since the man in the bed had done most of the work already, it was an easy brass ring to grab. Fred had probably told his new wife she could quit her job and look for a house in Chestnut Hill. And so the bribery had begun, the parade of gifts to distract the woman from the knowledge that her husband's job was more important to him than she was. Fred would probably be divorced with an ulcer within 5 years.

"Hang on, let me get it." Liz knelt under the hospital bed and located Ty's briefcase, a handsome one she had given him the previous Christmas. She opened it and stopped in the act of removing the sought-after files by what was lying under them.

"What the hell is that crap?" Fred asked, looking over her shoulder. "Books? When was he going to read? Letters? Who has time for that shit?" He started to reach around Liz, who slapped his hand away.

"That 'crap,'" she said icily, "is none of your god-damned business. Here," she thrust the files at him. "Get out. You don't deserve to be in the same room with him, even if he doesn't know you're here."

Fred snatched the files and ran, slamming the door behind him. Liz heard his snarled, "Bitch" even as the sound of his footsteps faded.

Liz didn't give a damn about Fred or the others who were scrambling to achieve what Ty already had. They'd try to do it faster or better than their peers and those who had gone before them. Most wouldn't succeed or would end up as casualties of legal warfare.

Liz reached into the briefcase and began to remove the items that had caught her eye, setting them on a tray near the bed. She found a framed photo of a man and a woman with a black eye sitting at a table and smiling together. She found the fortune from a Chinese fortune cookie, the lettering almost completely faded with age. There were two books, one of John Donne's love poetry that showed its near-daily readings over the past years. Liz could hear her husband's voice, warm and deep, reading passages as he'd held her naked body against his, her head pillowed on his shoulder and contented from their lovemaking. She quickly squashed the "maybe for the last time" that had come into her head. No. They hadn't been together long enough. She wouldn't let him leave. Not now.

Liz picked up a collection of short stories by one E.D. Gardner, as well-used as the Donne. Those, he'd insisted that she read to him. She smiled, remembering how self-conscious she'd been about it.

She found a bundle of old letters addressed to the man in the bed that also showed how often he'd re-read them. There was another photo of the man and the woman, this time holding two small children, everyone smiling. The oddest item was a hank of blonde hair, carefully braided and tied into a circle. It was attached to a reusable glitter tattoo of a rose. Liz smiled.

She found his clothes in a bag under the bed. Liz located the shirt he'd been wearing that morning and dug into the pocket. There was a small plastic disk that she turned it over in her hand, smiling even more. Her fingers had touched something else in the pocket and she removed a lavender-colored rose blossom, wilted and flattened, but still wonderfully fragrant.

"It's a wonder you had room for files," she said to the man. She didn't expect a response and didn't get one. "For a ferocious, fire-breathing litigator, you certainly are a sentimental bugger. Fred took it as a sign of weakness, but then Fred's going to find himself with an ulcer and a divorce in about 18 months, give or take. Fred's a prick. I think you ought to fire him.

"Look at this stuff. These are foolish things to lug around." Liz picked up the crushed rose. "All you need is the airline ticket to romantic places and you've got the song. Cleveland's not romantic. No cigarette with lipstick traces, though," Unaware, she began to hum the tune. She touched the items, different memory pictures crowding her mind. Some good, some bad, some exquisitely wonderful, some carrying excruciating pain that was almost physical. Liz looked at her watch. Still about 11 and a half hours to go.

"Since nobody seems to know for sure whether people in comas, excuse me, people who are unresponsive, can hear, I'm going to give you the benefit of the doubt. We've got some serious time to kill." Liz seated herself on the edge of the bed.

"You know, I'm looking at this collection. If an archaeologist found it a thousand years from now, he could piece together our story. Well, with a little help here and there. I'll show you right now. Don't worry, we have plenty of time."

Liz picked up the photo of the man and the woman with the black eye. "See? Here, we have the starting point."

8

Chapter 1

"Who're we playing?" Liz Gardner scanned the ball field as she dropped her bat and gear bag. Liz loved playing softball in the North End of Boston. The field was on the harbor and the about late day sun bathed the surrounding red brick buildings in golden light. A lively and loud conversation in Italian attracted Liz's attention to the bocce court near the ball field, where a hotly contested game was in progress. The air felt soft and warm, a breeze off the harbor blowing away the stickiness that is a trademark of summertime in the Hub. Liz's shirt, like those of the other members of the firm's softball team, depicted an alligator in bow tie and briefcase and was lettered with said "Liti-Gators."

"We're playing Brooks, Washburn, Hadley and Dunn," her friend Millie Wentworth answered, "AKA the 'Bad News Barristers'. It's a stupid name," Millie added with a sneer.

Liz stretched a little. "Just remember: people have been saying the same thing about us. Scouting report. Hey, Corey!"

A red-haired man with a runner's shape bumped into her from behind. "Jesus, Liz, you don't have to yell. I'm right here."

"Sorry. What's the lowdown on the Bad News Barristers?"

"Well, Dunn's been cheating on his wife with Washburn's wife. One of their star associates just got busted for possession, but they're keeping a lid on it, that's him over there chugging the beer…" Corey Lewis had the dirt. If you had to know, you asked Corey. However, sometimes he had too much information. Like right now.

Millie cut him off. "No. We just want the scouting report right now, not the scuttlebutt. That can wait till after the game." Several of their teammates had gathered for the report.

"Oh. Well," Corey cocked one hip and assumed a thoughtful expression. He played up his role as oracle to the fullest. "Let's see. That's not as much fun. Basically, the guys do the playing.

The women don't hit, don't run and field like they're afraid of breaking a fingernail..."

Liz looked at him quizzically. "Why is that?"

"Because they ARE afraid of breaking a fingernail. Honey, they're strictly window dressing. Secretaries, receptionists and a bi-curious file clerk." The other team was filing onto the field. "Look at 'em – all show, no go."

Indeed, the female members of the Bad News Barristers were immaculately groomed and made up from perfect coiffures down to immaculately white designer sneakers.Millie shook her head. "Don't tell me."

Corey nodded, "Uh huh. Tokens so that the team can play in this co-ed league. Plus, they're sick of the singles bars and this IS the lawyers' league. Really choice pickings if you want a sugar daddy."

Liz groaned. They'd encountered this sort of thing before, but usually the women either stuck to the sidelines or had *some* skills on the field. As she buckled on her catcher's gear, Liz spotted one man drinking beer with the cokehead and an artificially buxom, bottled blonde woman who was giggling, tossing her hair and hanging on him.

Liz laughed. "Hey, Corey, who's the guy getting the display from the Silicone Queen?"

Corey smirked. "I've trained you well. They ARE silicone and we won't be seeing HER slide headfirst."

"Yeah, yeah, yeah," Liz was impatient. "The guy, Corey, the guy."

Corey squinted, "Huh. What's Tyrone Hadley doing out here? I thought he lived at his desk. Boy, he must really want that tacky little trophy."

Millie did a double take. "Hadley? Are you kidding?" She looked again. "By God, it is. I saw his picture in the Globe a couple of weeks ago for that huge settlement he got. The Class Action King himself."

Tyrone Hadley. Liz watched him while she continued preparing for the game. He was sipping a beer and laughing with the younger man and the Silicone Queen. Liz had seen a lot of handsome men, had even slept with a few, but this one was different. He seemed unconcerned with or unconscious of his good looks. Most of the good-looking men Liz encountered wore their physical charms like a billboard and a shield, daring those around them not to be attracted. Liz heard Hadley laugh at something the Silicone Queen said. She liked the sound as it drifted across the field. It was deep and warm and masculine. Liz felt a tug in her groin that had been absent for quite a while.

Millie waved her hand in front of Liz's face.

"Yo! Reel in your tongue, Girl! You're drooling. Here." Millie pressed a beer into Liz's hand. Liz took a long swallow. "Ask him out."

Liz made a face. "No way. Even if I thought it, he'd probably send over a note turning me down." She sipped her beer. "Very easy on the eyes, though."

Millie shrugged, "Like what you see, do you?"

Liz nodded silently. "Maybe he's gay." With that, the Silicone Queen walked away from Hadley and the other man, back arched and hips swinging. Both were checking out her rear view.

"No such luck," said Liz, Millie and Corey in unison.

Liz went back to stretching. "Why is that guys can't see through that giggly fake act? Why don't they want someone who doesn't insult their intelligence? And why didn't we learn how to do that?"

"It helps to be waving a big set of jugs around when you do it."

Corey interrupted, "Yours would do nicely, Liz, especially if you lowered your neckline..."

"That's not happening," she snapped. "And you know why."

Corey looked ashamed. "I'm sorry. I forgot." He continued. "¬They can't see through it because the act is designed to move blood out of the brain and into another organ men use for making decisions. By the time the brain re-establishes control, it's too late and she's either on to the next victim or waving the ta-tas at a divorce attorney." Millie took a thoughtful swallow of beer. "You and I, my friend, were raised to rely on our brains and personalities. Life is very cruel. We're not bleached blonde trophies..."

"Excuse me," interrupted Liz, pointing to her own head, "Highlighted hair here."

"Yeah, but yours was natural to begin with. Don't interrupt, I'm on a roll," Millie replied. "Some smart perceptive son of a bitch will snap you up any day now."

"Andy Garcia?" Liz pretended to look hopeful.

Millie made a face at her. "Married. Don't change the subject. Not Andy, but there IS a great man out there for you, I know it."

Liz's face tightened, "How many years have I been telling myself that, Millie? I'm not in my twenties anymore. It's been years since I've been asked out. The only man in my life is a neutered cat and it looks like it's going to stay that way. I think I'm better off just dealing with being on my own than hoping for something that won't happen." She'd made peace with being alone, but it was a bitter, painful peace.

"Hey, did you use that gift certificate I gave you? You know, the one for the tarot reading?" Millie was deeply interested in metaphysics and psychic phenomena.

"Yeah. Last night." Liz started warming up her hands and stretching her fingers.

"And?" Millie looked around, not wanting this conversation overheard. The only one still within earshot was Corey and he knew that Liz and Millie would not hesitate to beat him senseless and then fire him if he talked. Corey was also into tarot and was all agog to hear this, too.

Satisfied that the conversation was as private as possible, Liz began.

"Okay. She said that I am fated to meet a dark-haired, dark-eyed man with a slightly darker complexion than mine."

Corey smirked, "That wouldn't take much."

"Shut up, Corey." Liz and Millie together.

"Anyway, she put him at around six feet tall, give or take a couple of inches, nice smile. Let's see, very successful, fit, nice dresser, thick hair he parts on the left, entrepreneurial, drives an expensive car. Um, great sense of humor, but some darkness, too. What else? Passionate, wonderful lover," Corey whistled. Millie smacked him.

"Really big..." Liz let her voice trail off deliberately. Neither Millie nor Corey said anything, but she could see their dirty minds fill in the blank incorrectly. "...heart. Gotcha. What did she say? Spiritual soul mates, we've been together in previous lives, I think. The Sox have their best shot at the Series this year and I was Teddy Roosevelt in a previous life. By the way, Millie, John

Lennon says 'Ullo,Luv."

Millie made a face at her. Corey snickered. Liz paused, searching her memory for the last iota of information from the reading. "There was stuff about shadows and armor. I don't remember, it's probably her standard line." She drank some more beer. "Yada, yada, yada, blah, blah, woof."

"'Blah, blah, woof?'" asked Corey. "What language does this psychic speak? Or maybe you've had enough beer." He made a grab for the bottle which Liz deftly kept out of his reach.

Millie stood, hands on hips, feet planted, glaring at Liz. "Listen, you, this woman is for real. She told me all about John before I even met him. So if she says there's a man coming at you, Honey get out your catcher's mitt." Liz held up her glove, grinning.

"Smartass."

Millie looked over at the Barristers. "You know," she mused, "Hadley fits that description she gave you. Even down to the way he parts his hair."

Liz looked again. Millie was right. "So? That proves nothing. How many men could fit that description? And that girl looks like she's already staked her claim." She worked her mitt thoughtfully. "Give it up, guys. I have." She continued to herself, "Got burned. I learned."

"What about that guy you were emailing?" asked Millie, "I saw those messages; he seemed interested."

"Turns out he was just passing time at work," said Liz, "I asked him for his phone number and he said he didn't want to go too fast. This was after 3 months and only contacting me during business hours." Anger crept into her tone. "He and his buddies must have gotten a huge laugh out of keeping me on the hook. I've decided it's the law of diminishing returns and the pain and humiliation now far outweigh the rewards. I'm done."

Corey sniffed. "Excuse me, you told me you had a great dinner with my cousin, Mel."

Liz laughed. "My dear, Corey, your cousin Mel admired my shoes and my purse, discussed faux painting with me and got the waiter's phone number before we left the restaurant. Don't tell me your gay-dar didn't pick him up."

Corey smiled and shrugged his shoulders. "I know, I know.

Aunt Hilda's gonna die when she finds out."

Corey sat down, putting his arm around her shoulders. "Look, you're too great to be alone the rest of your life. And I think you just got your notice to get out the red dress for party time."

"Tell you what, you introduce me to him, we'll have met, the psychic will have been right and life can go on," said Liz. "Thank you for the gift. I was highly entertained. End of story."

Millie scowled at her. "That's a shitty attitude. He might be interested in you. What if he walked over here right now and asked you out?"

Liz snapped at her, "I'd wonder what the hell was wrong with him that he'd think he couldn't do better than me. Millie, take a good look at the woman he's with. Now look at me. Can you honestly see that man preferring this to that? I sure as hell can't. I told you, I'm done." She worked the mitt some more, frustration giving added strength to her fingers.

The Bad News Barristers and the Liti-Gators were warming up on opposite sides of the ball field. Each side, while paying attention to its own activity, was watching the other surreptitiously. While the Gators were going easy and slow, the Barristers were throwing hard, especially, noted Liz, Tyrone Hadley. There was a set, hard look to his face as he hurled the ball. His partner grunted and yelled, "Jesus, Ty! Ease up, will ya?" Liz had an idea and motioned Millie in for a conference.

"Millie, what say we dog it a bit in the first innings?"

"Are you serious?" Millie was aghast.

Liz nodded, "Yeah. Look, they're going to be watching us warm up and won't be expecting much based on THEIR female players."

Millie was intrigued. "Go on."

"Okay, so you, Cassie, Rose, Nancy and I feed their expectations for a bit, let our guys 'cover' for us, let them suck up a few beers, then we lower the boom. You know, we get 'em with a sucker punch."

"I love it," said Millie. She beckoned Corey over and quickly filled him in on the plan. "Go tell Joe and the rest of the crew while Liz and I, ahem, 'warm up'."

The Bad News Barristers watched the Gators' pitcher and catcher warm up. They saw the softball thrown in big, soft, slow arcs, usually crossing the plate. They saw the catcher, in full gear, clumsily and weakly throw the ball back to the mound, barely making it sometimes. They heard a lot of giggling and "Oops! Sorry!" in girlish voices. The Barristers relaxed and had another round of beers. The Gators abstained. Finally, the umpire called, "Play ball!" and the Liti-Gators took the field.

The Barristers had placed their female members in the lineup where their skills would do the least damage and the male players had the best chance to move them around the bases. Whenever a Barrister girl came up to bat, the Liti-Gators would move in from the field expecting weak hitting if any contact was made at all. It proved to be a sound strategy.

The Barristers used the same tactic for the Gators' female players, coached into place by Hadley, who was the Barristers' shortstop. He was a powerful hitter and aggressive base runner. He'd smile, clap and yell, "That's okay, Honey" whenever a female Barrister struck, grounded or flied out. As part of the sucker punch strategy, one of the male Gators would run in to back up Liz for plays at home plate. She saw Hadley run full force into someone blocking the plate. Her teammate got up, shook it off and yelled, "Are you fucking crazy?" at Hadley, who shrugged and calmly replied, "That's how the game's played." He then accepted another beer from the Silicone Queen with a kiss and an arm around her waist.

After the fourth inning and before taking the field for the top of the fifth, Liz nodded to Joe who called the team into a huddle. Liz looked around and said just one word.

"Boom."

The Gators grinned and took their places. The fun was about to begin.

Millie looked hard at Liz before heading to the mound. "Are you sure, Liz? Did you see Hadley clobber our guy at home?"

Before putting her mask back on, Liz patted her chest protector and looked evenly into Millie's eyes. "Anything he can dish out, I can take." With that, she positioned her mask, squatting instead of standing behind home for the first time in the game.

"Batter up!"

Millie Wentworth, software engineer, patent attorney and member of the U.S. Women's Olympic Softball Team (injured,

15

reserved) struck out the side, including a dumbfounded Tyrone Hadley.

First up for the Gators in the fifth inning was Elizabeth Gardner, junior attorney, former catcher, team captain and batting champion for the 1983 NCAA Women's Softball Champions, Northeast Region. The Barristers moved in, their male pitcher smiled (patronizingly, thought Liz) and waited while Liz fidgeted in the batter's box. When she had adjusted herself into her usual stance, she smiled sweetly back at the mound. The Barrister pitcher threw the ball in a slow, high arc that went into the wheelhouse. Liz smacked it into a vicious line drive deliberately aimed inches over Tyrone Hadley's head, causing him to throw himself on the ground. Liz thought she had a stand-up double until she rounded first and saw the ball beginning to come in from deep left field. Liz ran faster and slid feet first under the tag Hadley tried to put on her, having pushed his own second baseman out of the way.

"SAFE!"

The Gators cheered wildly and the rally was on. Liz dusted herself off and made ready to run for third. She ignored Hadley staring at her. Or tried to. Having the man's undivided attention was unnerving. She kept her eyes on home trying to ignore the fact that Hadley's eyes were on her.

"Nice legs."

Liz tried not to smile. "Thanks." She glanced over to check out his. "And may I return the compliment? I've played this game before."

He chuckled and looked at her again. "That chest protector was hiding something pretty nice, too," he said.

Liz shot him a dirty look and said nothing. He was just trying to distract her.

"You're right, that was out of line. Sorry," he said. "You almost parted my hair with that hit." Tyrone Hadley had a deep voice with a subtle rough edge to it. The result was something akin to a growl.

"I didn't notice. Should I apologize?" Liz didn't make eye contact, but she tried to keep her voice sounding innocent. She yelled to home, "C'mon, Joey! Try not to hit any bocce players this time." Joe grinned.

She heard Hadley chuckle at that and again the sound made

itself felt in her groin. "Bocce players?"

She nodded. "Yep. This season, we've hit two. Last year, we got three, a bicyclist and an old dog." She glanced at him. "Not on purpose, of course."

"Of course." Their eyes met and Liz's stomach did back flips. She refocused on home plate and Joe DiNardo at the bat, but it required a huge effort to block out the thought of Hadley.

Joey took the ball deep into center field and Liz was off and running. She had thought that Hadley would try to block the base path, but he was back in the outfield yelling, "Goddammit! Get me the ball!" Liz increased her speed, legging it with all her might for home. Sensing rather than seeing or hearing what was going on behind her, Liz closed on home and hit the dirt, sliding in while the ball whistled past where her head had just been and past an astonished (and inebriated) Barristers catcher. Liz scrambled out of the way so Joe could cross the plate. Unfortunately, the catcher found the ball and lobbed it to Hadley, who had run in to cover home when the ball got away from the catcher. Before returning to his post at short, Hadley watched Liz high five her teammates. His expression was unreadable.

"Yo! Ty! C'mon!" Hadley jogged back to short stop.

At the top of the ninth, the Gators held a two-run lead. Two outs, a man on second and Tyrone Hadley was up for the Barristers. Liz called a time out and a conference at the pitcher's mound was underway.

"He's gonna swing for the fences and run the bases like a Pamplona bull," Liz stated. "The play's gonna be at home and on Hadley." The Gators nodded agreement.

Millie was offended. "You know, Gardner, I could strike him out."

Liz just looked at her. "Wentworth, I've been catching you for 20 years. It's late in the game and you're giving up more hits than a porno web site. You're out of gas." The Gators agreed again.

Joey spoke up. "Okay, Rocco, you run in and back up Liz at home." Rocco nodded. Liz looked at Joe scornfully, "Giuseppe, you insult me. NO backup." Joe started to protest. Liz overrode him. "Listen to me, Hadley's been playing full tilt all afternoon. He's got to be as tired as we are. He's been drinking and drinking hard all that time. And, do I need to remind you that I'm a girl and he seems to be a bit of a chauvinist? Joey, I can handle this. I don't need to be rescued."

Joe looked skeptical. Liz finished emphatically, "Believe me, he's not getting past me."

Joey capitulated, "Fine, Liz. It's your ass."

"And a very fine ass it is, Joe," shot Liz in a fierce whisper. "Besides, Rocco wouldn't hold the line. He's too chicken."

"Hey!" Rocco protested. Liz gave him a hard look. "Yeah, you're right. Go get 'im, Liz."

Loudly, she said, "Let's go, Gators!" and they returned to their positions.

As Liz hunkered down behind the plate, Hadley casually asked from just outside the batter's box, "Got your strategy all set?"

Liz didn't even glance at him. "Oh yeah. We decided to let *you* hit the spectator today." A small group had wandered over from the bocce pitch and gathered behind the third base line. Liz shook her head. These guys never learned. Hadley chuckled and again, the sound went through Liz, making her wonder how Hadley's kisses were. She shook off the intruding thought, muttering, "Like I'll ever find out."

"What?" Hadley had overheard the mutter.

"Nothing." That was close.

Millie wound up and the first pitch was a ball. Hadley got a piece of the second pitch and fouled it off behind third base, narrowly missing the bocce players. They responded with a chorus of Italian and Anglo-Saxon obscenities. Hadley smiled to himself, waved an apology to the old men and chuckled again.

On the next pitch, Hadley really got hold and hit a well-placed shot into deep left. Liz ripped her catcher's mask off and moved out for the ball to come in. The first runner scored and Hadley was running for all he was worth. The ball got to the cutoff at second just as Hadley rounded third. Rocco hurled the ball at Liz as Hadley began his charge towards home. A heartbeat after Liz caught the ball, Tyrone Hadley crashed into Elizabeth Gardner, sending them both to the ground in a heap.

Something deep in the pit of Liz's stomach gave a lurch as she felt his legs tangled in hers. His arms were on either side of her and his forehead resting against her face where it had hit. She stifled the impulse to rub her face against him and wrap her arms around

18

his body.

After a brief pause, Hadley rolled off Liz, looking at her and asking, "What the hell were you thinking?"

"Just doing my job."

Through her pain, Liz noticed his hand was touching her face, gently examining the spot where he'd hit, under where her right eye was swelling shut. His face was near hers, too, eyes anxious and searching. What the hell, thought Liz, who quickly sneaked a kiss before holding up the ball in triumph.

"OUT!"

She didn't dare look at Hadley, gingerly touch the left side of her chest and squeezing her eyes shut. She could hear running feet and a chorus of "Omigod! Liz! Are you okay?" "Hadley, you son of a bitch! What the hell were you thinking?"

From the bocce pitch, she could hear some of the old men yelling, "What are you thinking? You hit that little girl! Maybe I come over there and hit you, you son of a bitch!"

Liz never really remembered the rest of the evening. There was the trophy presentation and the usual post-game social hour at a nearby bar. The Gators kept congratulating her and buying her drinks, but her mind wasn't really with the party. The Barristers joined the Gators and even congratulated Liz on her play and tenacity. She held a makeshift ice pack to her right eye the whole time, smiling and nodding at the people talking to her. Her one open eye kept going to Hadley, who was always in the background. He, too, was drinking, chatting, the Silicone Queen hovering at his side, holding his arm.

It seemed that every time Liz looked at him, he was looking intently back at her. At one point, he sent over a beer to her, raised his glass of Scotch to her in a salute, smiling and nodding. Liz returned the gesture and they drank. The Silicone Queen looked daggers at Liz, then turned to Hadley, trying to pout prettily. For all the attention Hadley had paid to her before the game, he seemed completely unaware of her now.

When she got to her darkened and quiet home that night, Liz thought of her friends, all paired off and having someone with whom to share this triumph. Not Liz. She grabbed a plastic bag from the cupboard and filled it with ice. As she sat with the pack on her face, Liz wondered if she had just imagined it or if Tyrone

Hadley had kissed her back.

Chapter 2

"So, Attorney Gardner, you were willing to take one for the team. For risking life and limb for the glory of this law firm, I am grateful," Dan Dennis remarked from his perch on the corner of Liz's desk.

She looked at him out of her one good eye. "I think that's overstating things a bit, Dan. We got your damned trophy for you so we don't have to listen to you bitch and whine until next season." Liz went back to the papers on her desk. Her eye was throbbing to a ragtime beat. It wasn't as bad as it had been over the weekend, but it hurt like hell and was still swollen shut.

"You know, Dan, one would think that as a lifelong Red Sox fan, you'd have learned by now to handle disappointment with a little more grace and fortitude. However, we won and with only minor casualties." Liz leaned back in her chair.

"What do you want, Dan?"

Dan looked at her with mock innocence. "What makes you think I want something other than the opportunity to express my gratitude?"

"The named partners of a law firm do not drop in on associates for a social chat – it cuts too far into billable hours. Plus, my course of dealings with you leads me to believe that you've come here to hit me up for something especially big, probably difficult and conflicting with a potential golf game for you." Liz continued to gaze at him. "Am I right?"

Dan didn't even bother to look discomfited. He just continued to sit on her desk and grin.

"Elizabeth, you are remarkably astute and perceptive…"

Liz cut him off. "What do you want, Dan?"

"The Randazzo case."

Liz suddenly got a bad feeling. "What about it? I drafted the pleadings and the memos." She glanced at a calendar on her desk. "You're just scheduled to argue summary judgment today at

10:30… oh, no. No, Dan. You can't be serious."

"Liz, you know this case inside out. You're the one who came up with the arguments and case law. You can do this in your sleep." Dan had an insincere smile plastered on his face. "Besides, I'm supposed to be playing golf with two of the Bruins at that time. You wouldn't want me to miss an opportunity to sign a couple of great clients like that, would you?"

Liz put her hand over her bad eye. It was hurting even worse. "Dan, I don't care if you're playing with the Budweiser Clydesdales. You know how I feel about going into court. Get someone else or do it yourself. I'm not prepared."

Dan was smooth. "Sure you are. Like I said, you wrote all the memos and pleadings and they're great, Liz, really fantastic. Very tightly argued. Liz, you know this case better than I do. You're the man." Liz looked at him sharply. "Okay, you're the woman."

"You want me to go into a courtroom looking like this?" Liz pointed to her eye.

"Might be good for sympathy points." Dan was still grinning. Liz could have rammed her knee into his private parts, probably with the encouragement and cheering of Dan's long-suffering wife and any other woman who had ever met him.

Liz looked at her calendar again. "You're just trying to avoid Judge McCafferty, aren't you?"

Dan scowled. Bingo, thought Liz.

"He hates me," said Dan. "The man is a lunatic. F.L. McCafferty. Stands for "Fucking Loon" if you ask me. I can't set foot in his courtroom without getting some kind of bullshit contempt citation."

"Maybe that has something to do with you trying to hit on his daughter-in-law in front of him and his son a couple of years ago, Dan." Dan Dennis was a dedicated skirt chaser.

Dan's scowl deepened even more. "Yeah, well, I get sick of hearing 'Did you bring your toothbrush, Counselor?' every time I open my mouth. You go argue the motion."

Liz sighed. "Is that an order?"

"If it'll get you to do it, yeah." Dan unseated himself from Liz's desk and practiced chip shots with an imaginary golf club.

She shrugged. "Who am I arguing against?"

Dan shielded his eyes to watch an imaginary tee shot bounce a non-existent 250 yards straight down an 18th fairway at Augusta that was only in Dan's mind, along with a politely enthusiastic gallery and an imaginary Tiger Woods clapping him on the back. Liz wondered for a split second if she could get him committed.

"Tyrone Hadley." Dan eventually answered.

Liz was on her feet. "What? No way!"

Dan looked at her curiously. "What's the problem?"

Liz pointed to her shiner, its impressive swelling and extensive range of colors. "Who do you think did this to me, Dan? It wasn't the Easter Bunny." Not to mention, she didn't want to make her maiden argument in front of a notoriously picky judge. This was a nightmare. She hoped. All she needed was to look down and see herself naked and she could take comfort in knowing that she was just dreaming. Liz looked down.

She was fully clothed. Dammit.

Dan putted out on an invisible 18th green. Liz wanted to wrap the imaginary graphite shaft around his neck. Apparently, he sank it, because Dan looked up, smiling.

"Okay, so you beat him in a softball game on a very close call at home. What's the big deal? I mean it's not like you've slept with him and he never called you." Dan looked at her curiously. "Have you?"

Liz closed her eye. "No, Dan, I haven't slept with him." Dan shrugged. "Didn't think so. You're not his type." He frowned and looked hard at her. "Come to think of it, whose type ARE you? I never see you with anyone."

Liz cut him off, "You know, this is the kind of conversation that'll get me hundreds of thousands of dollars in a harassment suit." His words stung. "Besides, you've got me working too many hours for a social life."

Dan headed for the door. "Whatever. Go argue the motion. If White offers settlement, refuse. Frankly, I think they're both idiots, but as long as Randazzo's checks don't bounce, I don't give a damn. Oh and one more thing," Dan paused before he actually exited. "Make sure you remind Hadley he lost a bet to me on the game. He owes me $1,500. Get it." With that, Dan closed the door and he was gone. Liz sank down into her seat and gingerly buried her head in her hands. She had to go to court. Wonderful. That was cause for main-lining antacids. She had to argue the Randazzo v.

White case, which was basically a pissing contest between cousins-in-law. Bring on the aspirin. She had to do it with a black eye and no preparation. And, the frosting on the cake was that she was making her courtroom debut against Tyrone Hadley. If God was truly merciful, Liz reflected, He'd kill her right now.

She buzzed for Corey.

"Yes, Madam Cyclops?"

Liz scowled at the intercom. "Don't start, Corey or I'll hand you over to Dan as his new assistant. I need the Randazzo file in its entirety and I need it yesterday, along with a Notice of Appearance."

There was a pause. "You're serious."

"I'm due in McCafferty's courtroom at 10:30 AM and I'd like to be somewhat prepared. Move, Corey."

Within minutes, Liz not only had the Randazzo file, but Millie and Corey. Corey wouldn't have to be subjected to any torture greater than cutting up his Filene's card to get him to spill his guts, so naturally he had stopped to tell Millie on his way to retrieve the file. Millie's face registered astonishment.

"You're actually going to court. For God's sake, Liz, why?"

Liz looked at Millie. "I didn't volunteer, if that's what you're thinking. Let's look at this logically. Dan Dennis is the attorney of record. The presiding judge is F.L. McCafferty. I believe Dan's contempt fines in front of Hizzoner are equal to Rhode Island's annual budget. Dan claims he's scheduled to play golf at The Country Club in Brookline with a couple of Bruins, although knowing him, it could be a guy in a bear suit and miniature golf at that dinosaur place in Saugus." Liz smiled ruefully. "I must be stupid or a masochist because I keep working for the guy."

She smiled bleakly. "Want to hear the kicker?"

Both Millie and Corey nodded.

"I have to make this argument against Tyrone Hadley."

Corey clutched his chest and Millie clutched her head. "You're kidding." They looked at each other.

"The psychic was right," Millie said, wide-eyed. "Oh, my God."

"This is so cool," whispered Corey. "Liz got swept off her feet by her dream man and now she's going to see him again." He snapped his fingers. "Now, Liz. THIS is your novel. This is a million seller, guaranteed."

Liz shook her head impatiently, a move she regretted because it made her eye hurt even more. "That is such bullshit. It's a coincidence, that's all. Besides, he didn't sweep me off my feet. He knocked me on my ass. There's a difference."

"What are you going to do, Liz?" asked Millie.

Liz opened the file. "Kick the two of you out so I can prepare and pray. After court, I plan to drink. Heavily." The two took the hint and left. Liz buried herself in the file.

Close to the appointed hour, Liz paused outside the courtroom to which her case had been assigned. She'd done her best to focus on the case and the facts, but here she was outside a courtroom and shaking. The last courtroom exercise she'd had in law school, Liz had spent the half-hour before it in the ladies room, throwing up. She'd won her argument, but the stage fright never went away.

She took a deep breath, squared her shoulders and entered what she considered a private hell. It wasn't bad enough that she was about to make her first argument as an attorney. She was also alone, felt unprepared and couldn't see out of her right eye. Liz smiled at the bailiff who directed her to the defense table with raised eyebrows. He didn't say anything but stared pointedly at Liz's eye. She didn't offer an explanation, just busied herself retrieving files from her briefcase and trying to will herself not to throw up. All she needed was five minutes, clear, free and silent in which to gather her forces to meet her impending doom with courage and grace.

No such luck.

"Counselor."

The voice. Masculine, deep and with a rough edge. A fleeting thought went through Liz's mind: the only piece needed to complete this jigsaw puzzle of stress would be a fire breaking out in the courtroom.Liz turned toward the voice. He was standing on her blind side.

Elizabeth Gardner once again found herself face to face with Tyrone Hadley.

Instead of a baseball shirt, shorts and cleats, Liz found herself looking at a man clad in an expensive navy blue suit with a conservative silk tie. She wondered if his initials were monogrammed on the cuff of his shirt. Could be. His clothes fit him like they were all custom made, even the highly polished shoes. She felt shabby by comparison and the eye didn't help matters. Liz unconsciously rubbed the toe of her right shoe against her left leg, trying to add shine to it.

"Counselor." Liz returned the greeting.

"How's the eye?" Hadley asked the question casually. He was leaning against the plaintiff's table, arms crossed. Liz was aware that although the pose was relaxed, he was taking in everything. Including and especially her.

"It's just a black eye. How are you?" It was then that she noticed a cut on Hadley's lip and a faint bruise near his eye. "Oh, no. Don't tell me."

Hadley smiled tightly. "Two of your buddies escorted me outside the bar after the post-game and roughed me up. One was the guy you called Joey and I didn't get the name of the other guy."

"Rocco Metucci. Joey's best friend. I'm sorry. Those two get to be a little overprotective. If you like, I can have a word with Joey's Mom and she'll flatten both of them for you."

Hadley chuckled. The sound went through Liz in a pleasant zinging sensation. "That's okay. I guess we're even now. By the way, we weren't formally introduced the other day." He stepped forward and offered his hand to Liz.

"Tyrone Hadley."

Liz took his hand. He had a firm grip and a softness that showed these hands hadn't been used for manual labor. She remembered the touch against her face and felt herself getting hot. She wanted those hands on her, everywhere. But, for now:

"Elizabeth Gardner. Nice to finally meet you, Mr. Hadley."

He chuckled again. She felt the zinging and a desire to kiss him again. "My friends call me Ty."

"Liz."

He still held her hand and she wasn't about to end the contact.

"Where's Dan? I thought I'd be arguing against him today." Ty looked around, the action pulling his hand away from hers.

"He had an emergency and since we're just arguing motions..." Liz couldn't believe she could say that and sound casual. "He asked me to pinch hit."

Ty chuckled again. "Let me guess. Either he got invited to the

26

Country Club in Brookline or he finally realized that McCafferty's hearing the case."

Liz smiled in return. "Both."

"He give you any great advice this morning?"

"If I remember rightly, his parting words were to remind you that you lost $1,500 betting on the game and I should be the one to collect. Didn't that kind of thing get Pete Rose banned from baseball?" Liz tried to keep it light.

Ty nodded. "Sounds like Dan. He has his priorities."

Liz crossed her arms. "Well, I've done my duty and delivered the message." Damn Dan for putting her in this position. She could feel the shaking beginning, not from the impending proceeding, but from being so close to an attractive man. She stood up and perched herself on the desk. Liz's gut told her that it would be good to be at eye level with Tyrone.

Ty folded his arms. "So, was there a big celebration at Hoffman, Lovell and Dennis? Did they carry you around on their shoulders?"

Liz laughed softly, relaxing a little. "You were present for the only victory celebration we had. And thank you for the drink, by the way.

"No. Nothing special at the office this morning. Let's see. I had some people singing 'I get knocked down, but I get up again'. Another group broke into Queen's 'We Are the Champions' in a wonderful four-part harmony. The ultimate," she continued, "was a Johnny Mercer enthusiast who treated me to a chorus of 'Something's Gotta Give' in a very fine baritone."

Ty frowned. "How does that one go? I can't quite remember."

Liz laughed. "Something about 'when the irresistible force meets the unmovable object…'"

"'Something's gotta give, something's gotta give, something's gotta give'" they finished together and both laughed.

"Look, I'm sorry about your eye." Ty offered. "You'd be the unmoveable object. Do you always stand your ground like that? I thought for sure you'd have sense enough to get out of the way. I didn't intend for you to end up looking like Tony Conigliaro."

"Wrong eye," said Liz. She raised her chin and met his gaze with her good eye, saying quietly and firmly. "I stood my ground because I had to. I wasn't going to be the one who lost her nerve

27

and lost the game. Anyway, as the wise man once said 'that's how the game is played.'" She noticed that he looked uncomfortable. Good. "You don't hold back if you want to win." She saw a quick look flash across his face. Respect?

Ty smiled again and chuckled. He spoke. "No, you certainly don't but," He leaned in a little and spoke in a conspiratorial tone, "You and your friend held back, though. Dan got himself a couple of ringers. I checked up on you. College softball champ. Nice."

I could warm myself on the light in those eyes, Liz mused. She tightened her crossed legs to suppress the shaking.

"We're legit. Millie and I are both attorneys for this firm. You can check our billables. We played the entire season for the team, not just the one game. We just happen to be very, very good at softball."

"Are you a couple?"

Liz sighed. "Why does everyone assume that all female softball players are lesbians?" If I was, she thought, do you think I would have kissed you? "Neither of us is gay. Millie has a boyfriend and I'm…" her voice faltered as years of rejection tightened her throat, "working too hard for Dan. It doesn't leave me a lot of time," she finished lamely.

"Sorry. You're right. I'll remember that for next year. On another note," his voice became serious. "Any chance we can settle this thing right here, right now?"

Liz shook her head, remembering Dan's instructions. She knew that, had she not been dealing with two of the most pig-headed men on the planet, she could settle it without an appearance. However, Dan wanted his courtroom fees and the client was happy to pursue the suit all the way to the end.

"Today? I don't think so, but I'll be happy to take an offer back to Mr. Randazzo after court." Liz offered.

Ty looked at her thoughtfully. "Think you're going to win?" he asked.

Liz tried to be nonchalant. "I'd say my chances are good. My client and Attorney Dennis have made it clear that they wish to argue the motion. I'm just following my orders."

Ty laughed softly, another sound that had a disturbing, yet pleasurable effect on Liz. "They tried that line at Nuremberg. Didn't work."

Liz laughed. "You're equating a wholesale plumbing supplies contract with Nazi war crimes?"

"My client is," said Ty and they both laughed. Liz felt the familiar knot in her stomach she'd felt when he'd been tangled up with her. She couldn't let herself think along those lines. There was too much potential pain.

"Forgive my asking, but Tyrone is a name you don't hear very often. Are you named for a family member?" Liz couldn't believe she'd had the nerve to ask.

Ty smiled. "My mother had a crush on Tyrone Power. Ever hear of him?"

Don't assume I'm ignorant, Counselor. "Yes, I have. 'Witness for the Prosecution' is one of my all-time favorites, I've seen 'Prince of Foxes' and I believe he played Zorro at least once. In addition, he was a very handsome son of a gun and I see why your mother had a crush on him. Do I pass the test?" Liz's smile faded somewhere below her eyes.

Ty noticed the slight chill in her tone. "You pass. I'm impressed. Most people don't make the connection." He smiled. "I guess I should have learned not to assume anything where you're concerned, Liz."

The man's innate charm was not lost on Liz, who squeezed one hand into a fist. Don't let him distract you, Girl, she reminded herself. Liz smiled back at him. "A lot of people see the blonde hair and treat me as if I'm the village idiot." Her smile broadened. "Besides, I understand obsessed mothers and how it affects their children."

Ty looked puzzled. "I don't understand."

"My mother's grand obsession was Pride and Prejudice," Liz explained. Ty nodded. Liz continued. "I don't know how many times my mother read the book and saw the movie. I'm guess I'm just happy she went with 'Elizabeth' and not 'Greer Garson'." Liz chuckled herself. "If I'd been a boy, she might have named me Fitzwilliam or Darcy."

Ty said so softly, Liz wasn't sure she'd actually heard him or imagined it, "I'm glad you weren't a boy."

Before she could question him about the comment, the bailiff announced, "All rise."

Ty and Liz hastily took their appropriate positions behind their tables. The bailiff continued the announcement and Judge Francis L. McCafferty entered the courtroom and made his way to the bench.

"Be seated." They did.

The Honorable F.L. McCafferty was a large man, gray-haired and round-faced. He had a pair of reading glasses perched on top of his head which he flipped down to his nose as he settled himself onto the bench. McCafferty conferred with his clerk for a moment. Liz felt her anxiety beginning to rise again. She stole a look at the plaintiff's counsel. Ty Hadley looked as relaxed and at ease as she was nervous.

Dan's nemesis didn't look all that threatening. After all, he was wearing a fuchsia bow tie under his round face. Slap a beard on him, thought Liz, and you'd have Santa. And she wanted to laugh in spite of herself.

"Randazzo versus White."

Liz heard Ty stand up. He was still on her blind side. "Tyrone Hadley for the plaintiff, Your Honor."

Liz saw McCafferty look thoughtfully at Ty. "Not your usual caliber of clientele, Hadley. Kind of small potatoes for you, Counselor. He your cousin?"

"No, Your Honor. Just a client."

McCafferty nodded. He looked at Liz. She scrambled to her feet, heart pounding. "Elizabeth Gardner for the defense, Your Honor." Even as she said it, Liz was amazed her voice didn't crack or squeak from the stress.

McCafferty peered at her closely. "Where's Attorney Dennis?"

"He had an emergency, Your Honor and since I've been working very closely with him on this case, he felt a continuance was unnecessary and a delay was not in the best interests of the client. I did file an appearance." Where in the hell did all that come from?

McCafferty was unimpressed. "Uh huh." He looked at Ty. "Do you have any objection to Brother Dennis' shenanigans, Counselor?" Liz looked at Ty, who glanced back at her and said, "No objections here, Your Honor."

McCafferty nodded. "Very well. Let the record show that Attorney Elizabeth Gardner is here to represent the defendant. Tell me, Attorney Gardner, on what golf course or in whose boudoir is this 'emergency' taking place?" Before Liz could answer, McCafferty frowned and looked at her closely for the first time. He beckoned her forward.

"Counsel, please approach the bench." Liz did as she was told, hearing Ty do the same. As she stood before the judge, McCafferty leaned forward to study her right eye. Liz held still for the scrutiny. He sat back. "That's quite the shiner, Counselor. Very impressive."

"Thank you, Your Honor. Anything worth doing is worth doing well." She heard Ty suppress a laugh and cover it with a cough.

McCafferty smiled. 'You look like Tony Conigliaro."

"Wrong eye, Sir," Liz replied. "He got hit on the left."

McCafferty chuckled. "Quite so. Still," and he gestured to Liz's eye. "I'd hate to see the other guy."

"That would be me, Judge," Ty offered.

McCafferty's head snapped in Ty's direction. "You did that?" he barked. Liz turned her head in time to see Ty nodding.

"Didn't your mother tell you not to hit girls?" McCafferty roared, "I've half a mind to call the cops, Counselor!"

"Your Honor, it wasn't like that," Liz began, but McCafferty cut her off with a wave of his hand.

"Don't you defend him, Missy!" the judge bellowed. "Do you plan to protect him until he beats you to death?"

"Your Honor…" Ty began. McCafferty cut him off, too.

"Not a word, Attorney Hadley or I'll hold you in contempt!" This was too much for Liz and she matched McCafferty's roar.

"YOUR HONOR! WOULD YOU PLEASE JUST LISTEN TO ME FOR THIRTY SECONDS!"

Both men turned to look at her in astonishment. Liz's heart was still pounding and her mind racing, but dammit, the truth was going to be heard. McCafferty glared at her.

"You're courting a contempt citation, too, Counselor. Remember where you are. This is my courtroom and I will have decorum, Missy."

"I apologize, Your Honor, for the disturbance. But with all due respect, I didn't get this black eye from a lover's quarrel." Liz's voice was controlled, but loud and firm. "It's true that Attorney Hadley hit me…"

"AHA!" McCafferty was triumphant.

Liz continued. "But the 'hit' was a collision at home plate during a closely contested softball game, Your Honor." Liz finished.

She thought she'd successfully made her point, but McCafferty turned back to Ty. "And now you've got her defending you with some cock and bull story!" Liz saw Ty get angry. Without thinking, she laid her hand on his arm. Ty closed his mouth. Liz withdrew her hand and looked at McCafferty, who had noted the gesture with a raised eyebrow.

"Your Honor, I promise you that's the truth. I'm the catcher for the Liti-Gators and we won the league championship because I prevented my esteemed colleague here from scoring."

Apparently, she had made her point. McCafferty blinked. "You're the one? he asked. Liz nodded. "Brad Rogers said it was a big mama blocking the plate."

Yeah, he would, thought Liz. Ex-boyfriends can be pretty nasty.

"To the best of my recollection, Your Honor," Ty began, "Attorney Rogers was not at the game and therefore his information was not first hand." He gestured to Liz, "If he had witnessed the game, he could hardly have described my esteemed colleague," Ty slightly mocked Liz's phrase, "in such terms."

"Thanks," muttered Liz.

"Thank you, Attorney Hadley. I hope you packed your toothbrush because that's more than one more word and you are now in contempt," McCafferty replied calmly.

Both Liz and Ty were dumbfounded.

"Your Honor," Liz protested, "this is a gross abuse of judicial discretion! Surely you can't be serious!"

"Serious as a heart attack, Counselor," McCafferty responded, still calm. "Do you wish to join him?" Liz shut her mouth. "Good. Now, the only words I want to hear from the two of you are those related to the case at bar. After arguments, we'll discuss Attorney Hadley's sentence." McCafferty looked at the pleading before him.

"Now then, I believe the defense has moved for summary judgment in this case. I'll hear arguments, but first, tell me the truth."

"Your Honor?" Liz looked at him in bafflement.

"Dan Dennis didn't write any of these pleadings, did he?"

McCafferty asked.

Crap. "No, Your Honor, Attorney Dennis didn't write the pleadings in this case."

McCafferty nodded. "I didn't think so. I may be a fucking loon," Liz looked at him sharply as he emphasized the words, "but Dennis is an idiot. For the past eighteen months or so, his writing has shown a suspicious improvement. How long have you worked for Attorney Dennis?"

"About 18 months, Your Honor," Liz answered softly. She stole a glance at Ty. His face was unreadable, but he looked thoughtful.

McCafferty nodded. "Thought so. I remember you. I heard your moot court argument and you took my legal writing seminar at Essex, didn't you?"

Liz nodded.

"Speak up," McCafferty prompted.

"I hesitate to do so, Your Honor, as I do not wish to be in contempt of court if my words do not pertain to the case at bar." Liz looked him straight in the eye as she said it. She heard Ty suppress another laugh. One contempt charge coming up, she thought.

Or not. McCafferty leaned back and chuckled. "You got me. Okay, proceed with your argument, Counselor."

And Liz's first courtroom appearance was underway. As she verbalized the arguments outlined in her motion, Hadley did his part in attempting to shoot holes in her arguments. Liz stood firm, becoming so involved in the process that she forgot to be nervous or afraid, countering his arguments and objections. McCafferty asked one or two questions of his own, barked repeatedly at Ty and kept harrying him from the bench until the arguments were concluded.

"Thank you. Attorney Gardner," Judge McCafferty looked over his reading glasses, "I'm granting your motion for summary judgment. Both of you will have my opinion by the end of the week, although if I had my way, I'd have the defense write it for me. Why do you work for an idiot like Dan Dennis?"

Liz looked him squarely in the eye, fighting back the urge to kiss both men to celebrate her win, "Your Honor, Attorney Dennis gave me a job. Your office didn't." She turned to look at Ty. "And neither did your firm," she said to him.

McCafferty looked at her in astonishment. "You're kidding."

"No, Your Honor. I applied for a clerkship and got a rather snide letter from your Chief Clerk telling me, in not so many words, that my grades weren't good enough, I didn't graduate from the correct law school in the first place and I was too damned old. Apparently, whoever did the initial screening of applicants didn't get as far as my writing sample. Attorney Hadley's office was much along the same lines but more succinct."

McCafferty leaned back in his seat. "Well, I'll be damned. I've been looking for a good excuse to get rid of that snotty pain-in-the-ass Chief Clerk. I may have a job for you yet. And by the way, Young Lady," Here he plucked at his robe, "Only the one wearing the black robe gets to swear in the courtroom. Remember that for future reference."

Liz couldn't resist. "Does this mean I just earned a contempt citation, Your Honor? Will I be in the cell next to Attorney Hadley?" She heard Ty cough as he covered a laugh.

McCafferty didn't laugh. He didn't look angry, either. "You two wait here. I declare a 10 minute recess."

"All rise" as the judge left the courtroom and Liz's first day in court was concluded. With a win.

She went back to the defense table and covered up her shaking by carefully putting files back into her briefcase. Her eye and head were throbbing. Liz searched her purse for some kind of pain relief. All she found were breath mints and a pack of bubble gum. Sugarless.

"Here."

A masculine hand held out two tablets of extra-strength pain reliever, Liz's drug of choice. She looked up at Ty. He had a glass of water in the other hand. Liz took both the water and pills from him with a grateful, "Thanks. How did you know?"

"I didn't. But, I figured that if I was wearing that shiner, I'd probably be hurting, too. I can personally recommend this brand, especially for hangovers," He said it casually. "Congratulations on your first win, Counselor."

Liz washed down the pills with a good-sized swallow of water. "Thanks." She had no idea what else to say. "What happens next?"

Ty shrugged, "I tell White he lost. I didn't think the case had

34

much of a chance in the first place and I told him so."

Liz looked at him curiously. "So why'd you take it?"

Ty smiled. "He was my first client and he's brought me a lot of other clients over time. I owed him one. Besides, you'll learn that he and Randazzo have this ongoing legal feud. They've been at it for years. If it's not one thing, it's something else with those two and it's all trivial." His smile broadened. "Sal Randazzo will probably have you back in court suing my client within six months."

"Not me," said Liz. "I'll stick to my nice, quiet transactional stuff that doesn't require litigation."

Ty looked at her, puzzled. "But you're good." Liz started to protest, but he overrode her, "No, you have talent for litigation, why don't you want to do it?"

"Just because you're skilled at something doesn't necessarily mean you enjoy it. I was very good at the job I held before I went to law school and I hated every minute of it," Liz replied. "Anyway, I was talking about McCafferty when I asked what happens next. Is this sort of behavior normal?"

Ty actually laughed. "I don't think 'normal' really applies to Judge McCafferty. He has his own way of doing things. Usually, it's 'Thank you. Next case' and that's that. I wonder what he's up to." This last on a musing note.

Liz looked towards the door to the judge's chambers. "Maybe he's rummaging for a toothbrush for you." She heard Ty laugh as the door opened again and McCafferty re-emerged.

"All rise." They stood behind their desks.

Judge McCafferty looked extraordinarily pleased with himself. Smug, even. "Counsel, approach the bench." Ty and Liz approached the bench as instructed.

McCafferty spoke, "There's still the matter of Counselor Hadley's contempt of court. It is the decision of this court that Attorney Tyrone Hadley will serve a sentence of one night…"

"Your Honor!" Liz protested.

"Silence," McCafferty continued unperturbed. "Either in the Suffolk County facility or in Attorney Gardner's company." He looked at the two attorneys.

"What?" It was said in unison.

F.L. McCafferty beamed in a fatherly fashion at the two

astonished people standing before him. "You will, Brother Hadley, escort this young woman to dinner and any other amusements she may desire this upcoming Saturday or you can spend that night in jail. Your choice."

"Your Honor, I protest," Liz said forcefully, "This is a clear case of abuse of judicial power and a violation of First Amendment rights."

McCafferty blinked. "First Amendment?"

"Freedom of association, which is also freedom from association. You cannot use the power vested in you by the Commonwealth of Massachusetts to force people together in a social setting."

Liz heard Ty mutter behind her. "Good argument."

McCafferty didn't care. "Fine. Sue me. By the time it gets to the Supreme Court, I'll be dead and your," he gestured at the two of them, "grandchildren can argue it." He addressed Ty, "What's it to be, Counselor? An evening out with the lady or a night in the slammer?"

Ty looked at Liz. "Pick you up at 7?"

"Address yourself to the court, Counselor," McCafferty snapped.

Ty looked up at the judge. "Sorry, Your Honor. May it please the court, I'll serve my sentence with Attorney Gardner." McCafferty nodded. "Well done. Let the record show Attorney Hadley has received a suspended sentence. Here," he handed a disposable camera to Ty. "You will furnish proof satisfactory to this court that you provided Attorney Gardner with a fine evening of entertainment. Have someone take a picture of the two of you together. And here," he handed a piece of paper to Ty. "You will take her to one of these restaurants. They'll be expecting your call for reservations." Ty accepted the items without comment.

Liz was aghast. Before she could say anything, McCafferty rapped his gavel. "Court adjourned."

Liz found her voice. "Your Honor, permission to speak freely and off the record?"

McCafferty was rising from his seat, looked at her. "My chambers. Let's go."

Liz followed him into his chambers. She was fuming and allowed McCafferty to remove his robe and seat himself before she

36

spoke.

"Go ahead, Counselor."

"Where do you get off? Ty didn't deserve a contempt citation and he sure as hell didn't deserve to be forced into dating someone against his wishes. What the hell were you thinking?" Liz snapped. She pointed to her eye. "This was an accident that happened because he wasn't going to ease up in trying to score a run and I wasn't going to let him do it."

"I know. Brad Rogers lost $100 to me on the game. I saw you play. You're tough." McCafferty was smiling. "It was a close call. I was surprised when you came up with the ball. So was Hadley." He said, almost to himself. "Rogers is due for a contempt citation next time he's in here for calling you a 'big mama'."

"So, this whole contempt thing was a farce," Liz was still angry, "That was a rotten thing to do and humiliating besides. Undo it."

McCafferty smilingly shook his head. "Can't undo it, Lass. It's on the record and I can't have word get around that I've gone soft. Being considered a lunatic has its benefits." He leaned forward. "I thought I saw something between the two of you on the field. You should have seen his face after they untangled you. He couldn't keep his eyes off you."

"Your Honor, it's a good thing you weren't umping the game, because you're seeing things. He was surprised that he didn't get past me."

"I think he was even more surprised when you kissed him." McCafferty retorted calmly. "Yes, I saw that. I also saw a woman zealously defending a man who wasn't her client in my courtroom today."

"That's because of the injustice of the contempt charge, Your Honor," Liz snapped. "I hate bullies."

McCafferty raised his eyebrows. "So I'm a bully?" he asked softly.

"If you abuse your power in that fashion, you sure as hell are." Liz couldn't believe she'd said that.Surprisingly, he chuckled. Liz braced herself for whatever came next.

"May I call you Elizabeth? We're not in session right now." Liz nodded. "You know, Elizabeth, you remind me of my wife." A wistful smile crossed McCafferty's face. "She'd have stood here and read me the riot act just like you did and for the same reasons. And, you know, in the end we were both right. She just didn't like my methodology."

Liz calmed somewhat. "I'm sorry, Sir. Did she pass away?" Here, McCafferty shook his head sadly. "No. Worse. She's in a nursing home with Alzheimer's. It's been over two years since she's recognized me." He fell silent for a couple of minutes, head bowed. Eventually, he looked up again. "Anyway, go make your arrangements with Hadley for Saturday night. Stop," he held up a hand to stop Liz from arguing further. "The court has rendered judgment and it shall be carried out or the two of you WILL have cells next to each other. Go."

Liz turned and left, quietly closing the door behind her. Ty was still sitting on the plaintiff's desk in the courtroom, curiosity all over his face.

"What happened?" he asked.

Liz sighed. "The man wouldn't listen to reason. I tried, but you're still on the hook. I can't tell you how sorry I am."

Ty shrugged. "It could have been worse. Did you have plans for Saturday?" He was watching her face closely.

"I was just going to a jazz club for the second set. Diana Krall's playing. I have a ticket."

"Just one ticket?" Ty sounded surprised.

Liz looked at him. "Well, yeah, since I'm the only one who was going. I'd have gotten another, but my imaginary friend doesn't like jazz." Keep it light, keep it light.

Ty laughed. "You've got a comeback for everything, don't you?"

Liz smiled. "Just about. Sorry."

"Don't apologize," he was smiling. "I like wit." Ty held out a pad and pen. "Why don't you jot down your address for me and directions. I have to return a couple of phone calls. How's the head?"

It had stopped pounding, amazingly. Liz said, "It's better. Look, are you sure you wouldn't rather have me meet you somewhere?"

Ty stopped in the act of dialing a number, "Not if I want to stay out of jail." He continued what he was doing.

As Liz wrote, she thought that maybe McCafferty was right

38

and there was some kind of spark there. There had been a warm, happy light in his eyes as Ty talked with her. Just as Liz was beginning to think it was possible that McCafferty was not a lunatic, she heard Ty saying, "Hey," in a soft, warm lover's voice. She couldn't see his end of the conversation because he was on her blind side, so she focused on her task. McCafferty was a lunatic.

Liz finished writing. She screwed the cap back onto the expensive fountain pen, thankful she hadn't gotten ink on herself. She waited until Ty ended his conversation to hand him the pad and pen with a smile.

"All set." Ty looked quickly at the pad. "Salem? Isn't that a little far out?" He looked at Liz's face.

"Are we talking distance or attitude?" Liz asked.

Ty smiled again.

"Little of both, maybe. I was thinking distance, but," a look of mock suspicion crossed his face, "you're not a witch, are you?"

Liz chuckled. "Hardly, although I've been called that a few times by people who didn't want to use the 'B' word that rhymes with it. I just like the city." She began to gather up her briefcase to depart.

"So, you're not going to turn me into a toad if I'm late," Ty said teasingly.

"No, just a jailbird." She heard him laughing as she started to leave.

His voice stopped her.

"You know, Counselor, after your first courtroom win, it's customary to buy the losing attorney a drink."

Liz turned around, looking at him curiously. "I've never heard that," she said. Was he asking her out? "Besides, it's kind of early in the day, isn't it?"

Ty shrugged. "The sun's over the yardarm somewhere. And when I lose, a drink is in order. Like that softball game," he added with a smile.

Liz smiled back at him. "With your win record, you must be pretty dry by now. After that session, I could do with a double shot of something to calm my nerves, but I'll have to give you a rain check. Dan left me with a pile of work and I'll be staying late as it is."

"Wait."

Ty was coming after her with an envelope in his hand. "Here, you forgot something." He smiled as he handed her the envelope, his fingers touching hers. "I'll see you Saturday" and Liz felt that crazy zinging sensation down her spine again.

"Saturday it is." And she left.

Later, when Liz got back to her office, after giving the play by play of the morning's adventure to Millie ("I'm telling you, Elizabeth, the psychic was right"), she opened the envelope. Inside was a check payable for $1,500 to Elizabeth Gardner. The memo line read, "Screw Dan. You earned it."

Chapter 3

Liz thought she heard someone knocking on the front door, but couldn't be sure, since the sound was muffled by her distance from the door. Of course, since her dress wasn't zipped and she was still barefoot and without makeup, then, naturally, someone was most likely at the door.

"Just a minute!" she yelled as she raced down the stairs. A quick look around. No Beanie in sight, but that meant nothing. Liz opened the front door, praying she'd heard things.

Tyrone Hadley stood on the front step with the screen door opened.

"Hi. By order of the Honorable Francis L. McCafferty, I'm here to escort you to dinner and…" He didn't finish because a cat darted past him to the great outdoors.

"Aw, dammit! Beanie, get back here!" called Liz. "Excuse me, but he's an escape artist." She pushed past Ty, who suddenly found himself holding the door open to an empty house.

Beanie was trotting down the sidewalk, very pleased with himself. Liz could tell by the way he was switching his tail. God, the sidewalk was hot. Luckily, she knew how to win this game. "Who's the smart kitty? Who's the clever boy? Is it that Beanie?" She saw him stop and turn towards her voice, tail wagging.

"Who's a black and white menace to society?" This was in a sweet, light voice, but it made Beanie roll on the ground. Liz scooped him up.

"Gotcha, you sneaky little bugger."

Beanie didn't care. He kneaded Liz's shoulder and purred as she carried him back to the house. Ty held the door open and followed Liz into the house.

"Sorry about that! Oops! Hold still," Liz felt him zip up her dress, his fingers lightly brushing her skin. Even when he'd finished, Liz could still feel his touch.

She turned around, Beanie still in her arms. "Thanks. This is

Beanie, by the way," she said for lack of anything better.

Ty smiled, "Hi, Beanie." He put a hand out to pat Beanie's head. Beanie took hold of Ty's hand, licking his fingers and purring. Ty laughed. "Vicious animal."

Liz smiled. "Oh yeah. He's a killer." She put Beanie on the floor. Beanie lined his rear end up with Ty's leg and vigorously wagged his tail, looking up at Ty through big green eyes and purring loudly. Ty bent over and Beanie rolled to get a tummy scratch.

"Let me guess: He has some stupid name like Beanie Pawsworthy Ruffington the Third," Ty said as he scratched.Liz smiled tightly over Ty's head. Here come the cat lady comments.

"You're right, Beanie Pawsworthy Ruffington the Third is a very stupid name. However, Beanie Pawsworthy Ruffington the Fourth is not." She managed not to snap at him.

Ty looked up at her. "I'm sorry, I was just joking. I didn't mean to offend." He stood up, studying her face.

"I'm sorry, too. I just get defensive very easily. His name is B and E, but if you say it fast…"

"It sounds like Beanie,' Ty finished. "Why B and E?"

The scratching having ended, Beanie got up, trotted into the kitchen and pawed open a cabinet door. In a minute, all that could be seen was a furry white rump and fluffy black wagging tail.

Liz laughed. Beanie could break her bad moods without trying. "His specialty is breaking and entering and he refused to answer to Burglar." To Beanie, she said, "Get your furry ass out of that cabinet." He obeyed.

"See, Beanie understands that the phrase 'furry ass' means 'Cease and desist all unlawful activity or prepare to get sprayed.'" Liz explained.

Ty laughed, relaxed after the tense moment. Here he was, in her house, about to take her out on a date. Under duress, but hell, if you haven't been out in 3 years, a date is a date, even if there's a contempt charge attached to it. Then Liz came back to the moment.

"I'm sorry, I kind of mentally wandered off for a moment. Can I get you anything to drink? Water? Iced tea?" Thank God for the standard rituals of admitting a guest to the house. They effectively covered the tracks of a non-functioning mind.

"Got any Scotch?"

"No, I'm sorry."

"Then, I guess ice water's fine, unless you have a bottle of Mouton-Cadet 1947 handy," Ty was still smiling.

Liz laughed at the jest. "Oh, gee, the last guy who was ordered to take me out polished off the '47 by himself. After that, he sat there and blew "Louie, Louie" on the empty bottle. It turned out to be not much of a date and he had to do time."

Ty laughed, "I guess the ice water'll have to do, then." As Liz got the water for Ty, she saw him walk around the living area looking at photos and other pictures. He was closely examining one in particular when she handed him the glass of water.

"Thanks. Your eye's looking better."

"So's yours."

Liz's eye had opened but the bruise was still vivid in shades of purple and blue. Ty's, on the other hand, had healed completely, as had the cut on his lip. Liz had chewed out Joey and Rocco for inflicting the injuries in the first place. They had apologized, but vowed that if they had to do it again, they would. Liz had punched each of them in the arm as hard as she could and vowed that, she, too, would do it again.

Ty took a sip of water and gestured at the picture. "Very interesting picture. What is it? "

Liz looked. "That's a print from the Metropolitan Museum of Art, 'Pygmalion and Galatea." It's one of my favorite Greek myths." The picture showed a sculptor embracing a statue coming to life. From the waist up, the woman was alive, flesh-toned and returning the embrace. From the waist down, she was still motionless and white, locked in the marble from which she was carved. Ty glanced at Liz. "You've studied mythology?"

Liz made a deprecating gesture. "I wouldn't say studied. When I was a kid, I fell down a flight of stairs and broke my leg and ankle. My Mom went to the library almost every day to keep me busy. One day, she came back with a book of Greek myths and I was hooked." Liz mused, "I don't know how many time I read that book. For some reason, I really liked this particular story and when I found the picture…"

"…you had to have it." Ty finished. He glanced at his watch. "We should get going." He looked at Liz's feet. "This restaurant has a strict 'no shoes, no service' policy."

Liz became aware of her bare feet and bare face. "Shoes. Makeup."

"You don't need it." There was something in his tone that made itself felt all the way down her spine. She had to remind herself that he wasn't here by choice and the man was a natural charmer.

Liz smiled. "Thanks for the vote of confidence but this won't take long, I promise." She ran upstairs to finish getting dressed and to force her heart into a slower rhythm.

Liz was good for her word and was back downstairs within 5 minutes. Beanie had jumped onto a bookcase and rolled on to his back. Ty was scratching his chest and belly. Beanie had wrapped his paws around Ty's hand and was guiding it to the best spots. Judging by the smile and murmured "Oh, there but not there, huh?," Ty was enjoying it, too. He turned when he heard Liz approach and smiled even more broadly. "I think I have a new friend," he said. Then he added "Wow" in a soft voice, eyes riveted on Liz. "You look incredible."

Liz was flustered and managed to stammer, "Thanks. Am I within the dress code?" She was wearing a sleeveless raw silk dress in a soft purplish-blue shade. She noticed that Ty was dressed rather casually, jacket but no necktie. "I can change in a jiffy if you want."

Ty shook his head. "No need and I'd change reservations before I'd make you change that dress." He grinned and added, "It matches your eye."

Beanie made another grab for Ty's hand, rolling over and guiding it to his fluffy white belly. Ty obliged and began scratching again. He tried to withdraw his hand, but Beanie pulled it back, licking his fingers. "Hey, Fella, I've gotta go."

Liz said one word. "Beanie."

He stopped at the sound of Liz's voice and released Ty's hand. He looked at the two humans and wagged his tail, purring loudly. Ty took Liz by the arm and guided her forward.

Ty's touch was warm and firm. Liz could feel tingling where his fingers rested on her arm. She paused to collect purse and keys from a table by the front door. Beanie had scrambled down from the bookshelf and run for the door. He stood there, tail wagging, waiting for his opportunity.

"Beanie, don't even think about it. Get away from that door and nobody gets hurt, especially the cat." Hearing the stern tone, he obediently trotted back to the living room. Ty was smiling as he opened the doors. Both Ty and Liz watched to make sure there were no further escape attempts. There weren't.

"Here." He took her arm again and showed Liz to a large late model Mercedes. Again, Liz reminded herself that this was probably how he treated all his dates and not to read too much into it. Liz reached for the door handle but Ty stopped her. "Let me get that for you."

He opened the door, handed her into the car and closed the door when he was satisfied that she was settled. Memories of previous dates flashed through her mind, ones where she was lucky if said date remembered to unlock her door, let alone open it for her.

"Where are we going?" Liz asked after Ty got in.

He started the car and gave her a mysterious look. "You'll see," he said with a comical evil laugh.

They drove in silence for a few minutes while Ty navigated his way out of the Salem labyrinth. "Why do you live so far from Boston?" he asked. "I mean, this is a pretty good hike."

"The rents in and around Boston are ridiculous. If I wanted to live in something bigger than a shoebox, I could only afford to eat Jell-O." Liz replied. Ty smiled. "Here, I own my own home and a few rental properties."

She continued. "I like Salem. I like being near the water. I like the people, I like the mix of centuries among the buildings. I really feel at home on the North Shore."

"What did you do before you went to law school?" Ty asked. "I looked you up in Martindale-Hubbell and you haven't been practicing very long." He glanced at Liz. "Sorry, but I had to make sure you weren't…"

"…some kind of whack job?" Liz finished with a smile, "About the craziest thing I do is hope the Bruins will make a comeback. Don't worry, I'm not offended. I worked for an investment house here in town doing customer service. I hated every minute of it," her voice became tight with remembered anger, "It was especially hateful when I'd be instructed to deny something to a customer only to have the boss who gave me the instruction give the same customer what he wanted when the man got angry and demanded my supervisor." She shook off the bitterness. "That's the past. I don't have that problem anymore. My word is law."

Ty laughed at the joke. "Have you always been like this?"

"Like what?"

"Funny. Very quick with the one-liners. Why don't you have your own sitcom?"

Liz twisted in her seat so that she could see Ty. God, even his profile set off a reaction in her. "As for how long, I don't know. I'm pretty sure I had to learn how to talk first. No sitcom for me. I'd be unconscious from stage fright. I took an acting class in college and dropped out. I couldn't stop stuttering."

"That's too bad. You're funny. How'd you do in writing?" Ty was smiling.

"Solid B+ and astonishment." Liz waited for him to ask. She was enjoying her role as raconteur. Ty obliged.

"Astonishment?"

"Yeah. We had to type or write a descriptive paragraph on mimeograph paper so the professor could run off copies for the class,"

She saw the eyebrows go up again. "Yes, I said mimeograph paper. This was the dark ages before a PC in every dorm room." Ty nodded, chuckling. "Anyway," Liz continued, "I was late to class that day. The previous class, I had forgotten to bring my contribution and had to run back to my room to get it. This time, I had typed up the thing on the wrong side of the paper. My prof, a sweet Southern lady and said, 'Well, Liz, Ah guess you just fucked up again.'" Liz noticed that Ty was laughing softly. "Nobody had ever talked to me like that, so naturally I was astonished to hear it coming from not only a lady, but a teacher as well. Since then, I've had reason to hear that phrase quite a few times for different reasons."

"How'd she grade your paragraph?" He was still smiling.

Liz chuckled. "After all that, it got ripped apart. I don't think anyone liked the way I'd put even two words together. But I thought it was good and that they were morons."

"Atta Girl," The comment from Ty surprised Liz. "Were they morons?"

"Let's see, one of them's been writing for Rolling Stone since graduation and another just got a $3 million check for film rights to a book. I still say they were morons."

"Successful morons," Ty added supportively.

The lower deck of the Expressway was slower than usual, owing to late traffic headed for Cape Cod and the local combination of a sold-out concert on Boston's waterfront and a Red Sox-Yankees game at Fenway. "We're going to be sitting here for a while," said Ty. "How about some music?" He snapped on the car's sound system as Liz nodded. Within seconds, Miles Davis' trumpet softly filled the background. Liz smiled. "Kind of Blue" was a favorite album of hers.

"Good choice."

Ty was playing anxious host. "You know, I have other stuff if you prefer."

Liz shook her head. "This is classic stuff. Of course, I usually prefer Dave Brubeck myself, but Miles is great."

Ty chuckled. "Is there no end to your surprises?" He pushed a button and instead of trumpet, the car was filled with the Brubeck Quartet working their magic with "When You Wish Upon a Star." Liz laughed. "You have a few surprises of your own. Most people, if they think about Brubeck at all, begin and end with 'Take Five."

Ty spoke as he eased the car into an opening in the traffic. "Most of the women I know never heard of Dave Brubeck. They're more interested in dance and pop." The car moved forward and stopped. "To tell you the truth, I get bored with that stuff pretty quickly, but they get bored with this even faster."

Liz blurted out without thinking, "Maybe you should try dating women who don't have to be home by 10 on a school night."

She could have cheerfully bitten off her tongue. This was a one-time event and being catty was only going to hurt matters.

Liz saw Ty stiffen slightly and knew she had overstepped the boundaries. He said nothing.

"I'm sorry, Ty, that was uncalled-for and none of my business. You're not here by choice and I'm sorry if I just made things intolerable," Liz offered.

Ty still said nothing. His face was expressionless.

"If you saw my high school yearbook, you'd see I wasn't a great beauty. The photographer didn't have to beg me to shut up for my senior picture only because I had a mouthful of braces." Ty glanced at her. He said nothing. Great, thought Liz, I've blown the entire evening already. I'll be lucky if we don't end up at Denny's. Liz jumped when Ty spoke.

"That must have been awkward," he glanced at Liz, "having braces at that age."

"It's not as if I was the prom queen or head cheerleader," Liz said philosophically, "It's just that our town didn't have a decent orthodontist until then."

"He did a good job. You have a great smile." Ty pulled onto Storrow Drive.

"Thank you," was all Liz could manage.

Silence fell between them again, but it was not filled with tension like the previous one. They turned onto Boylston Street and Ty pulled the car over in front of the Prudential Center. "Wait here for a couple of minutes while I park. I don't think you want to start out the evening in a parking garage."

As Liz began to get out, she felt Ty's hand on hers. Again, it caused a warm wave of feeling to go through her. Liz turned towards Ty. His eyes were mischievous. He squeezed her hand slightly as he said, "Now don't run off. I've seen the inside of the Charles Street jail. I'd rather do time with you." He released her hand and Liz got out of the car. As she stood up, Liz had the urge to kiss him.

She found herself standing in front of a very pricey, very chic jewelry store. Their merchandise was still on display, although closing time was near. Liz looked at the artfully displayed treasures. Half of her brain was focused on the view, the other half was racing with nervous anticipation.

"Good, you're still here." Ty glanced over her shoulder into the window. "Engagement rings? A little premature, don't you think?"

Liz started to protest when she saw the glint in his eyes. "Well, I don't know," she said slowly, "What if McCafferty decides to make it a life sentence?" They both laughed.

"Seriously," said Liz, "Millie and I have this game we call 'Rock Hunt' for window shopping at a jeweler's. You identify the biggest, the most expensive and the tackiest pieces in the window. Sometimes, one stone wins all three."

Ty chuckled. "I see. Show me the winners."

As he turned to face the window, Ty moved to put his arm around Liz's waist, but stopped when she stiffened. He looked at her curiously, but said nothing.

"Um, let's see." Liz pointed to a large solitaire. "That's the biggest. There's the tackiest, which is kind of hard to find in a shop like this," she pointed to a gaudy, multi-stone cocktail ring.

"I can think of two or three women who'd disagree as to it being tacky, but I think you're right. Most expensive?" asked Ty.

Liz scanned the display. "The tags are hidden, so peeking is out of the question…"

Her voice trailed off as she focused on one particular ring. It was the most beautiful she'd ever seen and she'd never seen one like it. The center stone was some kind of rich blue, emerald cut stone with two smaller emerald cut diamonds on either side of it, all set in platinum. To Liz, the whole effect was timeless elegance. "Hey." Ty combined the single word with a gentle shake that roused Liz from her reverie. "You still with me?"

Liz blinked. "I'm sorry. One of the rings caught my eye." She pointed to it.

Ty leaned in for a better look. "That is gorgeous and very unusual," Ty commented, "What's that stone in the middle? It doesn't look like a sapphire." A clerk had begun to remove the displayed jewelry. Liz waved to get his attention. She pointed to the ring and mouthed, "What's the stone?"

The clerk mouthed back, "Blue diamond." He held up the ring so that she and Ty could see it better.

"Wow, I've never seen one before," Liz said. The clerk looked at her, then Ty, then back to Liz. She saw the question on his face and shook her head with a smile. The man nodded and smiled, then went back to emptying the window.

"What was that all about?" Ty asked as he guided Liz away.

"Oh, he assumed we were a couple shopping for an engagement ring and I just straightened him out." Liz was nonchalant.

"Should we be going?" Ty glanced at his watch. "Hmm. Time to head upstairs. You're not afraid of heights, are you?" Motioning for Liz to precede him, Ty guided her towards the Prudential Center and its elevators. Liz knew they were going to the Top of the Hub with that question. She remembered a group dinner from her previous career when two of the cockiest brokers had had to sit with their backs to the window in order to keep from passing out from fear. They had stayed marble white throughout the meal and only been able to walk by the windows again due to the large amount of beer they had to drink with their meals. Liz, on the other hand, had relished seeing Boston and Cambridge laid out before her.

They arrived on time for their reservation. The maitre d' greeted them warmly until he got a good look at Liz's eye. He looked twice at it, then at Ty with a disgusted expression. "Really. Didn't your mother tell you not to hit girls?" he asked haughtily. Without allowing an answer, he led them to a window table on the northern side of the restaurant and cut Ty off from seating Liz, doing it himself.

Ty sat in his chair looking bewildered and a little amused. "Why does everyone look at us and assume that I've been beating you?" he asked, genuinely confused.

Liz shrugged. "I guess it's easier to believe than the truth. Look at the two of us. Who'd believe I got the better of you at anything?"

She looked around at the view. The sun would be setting in about an hour. Right now, the city was bathed in the long, low rays of midsummer, very beautiful, but in them, reminders of the shortened daylight and falling temperatures to come.

"I guess you're not afraid of heights," Ty remarked as he watched her take in the sights. A one-man rowing shell made its way upriver, the rower maintaining a perfect rhythm. The sun caught the water on the oars, flashing in time with the strokes.

"I used to do that," Ty murmured, half to himself. "It's so quiet out there. You lose yourself in the rhythm and the movement. I started when I was a teenager. Got me out of the house and away from…" His voice trailed off as his eyes followed the shell. "I miss it." Liz heard the regret in his voice.

"Did you race?" she asked.

Ty smiled. "Won my class in Head of the Charles twice."

"I'm impressed," said Liz. She searched his face and asked quietly, "If you loved it so, why did you give it up?" She wanted to touch his hand, but didn't dare. Liz settled for leaving it on the table near his.

"I was building a practice and there wasn't time. Things took off for me and I started getting bigger cases, which meant more work." He looked at her. "You may have figured out that I don't get a lot of down time. But, success demands sacrifice. My father always said that. He knew." His voice had a bitter edge to it. He looked again out the window, silent.

Liz wanted to jump out of her seat and hold him. "Well," she ventured, "you must be doing something to stay in shape."

Ty's gaze stayed fixed on the view. "A bunch of us play hoops a couple of times a week."

"You and your friends?"

Ty looked back at her. "I don't have a lot of friends, but I play with the younger attorneys from my firm." He smiled ruefully. "Lately, they've been running my ass off. How about you?"

"How about me what?"

"How do you keep those legs so beautiful?"

Liz laughed, a little embarrassed. "Lot of walking but my legs aren't..."

Ty interrupted her, "Yes, they are. Trust me, I'm a connoisseur."

She ducked her head and blushed. "Thank you."

Ty looked at her oddly. "People don't tell you you're beautiful, do they?"

Liz looked back at him, eyes on his, "Why should they?"

"There are women who know they're beautiful because everybody tells them so," he said, "and they expect the world to acknowledge it. You can see it in their faces." Here, his voice became softer, "But a woman who is unaware of her glory puts them to shame."

Liz shook her head. "That's poetic. And very kind. But, the mirror doesn't lie. I'm not beautiful."

Ty opened his mouth to say something when the waiter approached, "I'm Marc and I'll be your server tonight. May I start you with a cocktail?" He didn't say anything about the eye or its possible cause, but Liz detected hostility towards Ty. She'd have felt sorrier for him if it hadn't been so damned funny.

They ordered drinks, wine for Liz and Scotch for Ty. Silence fell as they waited. The silence was broken by an electronic version of "Take Five" coming from Ty's jacket pocket.

Sheepishly, he pulled out his cell.

"I'm sorry. Gotta do some business." He rose to take the call at a more secluded area. Liz took the opportunity to head for the ladies room and a pause to gather her strength.

The cell tone had reminded Liz that this was not a real date. The caller was probably the girl she'd seen him with. She felt an almost physical pain at the thought of him with another woman and quickly stuffed the jealousy pangs down.

As Liz stood in front of the mirror over the sink, she didn't see her reflection due to the racing of her mind. What was going to happen? Did he expect a kiss at the end of the evening? Or more? Something in her hoped he did at the same time something else registered alarm at the possibility. Liz was aware of a vaguely electric feeling throughout her body, a warm, pleasant excitement that she'd never felt. She couldn't put a name to it, but she liked it.

No, you're done with all that stuff, she thought. You made your decision. This man is here under obligation and you should absolutely, positively not entertain thoughts of anything more than this evening with him. It's not going to happen.

Liz opened her purse and, for lack of anything else to do, checked to make sure she had her Plan B materials: enough money for a cab to North Station and her monthly pass for the train as well as the train schedule. Liz took out a lipstick to touch up and noticed the shaking in her hand. Using a two-handed grip, Liz reapplied her lipstick and rearranged her hair. She made her way back to the table and noticed that Ty not only rose to his feet as she approached, but also seated her. The waiter arrived two steps behind her to take their dinner order.

Ty assumed control, "We'll have the chateaubriand for two with..." Liz cut him off.

"Is Matty working tonight?" she asked Marc the waiter.

"Matty? You mean our executive chef, Matthew Sigby?" Marc looked offended at the familiarity. Liz ignored it.

"That's the guy. Go ahead with the chateaubriand, but tell him a la Vincenzo, no béarnaise, the searing had better be perfect. Tell him that this is for Elizabeth Gardner and he owes me his best shot or I'll call the Globe and expose him as a fraud." Marc lingered for a moment, uncertain. "Do it," she said. He hurried off.

Ty looked at her, brow furrowed. "Why are you terrorizing one

52

of the best chefs in Boston and why can you do it?"

Liz smiled. "I spent my summers at the Cape, but I wasn't on the beach. I was working in the kitchen of a lovely little trattoria and Matty interned there for a couple of summers." She smiled. "I'm not sure if it was more interning or getting underfoot, but he was there and I helped him get here. While he was there, though, he perfected grilling and Tuscan style flavoring. Trust me on this. The sides should be the best you've ever had."

"Really?" Ty asked. "So you know a lot of the chefs in Boston?"

"And New York and other locales. I know where to get a good meal wherever I go."

Ty leaned back. "Next time I go on the road, I'll call you first. Or maybe you should come with me." This was a warm note.

Before Liz could reply, Marc returned with two soups and a bottle of wine. "Chef says 'you'd better enjoy this soup, it's your recipe and he'll take it from here.'" Marc leaned over and kissed Liz on the cheek as he poured Hitching Post Big Circle into her glass. "He also sent that and apologized for not coming out but he's got a terribly bossy customer to feed." Liz chuckled. Marc straightened up and glared at Ty. "He also said I was to watch you in case you're the one responsible for the shiner. Something about a scaloppini mallet and your kneecaps."

They dug in on a chilled roasted tomato soup with basil oil and small dots of fresh mozzarella, served with a parmesan tuille. Ty broke the silence.

"Um, I noticed that you cashed the check. Did some of it go towards that dress?" Ty ventured. He smiled. "If so, it went for a good cause. You really do look great."

Liz grimaced, "Thank you, but Dan was so pissed, he escorted me to the bank to cash it and he took the money. Then he dumped more work on my desk."

Ty looked chagrined. "I'm sorry. I didn't think about what Dan might do. I'll talk to him."

"Don't!" It came out more sharply than intended. She caught herself and softened her tone. "He'll just think I complained to you and he'll make things even worse. I can tolerate Dan, but I still play the lottery."

"Still…"

Liz cut him off. "It's okay. Really. I would have returned it to you if he hadn't taken it." He started to say something else, but Liz cut him off. "I've learned how to handle Dan. I appreciate the offer, but I can take care of this. Honest."

Ty let the subject drop.

Halfway through the soup, his cell phone rang again. "Sorry, big case in progress and my associates have a ton of questions, Jimmy? Hold on a sec," Ty looked at Liz. "Excuse me." He excused himself and headed to the hallway again, the wait staff looking after him with disapproval.

Liz sipped her wine and shrugged. Oh, well. Apparently, he had higher priorities than entertaining her. This man was one of the best in the business and probably resented the time he'd had to take away from his job to comply with the court order. She shouldn't resent the intrusion.

Liz looked up and asked. "Crest or Colgate?"

He looked up, startled. "What?"

"Crest or Colgate, Counselor?" she repeated the question. "If the pace doesn't pick up very soon, McCafferty's going to ask you if you've packed your toothbrush and I'd like to give you the right toothpaste to go with it."

Ty looked at her. "You're planning to complain to the judge, Liz?" he asked. "That doesn't seem like you. "

Liz set down her spoon. "No, I'm not, but remember: he picked the restaurant, so I'm working on the assumption that His Honor has spies planted and…"

"If the pace doesn't pick up, I'll need to pack my toothbrush. Crest." Ty answered.

Liz pretended to study his face closely. "You look to me like someone who used to play Led Zeppelin albums until your mother was ready to break them over your head."

Ty smiled. "Oh yeah. And Deep Purple and Aerosmith."

Liz picked up her spoon. "Okay, so 'Kashmir' or 'Stairway to Heaven'?" Ty thought that one over. "I'd have to go with 'Kashmir.'"

"I'm sorry, Counselor, you lose. The correct answer is 'Fool in the Rain.'" Liz answered. Ty looked at her, not following. "Everybody loves either 'Stairway to Heaven' or 'Kashmir', but my favorite's 'Fool In the Rain.'"

Ty thought about it for a minute. "Chocolate or vanilla?"

"Chocolate. Vanilla is for actuaries," Liz answered.

Ty almost choked on his drink from laughing.

"My turn. Let's see," she pondered, "I've got it: Movies. Stay for the credits or not?" Liz asked as she spooned up more soup.

Ty shook his head. "I put in so many hours at the office that I can't remember what the last movie was that I saw in the theater." He looked thoughtful as he tried to remember. "I think there was a car chase and explosions and someone saved the world without mussing up his hair."

"That narrows it," offered Liz. "Could be Bruce Willis. He hasn't had hair to be mussed up in a while." Again, Ty nearly choked on his drink.

"One of us has to stop that," he finally said. "Let's see, my turn." He finished his soup while he considered the question. His eyes fell on a water glass. "Okay. Half empty or half full?"

Liz thought for a moment, chin in hand. "I'd have to go with half full in this case."

Ty raised his eyebrows. "Only in this case?"

"Yeah, it depends on the circumstances," she answered. "I am calling that water glass half full because I know that someone will come along to refill it at any moment." And, with perfect timing, Marc the waiter appeared and refilled the water glass. "See?"

Ty looked at her intently, amusement and something else in his eyes. Something that made Liz want lean across the table and kiss him. Under the table, she dug her nails into the palms of her hands to control herself. She could feel herself beginning to shake again.

"So, Liz. Why did you kiss me?"

The question caught her completed off guard. She didn't have a ready-made answer for that one.

Liz stared at her dinner plate. She couldn't look at his face. "I guess it was the head injury you'd just inflicted on me. Sorry about that."

Ty's answer surprised her. "No apology necessary."

Ty's cell phone rang again and he excused himself to go talk. Liz pressed her hands to her face, feeling the heat in her cheeks.

They continued to play "Either Or" throughout the rest of the meal, some answers providing jumping-off points for conversation.

Marc brought around the dessert tray. "Tonight we have chef's special tiramisu for the gentleman and pear and Stilton tart for the lady. Chef says he wants Miss Gardner's opinion on the tart."

Ty pushed his dessert plate towards Liz. "Care to taste it?"

Liz laughed softly. "No, thank you. I make the same thing, but mine is better, I guarantee it."

"I'll have to find out sometime," said Ty. He was looking into Liz's eyes. She thought she saw his hand start to move towards hers, but stop.

The sun began to set. The light changed from yellow gold to a deeper, more orange shade. A pianist had begun to play requests, singing old standards in a warm, honeyed soprano.

Ty was in the middle of a story when Liz heard the opening bars of "At Last" coming from the piano. She had been leaning on her elbow, chin in hand, looking at Ty when the song started and found herself focusing intently on his eyes. They were expressive and warm and she found her mind wandering while gazing into their depths. Liz thought that, with the light and life animating them, she could also see pain from old, unhealed wounds. She thought she would gladly and willingly heal that pain, given the chance. A bigger, more logical thought crossed her mind right behind it: nobody asked you to and it's not a good bet that you will be asked.

"...and I just made it over the fence before he got there," Ty finished his story. He listened for a moment, lifting his drink to his lips.

"'At Last,'" he said to himself, "one of my favorites."

"Mine, too," said Liz. "I love the standards."

Ty looked at her, eyebrows up. "Really?" he asked, "we seem to have a lot in common."

He looked at his watch. The sun had set and the darkness was thickening. Liz could see the first stars emerging.

"Did you make a wish?" Ty asked with a smile.

Liz came back to earth. "No, too many of them out there now." She was lying, but she wasn't going to admit to anyone, including herself, what that wish had been.

Ty glanced at his watch again. See? she told herself. He's looking to end this.

"We have time. Relax." He leaned back in his chair and sipped

56

some coffee. The pianist finished playing "Sophisticated Lady" to a smattering of applause and launched into a slow rendition of "These Foolish Things".

"Time before what?" Liz asked.

"The second set at Regattabar," Ty answered. "You did bring your ticket didn't you?"

Liz nodded, somewhat surprised.

"Good," he continued. "I had my secretary get one for me, too. This woman is good," he gestured towards the piano. "but, Diana Krall is something else."

Liz nodded agreement. The silence fell again, only this time, it was Ty who ended it.

"How'd you break your leg?" he asked.

"I beg your pardon?" Liz asked.

"You mentioned that you had broken your leg as a child, but you never said how it happened," Ty replied.

Liz toyed with the handle on her coffee cup, eyes on the table. "I fell down a flight of stairs at school," she answered tonelessly, hoping this would suffice.

She glanced up. Ty was watching her face closely. "Did you slip?" he asked quietly.

"No. I was pushed." Liz answered. She dropped her eyes to her coffee cup again.

"By whom?" The same quiet voice.

"One of the boys in my second grade class."

"Why?"

Liz maintained her focus on the coffee cup. "I made the mistake of telling him I liked him, in front of his friends, no less, and he answered by pushing me down the stairs. It was humiliating for him to have a loser girl show interest. I had to stay home for 4 weeks, he was expelled and my parents sued everybody in sight."

"Loser girl?" asked Ty.

"I lived in a different part of town from the other kids, I read too much and too far above their level. I wasn't one of the pretty girls. Loser girl." Liz's answer was toneless. She remembered her mother's "For God's sake, Elizabeth, if you don't lose some weight, no boy is ever going to want you! Honestly, don't you CARE about your appearance? Do you want to be alone the rest of your life?"

She looked up at Ty with a smile, trying to lighten the mood. "See? There's all this concern about kids bringing guns to school when the real menace is the architecture."

Ty didn't laugh. He didn't smile. Liz saw something in his face tighten up and she put her hand on his. "It was a long time ago, Ty and the kid was a kid. Really sociopathic kid, but it nothing more than a dumb kid action."

Ty turned his hand over to hold hers. Liz felt the thrill again.

"I'm sorry," he whispered.

Liz squeezed his hand. "Don't apologize. You didn't do the pushing." She withdrew her hand and covered its shaking by two-handing her coffee cup. The silence fell again, but this time, the vocalist filled it with another old sweet standard.

"So you've had a bad string of luck in the romance department, then?" Ty asked finally. His posture was relaxed, but Liz could see his attention was focused. Litigation mode.

"I didn't say that," Liz said. She felt like she was being cross-examined. "You know, this really isn't a favorite topic of mine. Can we change the subject?"

"You didn't answer my question."

"Do I have to? Why do you want to know?" Liz was beginning to feel uncomfortable.

"Well, I'm wondering why someone like you isn't married, engaged or involved. I didn't hear you telling McCafferty you couldn't go along with this because your boyfriend would be pissed," Ty continued calmly. Liz noticed that he was leaning back in his chair with his arms crossed, still looking very relaxed, but also very much focused on her.

"Someone like me?"

"You're smart, funny, very entertaining, you have excellent taste in music." Liz noticed he didn't say, "You're beautiful." She ignored the pang.

She tried to keep it light. "I'm waiting for Andy Garcia to come to his senses."

Ty chuckled. Liz continued.

"I thought the First Amendment freedom of association argument would carry more legal weight. Anyway, you're not married or engaged, either. And I didn't hear you telling McCafferty that your girlfriend would be pissed," Liz replied. Her words were heated, but she kept her voice low.

Ty just smiled. "The law is a jealous mistress."

"I hate that phrase," said Liz, attempting to deflect the conversation. "It's sexist for starters and implies that you are a slave to your job."

"So?"

"People should be more than what they do for a living," said Liz. "Unless, of course, you're one of those rare and lucky individuals who loves what he does for a living."

"I think I am," said Ty.

"Only 'think', Counselor?" Liz pounced on the opening. "You mean you're not sure you love your job?" Now who's cross-examining who? she thought.

Ty looked down at the table and started to laugh softly. "Very well done, Counselor," he said. "You shifted the topic and put me on the defensive." He looked at her. "I wasn't kidding when I said you'd make a good litigator." He looked down, thoughtful.

"I can't say I've had much more success with romance than you have," he said quietly, still looking down. "I've had some girlfriends, but things didn't work out. They never lasted more than a few months."

"Why not?" Liz asked gently. She was surprised that she'd actually voiced the question.

"I don't know," he said, "I work a lot of hours, that's always hard on a relationship. We'd have fun for a while, but it never lasted. I'd have to break plans or go out of town on business. Success demands sacrifice. I just figured that the right woman would come along and things would fall into place. Just didn't happen."

"Don't get me wrong; I have enjoyed my career as a litigator. I like the mental challenge and the adrenaline of being in the courtroom. It's like playing baseball: no matter how well you play, you're playing against another team. On the other hand, I'm a named partner in a law firm, did it in a fairly short amount of time and since I don't have judicial ambitions, I don't see myself climbing any higher in the legal profession." Ty shrugged. "At this point, it's maintenance, you know, keeping the top spot. I've been working so hard for so long that it's habit. And I don't have much reason to break it. So, there really isn't much more to me than my job, I guess."

"I'm sorry. It's none of my business and I didn't mean to put you on the spot," Liz said softly.

Ty looked at her and smiled. "Don't apologize. You didn't do the pushing." He looked at his watch again. "Why don't we get going?" He signaled for the bill.

"Wait a minute," Liz looked up to see a disposable camera in Ty's hand. "We have to get the picture, remember?"

Liz groaned. "My eye still looks like hell. I wish it was permissible to kick judges in the shins."

Ty chuckled. "No, it isn't. But you live in Salem. Can't you get someone to make a McCafferty voodoo doll for you?"

Liz laughed. "It's a thought."

As Marc the waiter came with the bill, Ty handed him the camera and asked him to take the picture. He then came around the table to pose with Liz, sitting very close and putting his arm around her. She felt the warmth coming from his body and the pleasure from being so close to him. They smiled and Marc took the picture.

Ty rose from his chair and assisted Liz in getting out of hers. As before, he started to put his arm around Liz's waist, but she moved out of reach. They rode down in silence, each lost in thought. Liz could still feel where he had touched her.

As before, Ty had Liz wait on the sidewalk as he brought the car around. The shops were closed and it was difficult to see stars with all the lights in Boston. A nearby florist was still open with flowers displayed on the sidewalk. Liz walked over to admire the roses, carnations and mixed bouquets. The lingering heat of the day brought out the scent in the flowers and she inhaled the sweet fragrances. Liz delicately touched a rose, feeling the smooth surface of the petal and inhaling its spicy floral fragrance. It was a sterling silver rose, silvery lilac and wonderful to smell. Liz jumped when she felt a hand on her shoulder.

Ty laughed.

"Sorry, I didn't mean to scare you, but you were kind of wrapped up in stopping to smell the roses." He took a few steps over to the florist who was sitting on a stool reading a newspaper by the light spilling from the shop.

Liz couldn't hear the conversation, but within a minute, the florist was handing her the rose she had been examining. "A pretty flower for a pretty lady," he said. "I have a soft spot for the sterlings myself. They're my wife's favorite."

Liz felt Ty's hand under her elbow as he guided her to the car. He dropped it when she visibly stiffened. As he had in Salem, Ty opened the door and seated her before getting in himself. The engine turned over and they were on their way to the nightclub.

"Thank you," Liz said as she sniffed her rose. "You caught me with one of my addictions back there."

Ty didn't take his eyes of the traffic as he replied, "You're welcome. It goes with your dress. For a minute there, I didn't know where you had gone. The thought crossed my mind that you'd called a cab and run off. Then I saw you at the florist. Tell me, do you always wander off like that on your dates? Has anyone considered a leash for you?"

"No," was all Liz said in reply. He didn't need to know how seldom she dated. "Certain kinds of shops just beckon me to go browse at them."

"Okay, so far we have florists and jewelers. Let me guess. Pet stores, book stores and music stores."

Liz raised her eyebrows. "Not bad. How'd you know?"

Ty waved a hand dismissively. "Elementary, my dear Elizabeth," and she felt a thrill as he said her name, "based on what I have observed, you've got that crazy cat, so you like animals. I noticed a packed bookshelf with a lot of titles that I like, which means you enjoy reading and I saw a very nice stereo system with a lot of classic jazz CDs, so you're into music."

Liz chuckled. "I salute your powers of observation and deductive reasoning." And she mockingly saluted him.

"It's why they pay me the big bucks," he said.

"That and the fact that you win all the time," she added. Ty turned his head for a second to look her in the eyes. "Not all the time," he corrected softly. "You've beaten me twice and that's about all I can stand."

At the jazz club, they were shown to a table near the front and the waiter asked for their order. Before Liz could answer, Ty had ordered a bottle of very expensive champagne for them. Liz tried to protest about the cost, but he overrode it with, "Why not? I can afford it and I want to do it."

The show began and Liz immersed herself in listening. Diana Krall and her combo cast a spell over the appreciative crowd. The champagne arrived and Liz was about to have her first sip when Ty indicated he wanted to make a toast. Leaning in close to Liz's ear, so as not to disturb the other customers, he whispered in her ear, "Here's to serving a suspended sentence" and gently touched his glass to hers.

Liz was so affected by having him this close, she almost forgot to drink. She started to set her glass on the table, but he stopped her. "Bad luck to set it down without drinking." Liz swallowed some champagne. Usually, she was not a great fan of the stuff, finding it having a nasty sharp edge to it and giving her intense heartburn. However, she noted tonight, there was a vast difference between the kinds sold in the supermarket and the high end stuff. What she was drinking was like liquid velvet, smooth and light. She sipped some more.

They listened for a while. The combo played a varied set of standards and new material, altering tempos and arrangements. After a break, the band came back and Diana Krall began singing "At Last."

She looked at Ty with arched eyebrows. He was smiling. "How about that?" he whispered.

Liz leaned back in her chair and smiled. Even if this evening was never repeated, the memories would carry her for a lifetime. Even if she never got to look back and say, "That's when it became our song."

Ty started to put his arm around her shoulders, but stopped. Liz felt a knot in her stomach. As much as she wanted it, this man was not hers and she could not permit herself to become overly familiar with him. The fight with herself caused her to shiver.

"Are you cold?" Ty rubbed his hand up and down her arm a couple of times. "Here." He removed his jacket and draped it over Liz's shoulders. She felt his face lightly brush her hair. "You smell wonderful," he murmured, "That perfume is fabulous."

She couldn't hear the rest of the music over the beating of her heart. She was acutely conscious that the warmth in the jacket had come from his body and it was almost impossible to resist the urge to lean her head on his shoulder or kiss his cheek to tempt him into kissing her.

After the show, Ty signaled a waiter over. He handed him the camera and he and Liz repeated their close together pose. Then, he slipped a cocktail napkin with a note to the waiter and within minutes, Diana herself came over to their table and shook hands. Once again, the camera came out and Liz found herself posing for a photo with one of her favorite jazz artists and a man she'd have given anything to call her own. And then it was over.

They were headed north on Route 93, traffic negligible at this hour. Liz sat with the blossom of her rose against her face and relived the entire evening in her memory.

"You're awfully quiet there, Counselor," Ty spoke quietly, but it startled Liz nonetheless. "Penny for your thoughts."

If you knew what I was really thinking, you'd probably push me down the next staircase we find, Liz thought. "I was thinking about this evening and how, when I didn't think it could get any better, you arranged for a picture with Diana Krall. I don't know how to thank you."

Ty shrugged, "There was film in the camera to be used up and you've kept me out of jail," he said indifferently, "but I'm glad you had a good time. I'll make sure you get copies of the pictures."

The rest of the journey continued in silence except for music spilling softly from the car's sound system. Liz mentally patted herself on the back for having resisted every urge she'd had to throw herself at him. In the dark and in the quiet, her mind was puzzling the question of what kind of lover he'd be. Even the slight physical contact tonight had gotten her juices flowing and she couldn't imagine what that most intimate of contact would do to her. Her train of thought was interrupted by their arrival at her front door. Again, Ty came around to help her out of the car.

As she got out of the car, Liz dropped her purse and the contents spilled onto the sidewalk.

"Here, let me get that for you," Ty stooped to pick up the items he could see in the light from her front porch. "What's this?" He held up her MBTA pass.

Liz tried to remove it from his hand.

"It's a T pass."

He kept it away from her and put it back in the bag. "Were you planning to ditch me tonight, Elizabeth?" Ty asked incredulously. "All set to make a run for it?" He sounded angry. "God knows,

63

you've been wound up and ready to bolt every time I touched you."

"No, I wasn't looking to ditch you," she said.

"Then why did you bring it?" Ty was looking hard into her face.

Liz squared her shoulders and returned the look. "Because I was taught, when going out on a date, to make sure you had the means to get yourself back to home and safety if it became necessary." She had been prepared to ditch him if things had gotten too uncomfortable.

She saw him relax a little. "I believe you."

"Good. Thank you. Would you care to come in for coffee?" And share my bed, if you want it. Mother's other rules about dating and sex be damned.

"No, thank you. It's a long haul back to Wellesley and I have to hit the road. I'll take a rain check, though." He stepped closer. Liz wondered if he was debating kissing her goodnight. He had her vote to do so. Ty leaned in and kissed her cheek. He leaned back and Liz saw a light in his eyes that only increased the heart pounding the kiss had started.

"I did enjoy myself, Counselor," he said. "I don't get out much. This really was a treat."

"So did I," she said. Ty just looked at her for a moment as if he didn't believe her, then abruptly turned and headed around the car to the driver's side. Without another word, Ty got in and drove off, pulling away from the curb, fast and noisy.

Liz headed into the house, blocking Beanie's escape route as she always did. She put her rose in a glass of water, making sure it was out of feline nibbling range ("You so much as lay a whisker on this, Beanie and you'll find your furry little ass at the Humane Society").

As she went through her preparations for bed, Liz kept pondering the same questions: was she imagining things or had Ty been aiming for her lips only to change to an alternate landing site on her cheek when he kissed her? And was his hesitation when she'd asked him in due to an impulse to accept the invitation?

Chapter 4

One rainy Saturday, a few weeks after the court-ordered date, tired from a full day in the office, Liz was digging frantically through her purse. T Pass, T Pass, where? Let's see, keys, receipts (need to enter those in the checkbook), makeup, Swiss Army knife, no T Pass...

Liz could hear a nearby car horn honking through the rain and her preoccupation. She ignored the sound while she continued the search for her pass. It was cold as is generally the case in Boston in late October. The leftovers of a late-season hurricane were dumping icy rain on New England, coming down hard, steely and relentless. It was going to be a mile walk to North Station to catch the train and a very uncomfortable mile at that. Murphy's Law says if you forget your umbrella, it will rain like there's no tomorrow. Her umbrella was back up in her securely-locked office and there wasn't time to fetch it. Liz froze as she heard a distant rumble of thunder. Oh, God, not that. As she felt her stomach clench, the car horn sounded again.

To distract herself from the growing terror of walking through a thunderstorm, Liz continued her search, turning her attention to pockets and briefcase. Still no pass. Great. She hadn't bothered to carry a lot of cash with her this morning and she wasn't sure if she had enough for both a cab and the train. And she was running out of time.

The horn honked again. Liz ignored it and looked towards North Station to nerve herself up for an incredibly miserable, terrifying walk. Within 10 strides, she was soaked to the skin and cold, but Liz pushed the thought aside. She heard her name being called. The Mercedes that had been honking had pulled alongside her. Liz peered through the downpour. Ty Hadley's head popped up over the top of the car, the driving rain quickly plastering his hair to his head. He snapped open a large umbrella and ran around the car to cover Liz. She saw that he was nearly as wet as she was from his brief exposure.

"Get in the car." He wrapped an arm around Liz and nearly carried her to the car. Once again, Liz felt a rush from his touch. "What were you thinking, walking in this?"

Before she could answer, Ty had muscled Liz into the car, taking her purse and briefcase. She quickly buckled herself in as he made his way around and got into the driver's seat.

As Ty started the car, he said, "You were really going to walk in this slop, weren't you?" as he gestured to the rain.

Liz nodded, "No cab fare, no choice. Besides," she added, "I'm only going to North Station to catch a train." She squeegeed some water out of her hair. "And I don't think I'd get any wetter. Sorry about your car upholstery."

Ty pulled the car into traffic. "It'll clean, don't worry. You headed home?" Liz nodded. She winced at a flash of lightning. Ty didn't seem to notice.

As the car waited at a red light, Ty glanced at Liz. "Long time, no see. How've you been?" The tone was casual.

"Busy. We got pulled in on a class action suit and Dan wanted me to research a couple of questions for him and have the answers Monday. Of course, he asked me yesterday at 4:00 PM."

Ty nodded, his eyes on the road. "Sounds like Dan. You're working on a Saturday and he's..." Ty left the question hanging.

"Scottsdale. Hilton Head and Bermuda took too big a hit from Hurricane Katie here," Liz answered ironically. The light turned green and the car rolled forward, windshield wipers furiously pushing away the driving rain. Between their rhythm and the warmth from the car's heater, Liz could have easily fallen asleep, except for the brevity of the ride and the presence of Ty.

"Is this Tillson v. Damon Industries? The price-fixing case? I know for a fact he's had that on his desk for at least a week," Ty asked. "Why do you put up with his bullshit?"

Liz held her temper. "Because he hired a C student from a fifth-tier law school when everyone else was fighting over the top ten from Harvard. Hey, you missed the turn to North Station, Ty!" Great. She was going to miss her train.

"If I was headed to North Station, I would have missed the turn," Ty answered evenly as he threaded the big car through traffic towards 93 North. "But I'm not going to North Station." He spared a quick glance at Liz. "If I recall, your home is in Salem."

Liz was floored. "But it's so far out of your way!"

"I have a full tank."

"The weather's crappy."

"The tires are good and the heater works."

The entrance ramp to the Central Artery was packed with cars and moving slowly. "It's going to take a long time to get there," Liz added in a vain attempt to dissuade him.

Ty gave her a long, hard look. "So?"

He turned his attention back to the road. "I'm driving you home whether you like it or not."

"Suit yourself," Liz answered and settled back into her seat. The sudden tension was almost unbearable and added to her physical discomfort.

As the car inched forward, Ty glanced at Liz, "Mind answering a question for me?"

"No."

"You act as if you'd rather be anywhere but near me. Do you dislike me that much?"

The question caught her off guard. "No, but since I never heard from you after our court-ordered date…"

It took nerve for Liz to say it, but she felt relieved. She'd had hoped that he would call or see her again. The disappointment had been sharp and she'd thrown herself into activities to forget it. Her house had never been cleaner. Liz was a great believer in occupational therapy for heartache. Keep yourself too busy. And people always admired a clean house. Since Liz had channeled a lot of unused sexual energy into it, her house was immaculate and well-decorated. And now, just as she was putting it behind her, here he was…

Ty looked at her incredulously. "Really? Well, Miss Gardner, I haven't even gotten an acknowledgement for the roses I sent you," he growled. "I thought that was rather rude."

"What roses?" Liz was puzzled and confused. "I never got any roses."

Ty looked at her quizzically. "I sent two dozen sterling silver roses to your office the Monday after our date. You never got them?"

"No. Honest. I got the pictures, but no flowers." The pictures had come through McCafferty's office.

He had sent her two dozen sterling roses? Must have been ordered by McCafferty. "What. You said Monday?"

"Yes, Monday. Ring a bell?" Ty looked at her, face and voice deadly serious. His look was penetrating, eyes searching her face for a straight answer to what would normally be a joking question. "Lose track of them amid all the shipments from your boyfriends?"

Liz smiled, trying to soften his mood. "I wish. I love roses, but I have to fend for myself in that department." He relaxed visibly, but still looked mystified, as if he couldn't believe that no one sent flowers to Liz. "But anyway, I remember that a perfectly gorgeous bouquet arrived without a card that day and the delivery guy couldn't make out the name on his clipboard. No one was expecting flowers, so we left them with the receptionist, except that I swiped three for my office. They were beautiful, smelled fabulous and it gave me a lot of pleasure to have them. Thank you."

Ty cursed under his breath, inching the car forward. "Monday morning, I'm gonna…"

"No, you're not," Liz surprised herself by interrupting him, quietly and firmly. "It didn't work out exactly like you planned, but those flowers brought pleasure to a lot of people. Even if I'd gotten the whole thing, I would have divvied them up and shared. Three were plenty for me."

Ty raised his eyebrows, "Only three?" he asked skeptically.

"Okay, you caught me. A dozen, but it would have been too obvious if I'd stolen that many," Liz admitted mischievously. She heard Ty's chuckle. Thank God. She didn't want to be around when he really got angry. There was some black, carefully walled-off rage she could sense in him and Liz didn't want to be the cause of its release.

"Ty, what did the card say?"

He was smiling as he focused on the dense traffic. "'Dear Fisk, Most roses are red, These are kind of blue, Want to go back and dine at the Pru?' I signed it, 'Rose.'" Ty glanced at Liz and laughingly shrugged, "I'm a litigator, not a poet."

"Wish I'd gotten it. I could have used the laugh." Liz relaxed. She couldn't fathom what Ty wanted but that didn't matter. Enjoy the ride and be grateful your transportation problem was solved beyond expectation.

Liz started to shiver. The harder she tried to suppress it, the stronger it got.

"Liz, are you okay? You look pale." There was concern in Ty's voice.

"Just wet and cold. No big deal. I'll warm up when I get home." She clenched her teeth to keep them from chattering.

Ty touched her cheek, remarking, "You'd have had double pneumonia by the time you got to North Station." He put both hands back on the wheel. "All right. Let's get you home."

He set his shoulders and the Mercedes cut off one of the millions of SUVs clogging the highway. Ignoring the furious horn-honking behind him, Ty kept exploiting the small spaces in traffic until it thinned out and was moving at a more normal pace around Winchester. Slow, because of the rain, but not the bump and grind traffic that it had been.

Keeping his foot firmly on the accelerator, Ty exhaled and glanced at Liz. "You can stop with the white knuckles now."

A crack of lightning and near-simultaneous boom of thunder made her jump. Liz glanced wildly out the window. "Maybe not." She tried to shrink into the car seat.

"Don't tell me you're afraid of thunderstorms." Ty looked at her.

She nodded. "Always have been. My mom used to tell me to get over it, but I never could."

He stole a glance at her. "And you were going to walk through it? God, you're brave."

Another boom made her catch her breath. "Not really. Just didn't have a choice if I wanted to get home." Another flash. Liz shut her eyes. Her shivering returned.

She felt a warm, strong hand covering hers, giving them a gentle squeeze. "Don't worry," she heard. "You're safe. I'm not going to let you get hurt. Just trust me." His voice was as warm as his hand. She could feel a warm flow of energy coming from it. It ended abruptly when he put both hands back on the steering wheel.

In no time, they were pulling onto Route 114 in Peabody and headed towards Salem. The rain hadn't abated, nor had the wind. Some hurricanes die harder than others and this one was going kicking and screaming. The roadway was a river. When the tires weren't hissing on wet pavement, the car was splashing through huge puddles. "This has got to be one of the worst nights I've ever seen," Ty commented.

"You're right," said Liz, "but I bet you Beanie makes a break for it, anyway."

"You're on. What's the bet?"

Liz was startled. "I don't know. I was speaking rhetorically."

"How about if I win, you pay for dinner and if you win, I get you another two dozen sterling roses and pay for dinner?" He glanced at her, "Hand delivered by me, if necessary."

"Dinner?"

"Usually I charge more to rescue soggy damsels, but seeing as how you kept me out of jail, I'll give you a discount this once." He winked. She felt an electric charge from it.

"Okay, but rain check on the dinner. I don't have a thing in the house." Another flash of lightning. "And I don't want to go back out in this."

"I know this is out in the boondocks by city standards, but I presume that the new-fangled idea of take-out and delivery has hit Salem? Or are you guys still stuck in the seventeenth century?"

Liz leaned back and closed her eyes. What was going on here? Surely this wasn't romantic, thought Liz. She had at least 15 years and 30 pounds on any of the girls he'd dated. Corey had filled her in on names and descriptions. Did he feel guilty over the black eye? Maybe he's just being kind. Or maybe he figures I'm an easy lay, Liz mused.

They pulled up in front of her house "Here's the plan," said Ty, "We'll get you inside first, then I'll get the bags, okay?"

Liz could tell her consent was not actually sought, but that didn't matter. Ty came around to her side, umbrella opened, and hustled her to the front door. A gust of wind caught the umbrella and blew it inside out a split-second before Liz found the house key in her bag. She froze at a particularly close and loud crash of thunder. Ty dropped the umbrella and pulled her close against his body. "Give me the key," he murmured as he took it from her nerveless fingers. "Breathe," she exhaled, "And again. Atta girl."

He had the door opened in seconds, but not before the downpour had soaked them both again. Beanie was poised on the threshold, positioned for an escape attempt. He started to dive for

70

the opening and stopped dead at the edge of the threshold, nose and tail twitching. A few raindrops hit his face and that decided the issue. Beanie ran for the indoors, Ty pushing Liz inside after him.

"Be right back."

Within a minute, Ty was back in the house, bag and briefcases in hand, dripping as if he'd just emerged from a swimming pool. Liz had an incredibly powerful urge to throw herself into his arms. Then she sneezed. Great. So did he. Peachy.

"Uh, look, take off your shoes and leave them to dry there. The bathroom's upstairs and I'll see what I have for dry clothes for you, Ty," Liz suggested, "Shower if you want to," Her voice trailed off as a mental picture of Ty in her shower leapt into her mind. Ty in the shower with her.

"You'd probably benefit from a hot shower yourself," Ty replied, "Care to…"

Liz sneezed again.

"Yeah. I'm going." Ty padded upstairs.

As she heard the shower begin to run, Liz found herself wondering what he looked like naked. She'd felt the strength in his arms as he'd held her; the rest must be just as muscular. Another lightning flash roused her. She shook her head and took off in search of dry clothes.

Keeping an ear on the bathroom activity, Liz found a flannel shirt and some shorts large enough to fit Ty. The water stopped. Just as Liz was about to knock on the door, she heard a "what the?" from inside the shower and a scrambling noise. Liz smiled as she knocked on the door. The door was yanked open and Beanie ran by at top speed, heading downstairs as fast as possible. Ty peered around the door, amazement on his dripping face and a towel clutched around his waist. "That was a first," he said. "Does he always get in the tub with you?"

Liz handed Ty the clothes. "Only for showers. He fell in once when I was taking a bath. We found out that cats don't like to dog paddle. He usually stays on the rim of the tub."

"He did," Ty answered, "I was just startled to see a face poking out from behind the curtain." He touched Liz's cheek and started to pull her in. Lightning flashed and she pulled back at a particularly big crack of thunder, willing herself not to scream. He started to come towards her and she backed away before she could think.

71

They stood and stared at each other for a moment. Liz broke off by turning away and mumbling about having to do something. He closed the door.

What the hell was he thinking? She leaned against the wall, hugging herself to calm the violent shaking.

Liz knew Ty thought she was shivering from being cold and wet and scared. She knew she was shaking from storm terror and from the huge effort it took to stop herself from removing Ty's towel and caressing his beautiful body. It was even better than she had pictured, slightly thinner, but fit, very fit. Liz admitted to herself that she had never wanted any man as powerfully as she wanted this one. And she had just refused an implied invitation to join him.

She headed for her bedroom and, dropping to her knees beside the bed, hastily hid the copy of the Kama Sutra Millie had given her as a gag Christmas gift. Just in case. Liz grabbed dry clothes for herself and returned to the bathroom as Ty emerged.

"My turn," Liz said a little too brightly. She pointed to the wet garments in his hands. "Clothes dryer or hangers?"

He studied her face, then answered, "Hangers, I guess. I think it's all dry clean only. Are you okay? You look ready to jump out of your skin."

"I will be. When this storm passes, I will be."

His hair was still towel damp, accenting the natural wave in it. Liz's hand itched to touch it, then stroke downwards to his face. She could see herself doing it. Under the bundle of clothes in her hand, she dug her fingernails into her palm. "Uh, there's a closet in the spare room over there. There should be plenty of hangers." The words came out a little too fast.

Ty nodded, still studying her. Liz wondered if he could see her intense desire for him. "Okay." He stepped aside to let Liz through the bathroom door, a little more than necessary, she thought. As she closed the door behind her, Liz heard him say, "See you in a few."

Liz stripped out of her sodden clothing and looked long and hard at her reflection in the mirror. Her hair was plastered down in snakelike strands, mascara trails ran from her eyes down her cheeks and she was paler than usual. Liz looked at the rest of her body, hating the sight. Nothing out of Playboy in here, she thought.

No flat stomach or defined rib cage. Just a 40 year old body. Of course, it looked a hell of a lot better than it had when it was a 35 year old or even 30 year old body, but still, Liz had to admit the Silicone Queen had her beaten as far as shapes were concerned. There was a knock at the door.

"Liz? You okay?" She could hear concern in Ty's voice.

"I'm fine, just moving kind of slow." She spotted the crumpled towel he had used and discarded on the floor. Liz had to suppress the urge to wrap herself in it. The door opened a crack.

"I'm not peeking, I swear," Ty said. "Want me to start a fire?"

'Uh, sure," she said unsteadily, picturing the two of them making love in front of a roaring fire, rain beating against the windows. She squeaked out, "that's a great idea."

As Liz soaped her body, her mind kept fixing on the image of sharing this with Ty, having those elegant fingers of his stroke and probe, her hands gliding over his chest and down, the two of them kissing.

The shaking began again. Liz shook off her daydream.

Liz rinsed off the last of the bubbles, warning herself that she had to keep her hands to herself if she wanted to see this man again on anything but a business footing.

Liz dried her hair and pondered the next step. Did he expect to stay the night? He couldn't possibly want to share her bed. She shook her head. Leave it alone for now. Let things unfold. The lights flickered. After donning another old flannel shirt and a pair of shorts, Liz hung up both her towel and Ty's, pausing to smooth his towel a little. She nearly fell on her face leaving the bathroom, tripping over Beanie who was waiting outside the door.

"Beanie, how many times do I have to tell you? There's no life insurance and you don't inherit dime one if you kill me." Beanie just blinked his green eyes and wagged his tail. Liz headed downstairs, Beanie at her heels. She found Ty in the living room, fire crackling as promised, examining her print of Pygmalion and Galatea and sipping a beer. He turned towards Liz as he heard her approach. Ty raised the beer. "I hope you don't mind. I found it in the fridge."

"Not at all," answered Liz, "Buying you a drink is the least I can do for you."

Too late, she wished she had re-phrased that. Ty's eyebrows

went up. "Oh? And what else would you do for me?" he asked softly, eyes gleaming.

You don't want to know, trust me on this, thought Liz as she blushed. "Actually, I need your help. The lights just flickered and that means the electricity is about to go. I'm going to dig out candles. Would you mind grabbing my boom box out of the spare room for me? We can have music, at least."

"As you wish," Ty disappeared, Beanie following closely.

Liz deliberately focused on the mundane task of hauling candles out of an antique breakfront. She shook her head. Sure, she could light every house in the neighborhood, but all the candles were scented like roses, apples or, worst of all, something called "Seduction." Oh, brother. She quickly sorted out enough in a single scent to provide light and took them back to the dining room table. She busied herself with lighting them. Rainy night, romantic light, incredibly desirable man within my sight, she thought and stopped. She reminded herself: a one-night stand with Tyrone Hadley and she'd never forgive herself. One night would not be enough, even if it was all she could have.

Liz heard footsteps and saw a blur of white dash into the room ahead of Ty. He was smiling as he watched Beanie's antics. Ty held out the boom box. "Your sound system and link to civilization. Where do you want it?"

Liz paused in lighting candles. She waved her hand. "Anywhere is fine. Let me get a take-out menu."

She lit the last candle and ran for the kitchen. Rummaging through her junk drawer, Liz located a menu from a Chinese restaurant. As she headed back to the living room, the lights went out. Before her eyes could adjust to the darkness, Beanie dashed under Liz's feet, causing her to lose her balance and fall into Ty hard enough to knock them both to the floor.

"Oof!"

"Dammit, Beanie!" Liz found herself sprawled on top of Ty. She looked into his face and said, "I am so sorry. Are you all right?"

Ty started to laugh. Beanie trotted up to his head and began to sniff his face, giving him a quick lick. Ty laughed even harder and Beanie sat back on his haunches, tail wagging.

Liz became aware of the full body contact with Ty and how

great it felt. When they'd collided in the softball game, Liz had been wearing her catcher's gear. Now, there was nothing between them save for clothing. She felt one of her legs between his, bare skin to bare skin, his hand in the small of her back, also on skin and a sneaky desire to stay snuggled up to this man for a long time. 40 or 50 years would be just about right. If she stayed much longer in this intimate touch, she'd kiss him again. Liz rolled off of Ty and leaned against the wall.

Ty raised himself on his elbows, still smiling and laughing quietly. "Tell me," he finally said, "When I plowed into you in that softball game, did I hit you as hard?"

"Harder maybe. I had my gear on." Liz gestured to Beanie. "Jack the Tripper there seems pleased with himself." She held out a hand to Ty, who sat up without her help and leaned against the wall next to Liz. She reflected that, although she'd really enjoyed being tangled up with him, apparently the pleasure wasn't mutual. Oh, well. It was fun while it lasted.

She withdrew her hand and covered up her awkwardness by picking up the dropped menu. "I like this place a lot. Food's great, they cook with natural gas, so a power outage doesn't affect them and," Liz sneezed, "they make a powerful won ton soup." She sneezed again.

"Since Beanie didn't make a break for it," she continued, "dinner's on me. I really don't know how to repay you for everything you've done today." Liz handed Ty the menu.

He gave her another unreadable look as he accepted the menu. "I hope your land line works," he said, "My cellular service isn't working right now. I think it's the rain. You don't have to thank me. If I didn't want to drive you home, I wouldn't have."

Liz was flustered, "But you must have had plans or had to be somewhere or with someone." This last hurt to say.

Ty frowned slightly. "No. No plans. My date cancelled. She was grounded for coming home too late on a school night," he said mockingly.

Liz buried her face in her hands, listening to him chuckle. She could feel herself flushing brick red. "God, am I ever sorry I said anything." Her voice was muffled. Ty hauled himself to his feet, then held out a hand to Liz.

"Oh, don't worry about it. I've had worse things said to me.

Besides," he said as he pulled Liz to her feet, "it's a lot of fun to rake you over the coals about it. You blush very nicely. Like you're doing right now," he teased. She ducked her head.

They headed for the candlelit dining room. Ty seated Liz in one of the chairs and pondered the menu. Beanie jumped into an empty chair near the humans, only his head showing over the edge of the table. "So, even on a lousy night like this one, these guys will deliver?"

Liz nodded, seizing on the change of subject. "Yeah. The Lins are not easily deterred. I've seen Fred out in even worse weather than this."

Ty shot her a look. "Fred Lin? The guy who owns the Chinese restaurant is named Fred Lin?"

Liz smiled, "No, his son is named Fred. Fred makes the deliveries."

Ty was curious. "Is that just a coincidence? Father's from the old country and just happened to name his son Fred?" Liz laughed as she looked at Ty. He relaxed, watching her and smiling.

"Not unless you consider Saugus the old country," Liz finally said, still laughing. "Roger Lin is the biggest Red Sox fan I have ever met. I don't know how he persuaded Celia to name their son Frederick Carl Lin, but she went along with it. Notice the name? "Green Dragon Wall"? Green Monster didn't sound Chinese enough. Celia drew the line at naming a dish 'Yankees Go Home'."

Ty was laughing as he listened. He picked up the menu, still chuckling.

"You know, Counselor, you've got some of the damndest stories I've ever heard," he said. They decided on a few items, including a double dose of soup. Since the only light was from candles, it was necessary for them to put their heads close together to both be able to read the menu. Liz could smell the soap on him from his shower. It was almost more than she could take. Another big crack of thunder and she nearly threw herself into his arms.

"Okay, we've got a plan," Ty finally said. "Now we need a phone. And I'm buying dinner," he added with authority.

"No, I lost the bet. Beanie didn't try to escape," Liz stated with equal authority as she looked hard at Beanie. He didn't care.

"He stuck his nose past the edge of the step and thought about it very hard," Ty answered as he, too, tried to give Beanie a severe look, "It's an escape attempt. End of discussion. Now where's the phone?"

"Kitchen," said Liz. She handed him a candle. "Here. I forgot where I left my flashlight."

Ty rose and pointed his free hand at Liz. "Just sit. I'll take care of this." He headed for the kitchen. Liz listened to him placing the order and after he gave the address, she heard him say, "A what? I don't know, let me ask." Liz?" Ty called from the kitchen, "What's a Beanie Box and do we want one?"

"Oh! Yes! I forgot! We need a Beanie Box!" Liz called back. This seemed to get Beanie's interest and he jumped up on the table to walk over and sniff Liz's face. "Down. Now." He got back into his seat.

Ty returned to the table, two beer bottles in one hand and the candle in the other. He passed one bottle to Liz and seated himself. "Fred says 'hi' and that it'll be about a half-hour." Ty raised his bottle. "Happy Birthday to me," he said softly.

"What?" Liz was stunned.

He looked at her. "It's true. Today's my birthday. Here," He showed her his driver's license. The date matched.

Liz stared. "My God. Why aren't you at a party or spending the evening with friends?"

Ty shrugged as he put away the wallet. "No friends to throw a party."

"What about..." she groped for the Silicone Queen's real name, "your girlfriend?"

Ty was puzzled. "What girlfriend?"

"The blonde I saw at the game."

"Ah." Ty didn't look her in the eyes. "Cheryl. She's not my girlfriend. I spend time with her, but, well...she's...she's just a...convenience."

Liz didn't know what to say. Part of her was jubilant he wasn't emotionally involved with the other woman and part was crushed at his loneliness. She tentatively reached a hand toward his, stopped herself and covered with a clumsy attempt at lightness, "Ah, well since it's your birthday, you get the biggest sparerib."

Ty chuckled, still looking downward, then looked at Liz, headed cocked to one side. "You know, Counselor, in this light, without all the hairspray and war paint, you look like you're about 17 years old," he mused, "Makes me feel like a dirty old man, especially today."

Liz smiled and shook her head slightly, ignoring the thrill his remark gave her, "17, huh? Must be the light or your eyesight should be checked because that age is well behind me now, but thank you."

Ty sipped his beer. "Actually, I had my eyes checked a month ago and this light is just fine. No complaints about the view. Here," He gently took her chin in his head.

Liz hardly breathed as he studied her face. "Your eye healed up nicely. I never got a good look at them before. Very blue, very pretty." She felt him rub his thumb against her chin and caught her breath. "Lovely smooth skin, too. For someone who doesn't think she's beautiful..."

Liz ducked her head. "That's the beauty of candlelight. It softens the flaws." She nerved herself up. "I don't have any complaints about my view, either." She looked away quickly, fearing the possible scorn she might see on his face. This was getting into dangerous territory.

Ty put his beer bottle on the table and regarded Beanie. "So, Counselor, what's the story with your little friend there? Where did you find him?"

Liz looked at Beanie with affection. "I didn't find him. He found me."

"Come again?" Ty asked."

"I was in the city waiting for a cab and I had a few bags with me, including a duffel bag," Liz began. She omitted certain details she viewed as non-essential. "This scrawny, filthy little animal comes sidling up to me, stands with his butt next to my leg and starts whacking me with his tail, just looking into my face and purring. I petted him, because he seemed to be nice enough and the cab arrived. I didn't pay any attention to the cat because I was trying to get my stuff loaded in the cab. I'd been pretty sick and it was a lot of effort just to get everything settled. I got home and he jumped out of the duffel bag. He lined his butt up next to my leg and started whacking me with his tail again. Millie says that the animal kingdom has me pegged as a sucker." Liz shrugged apologetically, "I've taken in a few strays. I couldn't throw the little guy out after he'd gone to all that work. He looked like he needed a little TLC and a good home," Liz laughed softly. "What is it Millie said? 'Gardner, you are a sucker for a furry face and a hard luck story.'"

Ty laughed at that. Liz continued, "He's been here ever since that day. Despite escape attempts and a raging obsession with squirrels, he's been a great pet and a good friend." She looked at Ty. "And that's Beanie's story."

Ty reached over and petted Beanie's head. "He is a nice cat." Beanie held up his chin for scratching and Ty obliged. "What were you so sick with?"

Liz tried to deflect the question with a joke. "Dutch Elm disease," she said lightly. "Comes from spending too much time around tree-hugging Wiccans."

Ty looked at her, face expressionless. "Uh huh. Hey, if you don't want to tell me, that's fine. I respect your wishes." He drank some more beer. "Can we get some music?"

Liz felt like she'd just insulted him. She still wasn't sure what his motives were for being here and she wasn't going unburden herself to a man she hardly knew. Something in her heart said that Ty could handle the truth. All of it. However, her brain overruled it and Liz busied herself with finding a good radio station on the boom box. "What's your pleasure?" she asked Ty without looking at him.

She didn't hear his reply because the radio crackled out with, "I want to know the name of the guys on the St. Louis team. Who's the guy on first base?" Liz looked at Ty, who nodded, and they spent the next few minutes listening to Abbott and Costello and "Who's On First?" Liz noticed that Ty was mouthing the words along with the radio.

"That's one of the college stations. One of the DJs plays classic comedy on Saturday nights. During the Series, he was playing 'Shakespearian Baseball,' which is a riot," Liz explained.

Ty nodded, "I know it well. One of my Dad's favorites." He gestured at the radio. "So was Abbott and Costello. I'd watch the movies with him."

"I see," said Liz. "Are you close?"

Ty looked at her, "No, never met Bud and Lou."

Before she could protest, he cut her off, "I know what you

meant. He's gone, has been for years and no, we weren't all that close. Tell you the truth, he was a workaholic bastard and a mean drunk. He came drunk to some of my Little League games. Said he'd had to entertain clients. He'd tell me to enjoy 'that shit' as a kid because it was all work as a man and twice as much when you married. Men made the money and women spent it, he said. My mother left when I was 15," Ty's voice was flat, but Liz could sense the pain. "She woke me up one night to kiss me goodbye and promised she'd come back for me. She never did." Ty looked down, eyes on a candle flame. "My father got sole custody and I never heard from her until after he died." Liz waited, her eyes never leaving his face. Ty continued.

"My father died the day I graduated from high school. I'd called to remind him and he'd yelled at me. 'Where do you think your goddamn tuition for your fancy-ass college is coming from? Maybe your mother, the whore, will show up.' And he hung up. The office cleaning lady found his body still at his desk with the phone in his hand and an order ticket for the big deal he'd just made all filled out. Aneurysm."

Liz wanted to wrap her arms around Ty and just hold him, but she couldn't. He wasn't hers to handle. She started to reach a hand towards his, but stopped herself.

"My parents were no picnic, either," Liz offered quietly. Ty looked at her. "They had a kind of hostile, silent relationship with each other and they weren't terribly warm and nurturing with me, either. I felt like a prisoner of war.

"Till the day she died, I always felt like my mother was disappointed with everything in her life and especially me. I got my taste in music from her. She'd listen to those old 'man that got away' torch songs by the hour. They may have been more than just a song."

"Oh?" asked Ty. He had his head propped up in one hand as he listened.

"After she died," Liz offered, "I was cleaning out her sewing basket and found a packet of letters to her from some guy."

Ty's eyebrows went up. "Do you think she was cheating on your father?"

Liz shook her head. "No, they were all dated before my parents married. The letter on top of the stack told her that he was marrying Michelle and he didn't want to hear from my mother anymore." Liz could hear her father as she said this, screaming at her mother, "Jesus Christ, Delia! He never wanted you; I did! Would it kill you to show me a little affection now and then?" Liz buried the memory and continued.

"I wanted to be a writer when I grew up, but she kept telling me I needed to be practical, that a writer must be extraordinary in order for people to want to buy their work. I won a state-wide contest when I was in school. Mom told me I shouldn't get my hopes up. And boys didn't like girls who were smarter than they were."

I was never pretty enough or thin enough or popular enough for her." Liz could feel the ache from the raw memory.

"Your mother didn't think you were pretty?" Ty was incredulous. "Was she blind?" In a quieter voice, he asked, "or jealous?"

The compliment caught Liz off-guard. She bit her lip and said nothing.

Ty asked, "What about your father?"

"I don't think he saw me as a girl. I never could get away with the big eyes and sweet face to get what I wanted. He'd get so angry." She could see, hear and feel it again. Liz blinked back some tears. "He was volatile. I never knew what would set him off."

"Did he hit you?"

She nodded. "A couple of times. Usually after he'd been drinking or had an argument with my mother. He had a vicious backhand that could knock me off my feet. Mostly, though, he just screamed and then wouldn't speak to me for days. Wouldn't listen to my apologies and wouldn't apologize if he was wrong. I didn't date, so there were never boys calling or coming around to take me out. One day, my father came out and asked me if I was a lesbian or just frigid like my mother," She dashed the tears away from her eyes. "That just about killed me."

She looked at Ty. "I guess we all have our demons, huh?" Ty just nodded silently.

They sat for a couple of minutes, the only sounds coming from the radio and the rain. Neither looked at the other until Liz stood up, reaching for a candle.

"Where are you going?" asked Ty.

"Kitchen. I have a gas stove and I'm going to make some tea. I think we could both do with some." Before Liz could get more than a couple of steps from the table, Ty was on his feet, gently pushing her back into her chair.

"Did I ever tell you that I was a Rhodes Scholar?" he said. "Believe me, you spend enough time in Britain, you learn how to make a pot of tea." He squeezed her shoulders. "I'll take care of this." Liz told him where to find everything and Ty disappeared into the kitchen again, taking the candle from her hand.

Liz put her feet up on the chair and hugged her knees. Rainy weather made the old healed breaks in her leg and ankle ache and tonight was no exception. It always reminded why they'd happened in the first place. She hugged her knees even tighter. She told herself that Ty was probably embarrassed and wanted to be alone in the kitchen right now. Liz would give him that space.

"Find everything?" she called out to him. "Want some help?"

"No, I'm doing just fine," he called back. "Just stay put."

Yeah, he wanted to be alone.

Liz fiddled with the dial of the radio, trying to find a station that was coming in clearly and with something worth listening to. She bypassed country, classic rock, oldies, rap, classical, talk radio, show tunes and folk in search of something suitable. She found a station she'd never listened to playing Diana Krall. "Popsicle Toes."

Ty came in from the kitchen carrying a makeshift tray containing a mug, teapot and another bottle of beer. He cocked his head and listened to the music for a minute. "Sounds like our friend Diana," he remarked.

"It is. I love this song. I don't remember her playing this one that night we saw her," said Liz. She was still balled up in the chair. Ty sat down and looked at her.

"Are you cold, Liz?" he asked. He leaned over and touched her forehead. "Got popsicle toes to be unfroze?" He playfully grabbed her toes. Liz immediately stiffed and he withdrew his hand as quickly.

"I'm fine, I swear. The weather makes my leg ache where it was broken. For some reason, this feels like the thing to do."

If Ty took these comments at anything other than face value, his expression didn't reveal it. He poured out tea for Liz.

"You know, not every man wants to hurt you." Ty said.

"I know." He had noticed. "The storm makes me jittery."

"Just the storm?" She looked at him. "You're sitting there in almost a fetal position, I notice you shake or remove yourself every time I touch you, you don't initiate contact unless you're unaware of what you're doing and you act like you're dying to get away from me. So is it all men or," he swallowed some beer, "just me?" He was watching her face closely.

Liz was silent, bracing herself against remembered pain. "No, not you," she whispered. She found herself continuing. "High school was a nightmare," she began. "I was the first girl in my class to develop breasts and," she motioned towards her chest, "that made me a target. From junior high on, the boys thought it was hysterical to try to grab them or grab at my crotch." She could still feel the hands, feel herself slapping at them. "When I was a junior, someone started a rumor that I'd said I'd take on the basketball team. Whether they believed it or not, I don't know, but some of the guys cornered me one day."

She inhaled, still feeling the terror and humiliation. Liz had tried so hard to forget this memory, but it was so deeply imprinted in her memory, she still relived it, sometimes waking up crying and screaming.

"What happened?" asked Ty. He reached for her hand. "It's okay. You're not in high school anymore. They can't hurt you now. Maybe it'll help if you tell me. I won't tell anyone, I swear."

Liz looked at him, seeing concern and compassion on his face. She continued. "They backed me into a corner in a hall where people didn't go very often. A couple of them started rubbing against me with their hard-ons. The leader had his fly unzipped and…" she closed her eyes, bile rising from the fear, "he grabbed my hand and used it to jerk off." Unconsciously, she tried to rub the non-existent semen from her hand. "He said if I told the principal, they'd come back and rape me." Her breathing was ragged, she was shaking.

Liz felt herself being pulled into his arms. She didn't resist. His embrace was powerful, crushing, warm and comforting. She buried her face into his shirt. Her shirt on his body. She thought she felt his lips against her hair. She shivered and he released her.

"I'm sorry, I shouldn't have done that," Ty said softly, "I wasn't thinking." He brushed his fingers against her face. "You didn't tell your folks, did you?"

Liz nodded. "Not everything. My mother said 'that's what happens when you wave your tits around.'"

"You never said anything to the principal, either, I'll bet."

Liz shook her head. "No, but Joey DiNardo heard them talk about it. He and Rocco beat the shit out of those guys one by one. The one who had," she groped for a phrase, "'used' my hand, they hit between the legs with a tire iron."

"I got off easy, I guess," said Ty with a smile. "Did that end it?"

"No," Liz said flatly, "The in-crowd girls toyed with me. When Senior Prom came around, they arranged for the boy I had a crush on to ask me to go. I was so excited," Liz could feel the tears rising. "I raided my savings account and bought a beautiful dress. I spent two hours getting ready." Liz looked at Ty, a bitter smile on her face. "My father just stood there and looked relieved. He'd asked me the lesbian question a couple of months earlier. I was waiting upstairs so I could make my big entrance. And I waited for 3 hours."

"Never showed, did he?" Ty asked quietly.

"No," Liz whispered. "But his picture was in the paper the next day because he and his real date had been crowned King and Queen. When I went back to school the first day afterward, the boys had stupid grins on their faces and the girls would look at me and giggle. They wanted me to cry. I wouldn't do it. I wanted to die, but I didn't want them to have the satisfaction of knowing it."

"No, you wouldn't, would you? When was the last time you cried, Counselor?" Ty was looking at her, studying her face.

"When the ball rolled through Bill Buckner's legs." Liz reluctantly pushed away and picked up her mug and sipped. "Good tea."

It was a way to let an unpleasant subject drop. Ty looked like he wanted to discuss it some more, but he let it drop.

The doorbell rang. Liz gave Beanie a withering look to keep him in his chair. He stayed.

Ty moved towards the front door. Liz heard him open the door and admit Fred. She heard the men exchange the usual sort of

84

conversation that people engage in when a delivery of food arrives. Liz went to the breakfront and pulled a number of painted glass dishes out of the cabinet. By touch, she found placemats, napkins and silverware. She and Ty returned to the table at the same time.

He looked at her burden. "What's that?" He spied the silverware and a disdainful expression crossed his face. "Forks for Chinese food? Unthinkable!"

"Look, no matter how I try, I've never gotten the hang of chopsticks and I thought 'what the hell, let's use the good stuff,'" Liz replied. "After all, Katie here could huff and puff and blow the house down."

Ty laughed quietly. He unloaded cartons from a plastic bag. One carton caused him to frown. "Hey, this one seems kind of light."

"That's the Beanie Box," Liz said. She quickly set out the placemats and china. Ty picked up a plate and examined it in the candlelight. "This is unusual. What is it?" He turned the plate over in his hands.

"It's Sydenstricker from the Cape," Liz answered. "I inherited a few settings from my mother and I've managed to collect a few more over time." She leaned in to point out a feature of the dish. "See? They paint the pattern on one piece of glass, put another piece over it, fire them both and you get the pattern inside a glass sandwich." Ty seated himself and began serving himself from cartons. Liz poured soup into an iris-decorated bowl for herself. She eyed one bulging box.

"Spare ribs?" Ty offered the box. Liz took a couple. Beanie started to get on the table.

"Hey!" Liz's yell was sharp. Beanie retreated, the picture of offended dignity.

Ty looked at him. "Is he going to sit there for the entire meal?" he asked as he licked sauce from his fingers, something Liz wanted to do for him. Instead, she covered with action.

"No. Watch this," Liz took the Beanie Box and opened it slightly, leaving the wire handle up. She placed the box nearer to Beanie than any of the other cartons. Beanie' whiskers began to twitch as he sniffed. Liz saw him lick his chops.

"Okay, now pretend you're not watching," she told Ty. Ty turned his head slightly, pretending to busy himself with egg rolls.

Liz spooned up a mouthful of soup.

Beanie struck. With a lightning-fast paw, he grabbed the Beanie Box and hauled it into range. He finished opening the carton with a combination of paws and teeth and seized his prize. He dove under the table with his spare rib. Liz could hear him chewing. Ty was leaning back and laughing. He applauded.

"Very good, Counselor. I wasn't expecting a floor show with dinner. What does he do for an encore, plate spinning?" The radio began to play Dave Brubeck's rendition of "These Foolish Things."

Liz scooped some rice and cashew chicken onto her plate. As she went to pick up her fork, Ty stopped her, his hand on hers.

"Chopstick school is now in session. No forks. Here. Watch closely."

He picked up a pair of chopsticks. "See how this one just sits? Now look."

He exaggerated placing the second stick between his forefinger and middle finger. "Just like holding a pencil. You try."

Liz awkwardly picked up the second pair of sticks, one eye on Ty's hand as she tried to mimic the way he was holding his chopsticks.

"No. You're gripping too hard. Just relax," Ty put down his chopsticks and took hold of Liz's hand. The touch caused her to inhale sharply. Ty looked at her and let go.

"All right, look, if this is going to bother you, never mind," he said. "The last thing I want to do is make you uncomfortable."

Liz reached for his hand. "No, look, please. You're right, not everyone wants to hurt me. I've just been on the defensive for so long, it's a reflex." She didn't mention that his touch had caused a shock wave of desire throughout her body.

Ty took her hand again and gently shook out the tension. "Okay, now, relax. Good." His tone was calming, gentle.

"Okay, now pick up that piece of chicken and give it to me."

Liz picked up the chicken, dropped it, then picked it up again. She started to transfer it to Ty's plate, but he took hold of her hand and guided it to his mouth. Liz felt him take the chicken from her chopsticks, their eyes locked on each other. This isn't happening, she thought. This is foreplay. He can't possibly…

Ty's voice cut her train of thought. "Sorry," he said with a grin,

"I got hungry." He still held her hand. "See? You can do it." He gently squeezed her hand. He let go to pick up his chopsticks and continue eating.

Liz's nerveless fingers almost dropped her chopsticks again. She didn't dare look up at him, focusing on her food instead.

"How'd you get to be such a chopstick expert, Ty?" she asked, tension raising her voice an octave.

If he noticed, he ignored it. "Lots of nights at work. I think we run a tab at the local take out place."

Liz blushed. "I'm sorry. I didn't think you might be sick of…"

He cut her off. "Actually, this is a lot better than the stuff I usually eat. What's the name of this place again?"

"Green Dragon Wall," Liz busied herself with the chopsticks, successfully putting chicken into her mouth. "I have to remember to ask Roger if they want to make another donation this year."

"Excuse me?" Ty looked at her curiously. "Donation?"

Liz nodded. "Yeah, for the auction at the Barrister's Ball. In fact," she added, "I was going to work on the stuff tonight."

"What stuff? It looked like there were items on your spare bed…"

"I have a bunch of the items upstairs," Liz said, "Dan volunteered me for the auction committee after they'd asked him to do it. We started getting donations early and I need to inventory them. You must have seen them when you hung up your clothes." She paused, wondering how far she dared to go. "I suppose I could do it tomorrow, but" she eyed Ty, "I'll need to clear off that for you, anyway." God, that sounded lame and prissy.

Eyebrows up, Ty asked, "Is that an invitation to spend the night, Counselor?" There was a teasing edge to his voice.

Liz didn't dare look at him. Eyes down on her plate, blushing, she said, "I'm not sending you out on a night like this. I take care of my friends."

"So," Ty said softly, "you see us as friends?"

Liz looked at him. She wasn't prepared to explain her feelings for him. "Well, I guess. You brought me all the way back to Salem when you didn't have to…"

"So you wouldn't think it might be because I had an ulterior motive?" Ty interjected. Liz looked at him, startled. He was watching her intently.

"No, I wouldn't," she said flatly. "I'm not the kind of woman who inspires ulterior motives."

Ty snorted and mumbled something that sounded like, "Guess again." He looked down at his plate for a moment, scowling in thought. Liz thought he looked a little frustrated, but she had no idea why.

Ty just stared at her. "So you honestly believe I'm here because of friendship and kindness?" he asked with an edge, "Not for any other reason?"

Liz's eyes never left his face as she nodded. "I absolutely do," she answered, almost as quietly. "From what I've seen, you're basically a good, kind man in a cutthroat profession."

Ty looked down for a minute and whispered something Liz didn't quite catch, but almost sounded like "No one's ever said that to me."

A thick silence fell for a moment. Neither could look the other in the eye. Liz decided she had to act fast before it became too awkward.

She waved at the storm still howling outside. "If the power's out, it could be a downed line and branches, the street lights aren't going to be working and it's just too dangerous. Here, you're safe, it's warm, we have food…"

"…the place smells like an apple pie," he interjected. "I accept. Truth be told," he said as he cut an egg roll in half and handed part to Liz, "I was hoping you'd ask. I'd have just gone back to my house and been by myself. It is rotten out there, we've got good food, the music's great and I like the company. This is as close as I've gotten to a birthday party in years. Here," he handed her the mustard, "this'll clear up your sinuses."

Liz gingerly dabbed the hot mustard on her egg roll. "What do you normally do on a Saturday night, Ty?"

He chewed for a moment, "Depends. Usually, I'm entertaining clients or attending office functions. Other than that, I work at home. How about you?"

Liz shrugged, "Not much, really. Once a month, the gang comes over for dinner and a movie. I'll go to clubs like Scullers if someone's playing that I want to hear, but other than that, it's pretty quiet."

"Maybe we could go together some night," Ty offered.

Before she could respond, the radio DJ announced "And we have a request going out tonight. The gold standard. The one, the only Miss Etta James performing 'At Last'." Liz and Ty glanced at each other. Ty wiped his lip and stood up.

"Dance with me," he murmured.

"What?" Liz wasn't sure she'd heard him correctly. He repeated himself.

Liz shook her head. "I'm not much of a dancer, really."

Ty grabbed her hand and hauled Liz to her feet. "Nonsense. I'll have you burning the dance floor in no time. Besides," he said as he pulled her close, "you'll need to know how for the Barrister's Ball, right?"

"I wasn't going to go," she said.

"What? After all the work you're doing? Why not?" he asked.

"My friends are all paired up and I'm not comfortable being the odd woman out at those things." She felt a hollowness in her chest as she said it.

Ty tilted her face up to look at his. "I've never been to one, either, but I'll go if you go." He smiled. "This'll be the prom you didn't have."

Liz hardly breathed. Ty held her away in formal dance fashion, one hand at her waist, daylight between their bodies, the other hand holding hers. Liz put her hand on his shoulder, feeling the muscles underneath.

"Now," he said, "look me in the eye. Don't watch our feet. If you trust me, this'll work. Unless Beanie trips us again, I promise I won't hurt you."

Liz looked into his eyes as directed and was mesmerized by the warmth she saw there. She felt his eyes searching hers, for what, she couldn't fathom. The urge to lay her head on his shoulder and let him pull her tight against his body again was enormous, but Liz reminded herself that he hadn't invited that intimate touch. They made a small circle around the floor, exhaled breath mingling, bare feet occasionally brushing each other. Each time, Liz felt a small shock from the contact and a desire to press a kiss on his lips. She bit her lip to keep herself in check. The song ended and they stopped moving, still holding each other. Liz was the first to step away. She was about to thank him when a particularly vicious blast of lightning struck, deafening thunder on top of it.

Liz couldn't tell if she threw herself against Ty or if he pulled her in, but his arms were wrapped around her tightly. She wound her arms around his body and pressed her face against his shoulder. He tightened his hold even more, murmuring wordlessly. She felt him slowly stroke her back. She began to relax. In a minute, she was able to step away from him. Reluctantly.

"Thank you," she said, almost in a whisper.

"You're welcome," he whispered back. He swallowed and assumed a light tone, "The advanced course includes a dip, but I don't think you're quite ready for that."

As he seated himself, Liz thought she caught Ty checking out her cleavage. She drew back quickly, lest he see too much. She quickly buttoned her shirt a little higher.

"Liz? Are you cold?" Ty had seen her cover up.

"Maybe a little."

"Here, more tea will warm you up." Liz held out her mug. "Yes, please." She looked into the mug and made a decision.

"Earlier, when you asked me about being sick, I wasn't truthful," she started, looking into the mug.

"I know," he replied quietly, "but I understand now why you're not very trusting. It's okay."

Liz took a deep breath. "When Beanie found me, I had just had my first chemotherapy treatment." She looked at Ty. "I had breast cancer. My HMO wasn't very good and the surgeon was inexperienced. The surgery scarred me pretty badly and the HMO wouldn't cover plastic surgery to repair the damage."

He was sitting still, staring at her. "Are you okay now?"

Liz nodded. "Clear as a bell, but…" she motioned to her chest, "nothing Hugh Hefner would want in his magazine. It's been an issue a couple of times."

"An issue? With…?" Ty left the question hanging.

"With dates," she looked at Ty, almost defiant. "The scars have ended more than one relationship for me. The man I thought was my boyfriend bailed when I was diagnosed." Her expression became bitter, "Real cute. Had this stupid-ass grin on his face, you know, thought he'd be funny and I'd forgive him. Said he'd always preferred double-breasted suits and that went for women, too." She looked away. "I remember I was thinking about that remark as the anesthesia began to work." She shrugged off the memory and continued. "I found out that I was just 'convenient.'" She deliberately chose the word and watched Ty wince. "He had another girl who meant more to him, I guess.

"Afterwards, one date accidentally saw the scar when my sweater slipped and he left me at the restaurant we'd gone to. It took me until now to realize that maybe being on my own isn't so bad. When I was younger, you know, I'd always seen myself as being married and having a big, happy, noisy family at this point..."

"You still could, maybe not big, but..." Ty interrupted.

Liz shook her head, "I guess it just wasn't in the cards. I've had enough pain and rejection in my life. I don't want to risk any more."

They sipped their tea until Ty broke the silence again.

"Tell me something," he asked as he poured out some more, "Is there something going on between you and your friend DiNardo?"

"No," Liz shook her head.

Ty set down the teapot, "Was there?"

Liz made a face. "Ew, no."

"Why?" Ty asked. He was leaning on one elbow as he listened. Beanie, having devoured both of his ribs, tried to sneak onto the table for more. Ty pointed a finger at him and Beanie settled himself onto his chair, cleaning sauce off his face.

Liz laughed. "Joey and Tony DiNardo are the closest thing I have to brothers. We grew up next door to each other. Their mom taught me how to cook. I spent my summers and weekends working in their restaurant down in Hyannis after they moved; the whole family did." She smiled. "Angie just gets bent out of shape when I improve on her recipes. Of course, she sticks with the changes I make." Liz sipped her tea. Thinking about her adoptive mother always made her smile.

"At least it's got you smiling again," Ty commented, "I was afraid I was going to have to do a walrus impression with the chopsticks to make you laugh. I don't even want to think about splinter risk. Here." He handed Liz a fortune cookie. "It's my birthday, so I chose first."

Liz broke open her cookie and read it out loud, squinting in the soft light, "'your destiny lies before you. Choose wisely'."

"Sounds promising. Let's see what I got," said Ty, "Hey, I got the same one."

"You did not, let me see," said Liz.

Ty held out the slip of paper triumphantly. "There. See?" he said. "Nyah." Ty stuck out his tongue at her.

Liz giggled as she read the paper slip. Indeed, his fortune was the same. "Son of a gun," said Liz, "I wonder what the odds are on that." Was this a sign?

"Still hungry?" she asked Ty.

"Maybe," he said cautiously. Liz rose. She gathered up the dishes to take into the kitchen and realized that she couldn't handle them and a candle. "Want some help?" asked Ty. "I notice you don't ask for it, even when you need it." He was on his feet already, gathering up cartons and candle. Beanie took a swipe at the now-empty rib box, hoping to make one last big score before calling it quits. He missed. Liz and Ty went into the kitchen. She rinsed off dishes and he piled the cartons on the counter. With a smile, Liz took the empties and put them in the garbage. The ones still containing food were off-loaded into plastic storage boxes. Liz noticed that Ty didn't really seem to know what to do. She took the candle from him and opened the refrigerator door, quickly slipping leftovers in, removing a small covered dish and fending off Beanie all at the same time. "Why don't you start some more tea?" she suggested to Ty.

He looked at the dish. "What's that?" he asked as he refilled the tea kettle.

"Dessert, if you want it," she answered.

"I do." He put the kettle on a lit burner. "Who does your cooking for you?" he asked.

What an odd question. "I do," said Liz. "What about you?"

Ty shrugged, "I spend most of my time at the office so I eat out a lot," he said.

"I see," she said, "And when you're home?"

"I have 5 cuisines on speed dial."

"Cleaning lady?" Liz probed.

"Full-time housekeeper," he answered. Ty shrugged again. "I'm not really all that domesticated, I guess."

"Well, you're busy. I can see needing the help." Liz said.

The kettle began to whistle and Ty prepared another pot of tea.

"Hey, at least I can boil water and soak leaves," he said with a smile. Liz laughed. They returned to the dining room and seated themselves.

"Okay, Counselor," Liz said as she uncovered the dish and scooped out a generous portion. She passed the dish to Ty, who examined it warily.

"This is my tiramisu," said Liz. "I was going to take some into the office on Monday, but with the power being iffy, I'd rather feed it to someone than have to dump it."

Ty spooned up a bigger portion. "So this is the stuff you claim is so much better than the top restaurants in Boston, huh?" He was digging in with gusto.

"Did I lie?" Liz asked.

Ty looked at her and smiled, "No, by God, yours is better. This birthday's getting better."

Liz grabbed the nearest candle. "Here," she instructed, "make a wish and blow it out. I'm not going to sing or YOU'LL end up crying."

Ty laughed, paused and blew out the candle. He scooped up another mouthful of tiramisu.

"Want to be my personal chef? Gotta beat the hell out of being Dan's ghost writer," Ty offered.

Liz laughed even harder. "I think I have as much as I can handle, job-wise, right now. But I'll tell you what, it's no fun to make something special just for myself. I'd be happy to make dinner for you sometime."

Ty was thoughtful as he mouthed the dessert. "Let's see, I taste coffee, brandy, I think, chocolate and something I can't identify." He swallowed. "What's the secret ingredient?"

She noticed he ignored the dinner offer. "If I told you…"

"It wouldn't be a secret. I know," he finished. Ty took another mouthful. "I love this stuff."

After they'd cleared dishes and secured the fire, Liz led Ty upstairs. In the spare room, Liz set down her candle on a night table and Ty followed suit. The light cast long, flickering shadows over the room and over an eclectic assortment of items on the bed. "And here we have the loot for the auction," Liz announced.

"What's the charity this year?" Ty asked as he picked up a framed piece.

"Breast cancer, so this one's close to my heart," Liz replied. "We're supporting the Bay State Breast Cancer Foundation and I see you have what I think is the star item in your hand."

Ty cocked an eyebrow at her. "Really? Looks like a framed album cover."

"It is, but do you see all those black squiggly lines?" Liz asked. Ty nodded. "Aerosmith."

Ty was clearly impressed. "Really? How'd you do that?"

"Corey used to babysit for either Steven Tyler's kids or Joe Perry's kids. I forget which and I shouldn't because he brags about it often enough. Anyway, Steven Tyler was wicked funny. He said that they'd seen plenty of breasts over the years and it was a pleasure to support them." Ty laughed so hard, he almost dropped the cover.

Liz picked up a fielder's glove and bat. "Check these out."

Ty carefully put down the album to examine the gear. "Whose?" he asked. Liz thought he was beginning to look like a kid in a candy store. "The ball is signed by the 2004 Sox, the glove by Yaz and the bat was given by Carlton Fisk. The grandmother of one of the guys in our firm lived next door to the Fisks in New Hampshire." Liz saw Ty's face become reverent as he handled not only the baseball gear, but also a basketball signed by Larry Bird, a Cam Neely hockey puck with Ray Bourque stick and a John Hannah helmet. "What's that?" he pointed to more framed artwork in the corner. Liz carefully removed one item.

"Let's see. This is a poster from that movie that was shot here." She looked at Ty, "You know, I love how in touch Hollywood is: the writer makes a reference to Scollay Square. The knucklehead actor didn't even learn how to pronounce it right." She smiled and shook her head. "However, I think he did manage to spell his name correctly when he signed the poster with the rest of the cast. On the block it goes. We have a couple more from other movies shot in the area." She returned the poster and put the album in the corner with it.

Ty was looking through a packet of envelopes. "What are these, gift certificates?"

"Yup. Restaurants, weekend getaways, tickets for some of the museums…"

"This one says an afternoon of shooting," Ty was frowning at the envelope.

"Oh, that must be Dean, Dodge and Weis," Liz said quickly. "I believe they represent Glock and Gun Owners of America. Someone bids high enough, you've got the Warren Zevon package." She waited for the question.

It didn't come. "Lawyers, Guns and Money. Very good," said Ty with a grin. "It's an impressive collection you've assembled."

"I am Woman. I get shit done," quipped Liz.

Ty smiled."Maybe you should put that on a T shirt." He looked at another envelope. "This one says tiramisu from Elizabeth Gardner."

Liz nodded. "Last year, it went for $50. My co-workers buy it and we have a little party with it."

Ty nodded, but said nothing. Beanie jumped up on the bed and sprawled to his fullest length in the middle just because he could again. Liz gently removed him. "C'mon, You. I don't think Ty wants to share his bed tonight." The thought caused a pang.

She heard Ty murmur something behind her that sounded somewhat like "not with the cat, but…"

She turned around. "I'm sorry, did you say something?"

"Just thinking out loud," he said. "Don't worry about it."

Liz picked up her candle. She wanted him, badly. But there was no way she would risk the rejection. "The extra toothbrushes are on the second shelf of the medicine cabinet. Goodnight Ty. I guess I'll see you in the morning."

"Are you going to be okay with the storm going on?" She nodded. "Good. I think I can do this now without throwing you into a panic," Ty put one arm around her and kissed the side of her face. "Thank you for a great birthday." He kissed her cheek again, but closer to her mouth. "Thank you for looking out for me. And," this time he brushed his lips across hers. "thank you for being my friend. Goodnight, Liz. Sleep well." He closed the door after her.

Rather than go to her own room, Liz stood outside the door. It was almost physically impossible to make herself walk down the hall to her own bedroom, so powerful was the drive to reopen that door and make love to Ty. Thunder rumbled distantly and Liz made her way down the hall to her own room. The night passed in fitful sleep, interrupted by vague dreams and noise from the receding storm.

By the time Liz woke, the storm was gone and so was Ty.

Chapter 5

Liz looked around, eyeing the Christmas decorations. Unadorned, the Great Hall of the World Trade Center was a chilly, homely, industrially bleak space with slick gray concrete floors, sentinel-like support beams and walls of a bland white shade. Most of the time, it was a depressing and intimidating place and therefore made the perfect location for the annual July administration of the Massachusetts Bar Exam.

But tonight, the Great Hall was decked out in Christmas finery. The columns had been surrounded either by beautifully decorated Christmas trees, for those near the temporary parquet dance floor, or been wrapped in fresh Christmas greens and twinkling lights. The smell was heavenly. The walls had been covered in black cloth that had been rigged with tiny lights to give a starlit night effect. More lights hung from the ceiling or were hung in ficus trees scattered around the floor. Various bars and food stations with different cuisines were set up around the perimeter of the party area (of course, the all-you-can-eat shrimp cocktail station got the most business). A dance band was busy warming up on a stage erected next to the dance floor. This was where the auction would be conducted.

Liz nodded as she looked around. The transformation could almost make her forget sitting here for four days in two successive Julys, sweating bullets and staving off panic. Almost.

Liz made her way to the area behind the bandstand. Partitions had been put up to store the auction items until they were put on the block. Now that they weren't occupying space in her house, she was impressed with the loot. Liz nodded to the other committee members who were cataloguing and tagging last-minute donations. One of the men looked up, surprise on his face. "Look who made it this year," he remarked, smiling. "I don't know how you did it, but we've got more and better stuff this year than we have in five years."

"Thanks, it does look like a good haul," Liz said, "Has anyone heard from our emcees? They should have been here by now."

"I got a call about an hour ago. They wanted to stop off for a quick bite to eat first. Don't worry, Liz, they'll be here, it'll go off without a hitch and we'll raise a ton of money."

Liz smiled at the speaker, "Thanks, Jack." She had arranged for a popular local morning radio team to act as emcees for the auction. The AMbeciles, hearing that the auction was to raise money for breast cancer research, volunteered their services free of charge. They were also able to persuade some local celebrities to donate additional memorabilia.

Looking at a table laden with items, Liz's eye fell on a gift certificate envelope. Dinner for two at the Top of the Hub. She got lost in the memory of a beautiful sunset, a female voice singing "At Last" and staring into Tyrone's eyes.

The thought made her look around. He had promised to be here tonight, she thought. She'd believed it enough to spend a small fortune on a dress and shoes. Sometimes, you had to show a little faith.

"Okay, Larry, Jack, Annamarie, I spent too much on this dress to hide back here with you, so I'm going to mingle, make sure people have had enough to drink so that they'll bid recklessly and wait for the fun to start. Find me when the AMbeciles get here."

Larry saluted. "Will do. And you are lookin' good tonight, Liz. Save me a dance."

Liz beamed, "Thanks, Larry. I will if it's okay with your wife." And she left in search of Millie, John, Corey and her gang.

The crowd was getting thick enough to make spotting people somewhat difficult. Liz was scanning the crowd when she heard the voice behind her and felt a strong, masculine hand on her bare shoulder. Even if he hadn't spoken, she'd have known Ty's touch.

"Counselor."

Liz turned to see Ty standing behind her.

"Counselor. You kept your word." She returned the greeting and took in the sight. The Barrister's Ball was a black tie event. As good as this man looked in a beat-up flannel shirt, grass-stained softball clothes or blue business suit, he was devastating in a tux. However, in addition to the tux, it could be said that he was wearing the Silicone Queen since she had both hands wrapped around his right arm possessively and, as usual, was staring at Liz with naked hostility.

"I did, Liz," Ty said. His eyes took her in from head to foot. "And I see you held up your end. You look beautiful."

Liz watched the Silicone Queen's eyes narrow and her grip on Ty's arm tighten.

Ty responded by gently prying her hands loose and saying, "Cheryl, I want to talk to Attorney Gardner. Why don't you go get a drink? I think I saw Jimmy over by the bar."

The Silicone Queen started to protest, stopped when she saw his face and shot one more murderous look at Liz before sashaying off to the nearest bar. Liz glanced at Ty and noticed that, unlike the softball game, he didn't watch her leave. His eyes were on Liz.

"So tell me, Liz," Ty began, "How did you do with donations for the auction?"

Safe topic, thought Liz. "We did extraordinarily well," she said, "In fact, I was surprised at some of the donations that came in during the last couple of weeks because I hadn't approached the donors. I don't suppose you had anything to do with that?"

Ty ducked his head and chuckled. As always, the sound generated a nifty little thrill in Liz. "Guilty. It was my fault you got stuck with this. I wanted to help."

"I see Ray White donated tickets for the Celts / Lakers game next month. How'd you pull that off?" Liz asked.

Ty grinned, "That was Mrs. White's doing. She's had enough of Ray and Sal Randazzo's running courtroom drama, so when Ray's season tickets came in, she took the Lakers tickets. Carla says he only whimpered for two days," Ty explained. The grin receded as he added quietly, "Besides, Carla White's a breast cancer survivor."

"I see. I'll have to thank her personally," Liz replied. She smiled, "She and Barbara Randazzo think alike."

Ty cocked his head, "What did Sal, uh, 'donate?'"

"His brand new set of Calloway golf clubs. Barbara said he sulked for a week. Guess he's not as good a sport as Ray White."

They were still laughing when the Silicone Queen returned armed not only with drinks but with a small crowd of people whom Liz recognized from the softball game, mostly women. They quickly moved in between Ty and Liz and effectively ended their conversation. As Liz turned to walk away, her eyes briefly met those of the Silicone Queen, who smiled in catty triumph. Liz smiled pleasantly at her, looked back at Ty, caught his eye, waved and left.

You know, Liz thought, a drink might not be such a bad idea. Liz spotted John, Millie and Corey standing in front of a bar not too far away. Corey was holding an extra drink in his hand which he held out to Liz as she approached.

Champagne. With a memory of Diana Krall, an intimate set at Regattabar and Ty wrapping her up in his jacket because he thought her shivers were from being cold. That memory was quickly replaced by the Silicone Queen's victorious sneer.

Liz remembered her manners. "Corey, thank you. Any good?" She sipped. "By the way, I love the tie. Clearly, black tie is open to interpretation these days."

Corey adjusted his royal blue and gold star-patterned bow tie with a smirk. "My cummerbund is black and that's tied around my waist. As for the wine," he waved dismissively, "Don't get excited. It's from upstate New York."

Liz laughed. "Snob."

Corey snapped his fingers, "Honey, I go first class or not at all. Speaking of which," he walked around Liz inspecting her thoroughly, "You do make an entrance, Ms. Gardner. You are first-class, deluxe, Who-Wore-What-to-the-Oscars looking fine, Miz Liz. Your fairy godmother must have worn out her wand beating on you. I'd approve, but you went shopping without me."

Liz's new gown was a midnight blue velvet strapless sheath, chosen after three Saks Fifth Avenue saleswomen had ganged up on her and emphatically vetoed the gowns she'd selected. It was cut high on the bust and dipped modestly in the back to a full-length skirt. She had complemented the dress with elbow-length gloves, a tasteful amount of rhinestone jewelry and a sequined clutch to add sparkle without going overboard, chosen by a fourth saleswoman who'd been attracted by the commotion. The deep blue in the gown set off her white skin and brought out the color of her eyes, they'd all told her. Perhaps they'd been right.

Millie nodded agreement, "He's right, Liz. If I didn't know you, I'd lay a death grip on John the way our friend there," she jerked her chin towards Ty's group and the Silicone Queen, "grabbed onto Hadley."

John added, "She made a beeline for him as soon as she saw him touch your arm."

Liz shrugged. "We were talking about the auction and suddenly the Berlin Wall of Bimbos went up between us." She looked at Millie, whose attention was focused elsewhere and mouthed, "It's a go" to John. He nodded and grinned, touching the pocket of his jacket.

"So," Corey asked "Did you hear from him after the night you didn't sleep together? Girl, you wasted such an opportunity."

"Shut up, Corey," said Millie. "Don't be a pig. But you should have jumped at the chance, Liz."

"It wasn't that kind of evening, guys," said Liz. "And not all intimacy is physical."

"Hmpf," snorted Corey. "Maybe not, but that's the best kind. You know," he said, looking at the Silicone Queen, "I don't get it."

"Don't get what, Corey?" Millie asked as she lifted her glass for a sip.

Corey gestured to Liz. "Well, our Liz here is class, brains, beauty, everything, dressed to kill and yet he's with that."

The Silicone Queen was wearing a blood-red halter mini-dress that showed almost more skin than it covered.

Corey murmured, "She brings three words to mind: tacky, tacky, tacky. Do you think there's a can of Aquanet Extra Hold left in the city? I mean, come on, that is big hair. The whole look is Trailer Park Barbie lives her Pretty Woman fantasy. Especially the streetwalking part."

Millie almost sprayed her drink while Liz was choking on hers. "Corey," Millie managed to rasp, "are you done being mean and spiteful for the moment?"

"Hmm," Corey thought about it for a moment, "One more thing and then, yes, I can do the peace on Earth, goodwill towards men jazz. Girls, have I got the dirt for you." Millie and Liz leaned in for the report. John gave an exasperated shrug and went back to the bar for a refill.

Liz whispered to Millie, "You know, we should be ashamed of ourselves for gossiping like this. It's unkind and un-Christmas and nosy."

Millie pretended to sigh, "Yeah, but it's a helluva lot of fun.

Make a note in your calendar to be ashamed later. Spill it, Corey."

He looked around, "Well, my sources – and they are of the highest reliability – tell me that our girlfriend, the SQ, hasn't been anywhere near Liz's man…"

"He's not my man, Corey," Liz protested.

Corey ignored her and continued, "since the softball game and she is PISSED. Seems he's cut off her access to his credit, his house, everything. And she blames Liz."

Millie and Liz regarded each other with raised eyebrows. "I don't know why she'd blame me," said Liz. "He's never made a pass at me."

"Sure about that, Liz?" asked Millie. "Maybe you just don't recognize them."

Out of the corner of her eye, Liz saw Ty, by himself, step up to the bar and exchange small talk with Judge McCafferty. Both men were smiling and seemed to be enjoying the conversation. Apparently, unlike Dan, Ty didn't hold grudges.

Liz felt a tap on her arm. She turned to find Joey and Jenna DiNardo, Rocco Metucci with his girl and several other friends from the firm. Liz forgot about Ty as she greeted people, chatted and laughed.

Feeling another tap on her arm, Liz turned to find herself face to face with Judge McCafferty. He had another older man with him whom Liz recognized as a Justice of the Supreme Judicial Court.

"Your Honors, this is a pleasant surprise. Good evening, Judge McCafferty," Liz greeted him, "and Justice Friedman, I believe." She shook hands with both men.

McCafferty held onto her hand and addressed Justice Friedman, "Bob, this is the little girl I've been telling you about. First, she took down Hadley on the ball field. Then she out-argues him in my courtroom and I find out she's the one who's been doing that idiot Dennis' writing. The kicker was when she let me have it for not hiring her." McCafferty sounded like a proud parent.

Justice Friedman looked at Liz. "You've been doing Dan Dennis' writing for him?" Liz just nodded. "Shoulda known. He spends more time on the golf course than in the courtroom. You do good work, young lady."

"Thank you, Sir, I think," said Liz.

Justice Friedman grinned. "Next time I have an opening for a clerk, I want you. You'd make me look awfully good."

McCafferty put his arm around Liz's shoulder. "With all due respect, Mr. Justice Friedman, buzz off. I saw her first." With that, Friedman excused himself and McCafferty turned his undivided attention to Liz.

"Well, my dear, I see the eye healed up nicely and I didn't throw Hadley's butt in jail. Not bad for a bully, eh, Lass?" McCafferty looked pleased with himself.

"With all due respect, Your Honor, you are outrageous and I'll probably deeply regret giving you hell," said Liz shaking her head and laughing. "Can I get you another drink, Judge?"

"No, thank you. I just got myself a ginger ale and I'm all set. As for regretting giving me hell, maybe, maybe not: time will tell," said McCafferty.

"Oh, come on, Judge, Ty and I are on friendly terms, but I don't think there's anything more to it than that nor will there be." Liz succeeded in keeping the disappointment out of her voice.

McCafferty studied her face with a shrewd, knowing expression and changed the subject.

"Listen, my dear, I know you probably don't want to talk shop right now…"

Liz smiled, "I'm probably the only one here who isn't trying to cut some sort of deal tonight, so please, go ahead. I don't want to feel left out."

McCafferty laid a hand on her shoulder, "How would you like that clerkship with me? I've got an opening coming up in the beginning of January and I want you to have it."

Liz was astonished. "You're kidding. Don't you have to conduct interviews or something like that?"

McCafferty waved his hand, "I'm a fucking loon, remember? I do as I damn well please and I want to have you on my team. Listen, you work with me for a year or two until I retire and I guarantee you can write your own ticket. I know, I know, most lawyers look at this as entry-level and it is. But, you're going nowhere with Dennis, he's not paying you anywhere near what he should – I know, I checked and he's exploiting you. I'd be exploiting you, too, but at much better pay, you'd be more visible as my clerk and actually laying the foundation for a good career instead of a dead-end job covering Danny Boy's hairy white ass for a wage that's downright insulting. What do you say?"

Liz blinked. "I'd need to think about it. Judge, to be honest, I'm really not all that fond of practicing law."

McCafferty was not dissuaded. "How about teaching? Think you could train the up-and-comers to do it right? You'd still be in the catbird seat if you come with me." He patted her shoulder. "Think about it, Lass. You'd get to do the parts of the law you enjoy, leave the dirty work to me and you'd have fun on the job. One more thing," he pointed upwards. Liz followed the line of his finger and saw the mistletoe. McCafferty gave her a quick peck on the cheek. He leaned back, "You look lovely tonight, Elizabeth. I hope that man's got the eyes to see it." And he left.

Liz stood still for a moment and absorbed what had just happened. Instead of the door-to-door begging she had done to secure the crappy position she had, someone in a position of power and influence had just offered Liz a golden opportunity. The thought crossed her mind that maybe she ought to buy a lottery ticket.

Liz made her way back towards the bandstand only to be intercepted by excited and agitated committee members.

"Liz," Larry began, "we've got a problem." Liz felt cold dread clutch her stomach.

"What kind of problem? Is the auctioneer here?"

"Yeah," said Jack, "all set, warmed up and ready to go. It's the emcees."

"What about the emcees? Didn't they make it?" Liz asked warily.

Larry had been upset before, but now, "They're here, all right, but they're puking their guts out in the men's room."

"Bad sushi," Jack added.

Liz closed her eyes. "Oh, God. Where are we gonna get someone else? The auction's supposed to start in five minutes. One of you guys'll have to do it."

Larry turned grayish-white, "Liz, you're joking. Just the idea has me ready to go into the men's room and join the hurling." Liz looked at Jack, who shook his head. "No way, Liz, I'm not good at thinking on my feet."

"Jack, you're a trial attorney and you can't think on your

feet? How do your clients feel about that?" She was amazed at the cowardice. Nevertheless, Jack was adamant. "I'll stutter. You do it, Liz."

Liz was even more amazed. "Me? I wasn't planning on attending until a few weeks ago." The cold dread got colder. "No, no, a thousand times no."

"You can do it," said a familiar deep voice behind her.

Liz spun at hearing Ty, startled. "What?"

He smiled. "I said, 'you can do it.' Hell," he sipped from the glass in his hand. "You just smile and flash those baby blues of yours and all those hard hearted shysters will be eating out of your hand."

"Not after they watch me throw up on stage," Liz retorted. She shook her head. "I can't. I don't want to. Please, find someone else and leave me alone."

She started to turn back when he spoke again.

"I'll go up there with you."

"What?"

Ty repeated his offer with Jack and Larry adding their encouragement. "C'mon, Liz. You can do this." "Look, we really need you right now." "Seriously, Liz, you've gotta get up there."

It took a few minutes, but they wore her down and Liz finally agreed to go onstage with Ty.

She looked at Ty as he downed the last of his drink and handed off the glass. "You give me your hand and we'll do this thing together. Okay? Trust me." He took her arm. She felt the charge from the touch of his skin to hers, so powerful her knees almost buckled.

Liz gulped and nodded. "I guess so."

"Right." And he led her onto the stage.

Ty laughed and Liz relaxed somewhat. Maybe this wouldn't be so bad after all.

They met with the auctioneer and reviewed the procedures for conducting the auction. The guests of the Ball began to move from the various corners of the room to the area in front of the bandstand. While discussing logistics with the auctioneer, Liz watched the throng out of the corner of her eye. It looked like the entire population of Boston was in the room. Larry handed Liz a packet of cards with lot numbers and descriptions of offered items.

As she glanced through them, Larry whispered, "Thanks for doing this, Liz. You'll be fine." Liz fought the wave of panic that hit her.

She paused in her reading just long enough to give him a dirty look to go with, "Payback is a bitch, Larry. How are the AMbeciles?" She held out faint hope that they'd recovered.

He shook his head, "Still in the men's room and still sick as hell."

Ty put his arm around Liz and gave her a squeeze. "We don't need them," he said, "We can handle this, right, Counselor?" Liz didn't even look at him as she said, "From your mouth to God's ear, Counselor."

Since Liz wasn't looking at Ty, she felt instead of saw him brush his lips against her cheek and put his mouth near her ear to whisper, "Lighten up, Elizabeth. You're not facing a firing squad and I know you can do this. If you lose your nerve you lose the game, remember?" He kissed her cheek, softly and warmly, and said aloud, "For good luck. Ready?"

Liz had felt the first light kiss all the way to the soles of her feet. The second kiss had made itself felt in her stomach and heart. The arm around her shoulders was just a warm and friendly gesture, Liz told herself. She was fighting an urge to turn and wrap her arms around Ty and return his kiss.

"Okay, it's time," from the auctioneer.

Microphones were handed to Liz and Ty and they were on. Liz stepped forward and smiled at the faceless crowd. "Good evening and welcome to the 5th annual Barrister's Ball and Auction." This brought applause from the crowd and she was able to relax slightly.

"For those of you who were expecting the AMbeciles, we're sorry but they're under the weather..."

Ty jumped in, "...and probably in need of an attorney. Is there a personal injury lawyer in the house?" This got laughs. He continued, "For those of you who don't know us, I'm Tyrone Hadley of Brooks, Washburn, Hadley and Dunn and my lovely colleague here," There was thunderous applause, especially from the women present. He gestured to Liz, "Is Elizabeth Gardner of Lovell, Hoffman and Dennis." This got even more applause. Liz picked up the patter, inspired. She turned to Ty.

"You know, Counselor," she said, "This is where they've been holding the bar exam for the past few Julys."

"That's true," Ty replied. He looked at her curiously, knowing she had a point, but unsure of what it was.

"Well, I noticed some folks out there pointing out where they'd sat to take the exam," Liz continued, "Some of them were taking their friends to more than one spot, saying 'Okay, I was here the first time and the second time...'" she imitated someone giving a tour of spots on the floor. The audience laughed. "I noticed one guy, however, who almost covered the entire floor, but, you made it finally, didn't you?" She looked up and pretended to peer into the crowd for one particular face. Surprisingly, one man yelled back, "You're damned skippy! Five times and I made it!" This was met with more laughter and applause for the determined lawyer. Ty was chuckling beside her. Liz turned to him and he picked up the cue, reading from a card.

"The proceeds from tonight's sale will be going to the Bay State Breast Cancer Foundation. One in eight women will be diagnosed with this disease and the rate is increasing. Please bid high and bid often." The applause was louder. Liz exhaled slowly. This wasn't going to be so bad, after all. Then she heard the shouts.

"Hey, if this is for breast cancer, we want to see boobs! Show us your boobs!" came the drunken voices from the back of the crowd. Liz recognized one of them as Jimmy, the young lawyer from Ty's office. Ty started to say something but Liz cut him off.

"You want to see boobs, I'll get you boys a mirror," she retorted. This got appreciative laughter, applause and whistles from the rest of the crowd. The hecklers fell silent but Liz heard "Bitch" come from the back of the room. It was a female voice.

"Atta Girl. Don't mind Jimmy, he's loaded." Ty said in her ear. She felt him inhale deeply. She also smelled the Scotch on his breath. "You're wearing that great perfume again." His nearness was overpowering.

"Okay, Lot #1," Liz read from her card, voice shaking, "Donated by Cetaceans Unlimited of Gloucester, is a whale watch for four out of historic Gloucester Harbor. Let the stars of Stellwaggen Bank put on a show for you," Liz looked up from the card, "Bid high enough and they'll throw in the Dramamine." More laughter. And the auction was underway.

For the next two hours, Liz and Ty introduced items for sale, usually with some quip or joke to go with the item. Judge McCafferty, who had positioned himself near the foot of the stage, added to his donation at the last minute. He had originally given a trip for four, joining him in his box seats, for a Boston Red Sox home game against the New York Yankees. When Liz was announcing the package, McCafferty motioned Ty over and handed him an envelope. Ty grinned as he read what it contained.

"If the highest bid on this package goes over $2,500, His Honor, Judge Frank McCafferty, will include a free pass good to excuse the bearer from one contempt charge in his courtroom." This was met with enormous laughter and the Judge looked pleased. The lot went for $5,000 to a young lawyer who blurted, "I hope to God I don't need this" and Judge McCafferty said, "You will, Son, you will." The audience laughed and applauded.

Ty introduced the next item. "Lot Number 24, donated by Elizabeth Gardner," he looked at Liz who nodded, "is a tiramisu made by Attorney Gardner," here he looked at Liz again, "with her own two lovely hands." Ty picked up Liz's hand and kissed it. Photo flashes went off, capturing the moment. The audience whistled and hooted its approval. Ty kissed her hand again. Liz was too startled to do anything but smile.

Liz expected the tiramisu to fetch somewhere around $40 or $50, the usual. Liz stood back, expecting a brief round of bidding. Someone handed her a glass of water and she sipped while she waited.

As expected, the bidding started at $25 from someone Liz didn't know. Joey advanced the bid to $40.

"$100," said Ty in a firm voice. Liz almost choked on her water.

"Hey! You can't bid!" Joey protested. He glanced at Liz, who shrugged and looked bewildered.

Ty looked at him coolly. "I'm not the auctioneer, so yes I can."

"Guys, don't do this, please," she pleaded. Joe ignored her.

"$125," he said. He and the other members of Liz's gang had clearly banded together to ward off this interloper. She could see them discussing strategy.

"$150," from Frank McCafferty. There was a murmur from the non-bidding members of the audience. McCafferty's face said he was up to something, although exactly what, Liz wasn't sure.

"$250," answered Ty. "It's worth far more than that."

"$300," from Joe.

"$400," from McCafferty. Liz could hear gasps in the audience.

"$450," from Joe with the approval of his cohorts.

"$500," Ty announced. Liz and the auctioneer looked to Joe, who shook his head, but, Liz noted, he looked pleased with himself instead of disappointed at losing the bidding. McCafferty, too, shook his head with a smile. "Going once, going twice." No challenges. The auctioneer brought down his gavel with a crash, "Sold to the gentleman for $500. Congratulations, Sir."

The remainder of the auction was a blur as Liz kept asking herself why Ty had done it.

One item came up that Liz had wanted for herself since the donation was made. One dozen roses per week for a year. Following Ty's lead, she made a bid on it, but the item quickly went over her range to someone who had made arrangements for bidding by proxy. She applauded with the rest of the crowd and caught an odd look from Ty as she smiled.

Getaway weekends were sold and sports memorabilia. Corey's donation of a homemade sushi dinner for two caused the AMbeciles, who had managed to recover enough to watch the auction, to run back to the men's room at top speed, with an attorney in pursuit.

Without so much as a flicker of guilt, Dan Dennis bought Sal Randazzo's golf clubs. The Bad News Barristers pitcher won Millie's pitching lessons ("Good job!" yelled Ty, "Maybe we'll actually win next year."). As expected, the Aerosmith album cover went for thousands of dollars.

There was only one small sour note as the auction wound down. The last lot was a getaway weekend for two to a romantic Cape Cod hotel. The Silicone Queen had managed to work her way to the foot of the stage and had mouthed "get it for us" at Ty. Liz couldn't tell if he had noticed. The bidding was spirited, particularly among the men surrounding her, but Ty remained silent. Liz saw the rage building on the Silicone Queen's face until the auctioneer's gavel fell and Ty had not bid at all. She looked at Liz who noticed how ugly the Silicone Queen's face became when it reflected a nasty mood. Liz saw the woman mouth one word at her. "Bitch." Liz turned her attention to a tally sheet handed to her by one of the runners. She smiled and turned back to the audience.

"Ladies and gentlemen, it gives me great pleasure to announce that, due to your generosity tonight, we have raised $75,000 for the Bay State Breast Cancer Foundation. Thank you, thank you and thank you." The applause was thunderous. Ty held up his hand.

"In a few minutes, we'll begin dancing. Until then, the bar's open." There was more applause and the crowd began to disperse to the food and drink stations.

Liz gratefully handed her microphone over to the auctioneer. "Thank God that's over." She felt a warm hand on her shoulder and knew it was Ty's. She turned to look at him. He was smiling at her and gently rubbing her shoulder. There was an affectionate warmth in his eyes as he looked her over. The pleasure of his touch went far beyond the kindness of it.

"See, I knew you could do it, Liz," he said. Before she could ask him why he had bought her tiramisu, Millie called to Liz. Reluctantly, Liz stepped away from the caressing hand. She offered her hand to him.

"Thank you so much for backing me up. Truly, I don't know if I could have done it without your help." Ty took her hand, but instead of shaking it, he lifted it to his lips and kissed it. On the stage, she'd been too distracted by the auction, but now, Liz had a hard time controlling her breathing.

"My pleasure," he said, "By the way, Counselor, I meant to tell you, you look incredible tonight." He kissed her hand again. "Is your dance card full or could you fit me in somewhere? I really want to talk to you." His eyes were focused on her face and there was an intensity to his expression that Liz found both exciting and unsettling. He raised her hand back to his lips and said, "Please" against it, the word causing him to kiss it again. Liz's heart nearly stopped.

"Of course," Liz was surprised to hear how husky her voice sounded. Her heart was hammering and she could feel the blood rising to her cheeks. She gently pulled her hand away from Ty. "I really need to freshen up right now, but I promise I'll come back."

As she stepped away to join Millie, Liz heard Ty say, "The last dance is mine." The two women made their way to the ladies' room, their progress slowed by people wanting to congratulate Liz on a successful auction. Luckily, this had the happy effect of delaying their entry into the ladies' room until after most of the crowd had left it.

"What was all that about?" Millie asked Liz. She handed Liz the purse she'd been holding for her. Liz was about to answer when they heard a loud sniffing sound coming from the handicapped access stall. This was followed by two more. Liz looked at Millie who held a finger to her lips. They remained silent and eavesdropped.

"Do you believe that bitch?" came the voice of the Silicone Queen. "That fat cow gets him onstage with her, he buys her shit, he won't even look at me. I mean, what the fuck?" The snorting continued. "That is my man and she's trying to steal him."

Another voice piped up from the stall. "I know, what's she got that you don't?"

"Wrinkles," someone said. They all giggled.

"I see her again, I'm gonna totally beat her ass," said the Silicone Queen. "I'm tired of her fucking with me." More sniffing. "This is really good shit. Jimmy gets totally awesome blow." The other girls murmured agreement.

Liz had turned and started to leave as the stall door burst open. The Silicone Queen and her friends quickly blocked her exit. Liz had a sudden flashback to a darkened high school hallway. Somewhere, deep down, she found courage for the confrontation. Best defense, she thought.

"So, you're going to beat my ass. Here?" She asked. "Your name is…" she groped for it, "Cheryl? I'm Elizabeth." Liz held out her hand.

The Silicone Queen took a step forward and slapped away Liz's proffered hand. Liz could see how raw the underside of the other woman's nose was and how her heavy makeup was beginning to smear. Liz felt Millie step in behind her.

Cheryl pushed Liz, who was stopped from falling by Millie. "I don't give a shit what your name is," she hissed. "That is my man and you just keep your fat ass away from him or I will fuck you up. He's mine, got it?"

"That's not what he told me." Liz heard her own voice but it was as if someone else had spoken. Even Millie blinked.

"What? Bullshit. When did you talk to him?" Cheryl

111

demanded.

"On his birthday, when he spent the night at my house. Actually, weather aside, we had a great time."

"Did you fuck him?" Liz heard panic behind the aggression. It gave her confidence.

"That's none of your business."

This stunned the younger women. As quickly as the shock hit, it wore off and Cheryl's face became red and angry.

"I don't believe you."

"Ask him." Liz said quietly. "He drove me home from work and spent the night."

"Don't think I won't, you fucking liar!" Cheryl and her posse turned and barged out of the bathroom, knocking women aside as they left. Liz and Millie watched them go, not daring to move. Liz exhaled and turned to Millie.

"I can almost feel sorry for her. I mean, she doesn't really understand that he just sees her as ..." She couldn't finish the sentence.

Millie snorted, "Oh please, from what Corey tells me, she's been treating him like an ATM. Don't waste too much of you sympathy on her. But you be careful, too."

"About what, Mil?" asked Liz.

"I noticed that Hadley's knocking back the Scotch at a pretty good clip tonight. And I hear he gets a lot of practice. Are you sure you want to get involved with a drinker?"

Liz looked at her. "Mil, nobody's getting involved with anybody else. I told you, I'm done with dating. Beside," Liz started putting items back into her bag, "When have you ever been to a Bar Association event that didn't have a bar? Lawyers drink."

"Well," said Mil, "If he's as good at drinking as he is in court, he's got problems. And by the way, you aren't seeing what I see. That man is looking at you like a hungry dog looks at a bone. I mean it, Liz. He wants you."

"If that's true, Millie," said Liz innocently, "then I guess he'd be the one with the bone, huh?" She elbowed Millie and the two of them broke into giggles. Liz sobered. "He just feels guilty for the black eye and he's been trying to make up for it ever since."

"Jesus Christ, Elizabeth, will you open your eyes?" Millie exploded. "Just because you don't recognize flirting doesn't mean it's not going on. If you weren't so damned stubborn, you would see this. And by the way, you should see what he sees."

"What's that?"

"The glow in your eyes when you talk to him."

As they returned to the party, Millie receiving a warm kiss from John. Liz caught a questioning look from John and nodded at him. She ignored Millie's frown as she looked between the two of them, just smiling cheerily.

Liz walked to the bandstand, again stopping from time to time to receive congratulations for a job well done on the auction. As she reached the foot of the stage, she motioned the bandleader over and exchanged a few words with him. He nodded and spoke to the band. As previously planned, they began to play "Someone to Watch Over Me." Liz saw John escort Millie out to the dance floor and pull her in close.

"May I have this dance, Counselor?" Liz heard Ty's voice next to her ear. "I know you've had lessons."

She smiled at him.

"You asked for the last dance, Counselor," she teased. "This isn't it."

Ty chuckled and Liz caught herself. "Touché," he said, "but I want this one, too."

"In a minute. I want to watch this," she turned her attention back to John and Millie.

"What's going on?" he asked.

"Watch."

John knelt in front of Millie and took her hand in his. Liz couldn't hear him, but she knew what he was saying. "Is he proposing?" Ty asked.

"He certainly is." Liz watched John take a small box from the pocket of his tuxedo and watched Millie gasp. "YES!" Millie's excitement overrode her volume control. The watching crowd laughed and applauded as John slipped the engagement ring on Millie's finger and rose to kiss her. The band struck up "Wonderful Tonight" and the couple began circling the floor in each other's arms.

Liz felt Ty pull circle her waist. "You helped him do that, huh?" he asked.

She finally turned towards him. "I did. I arranged things with the bandleader, I advised John about the ring and tricked Millie into telling me her ring size." She felt an urge to kiss him.

Ty led Liz out to the dance floor. "Now remember, just keep looking me in the eye and you'll do just fine."

Liz put one hand on his shoulder and let him take the other in his hand. They began to move in time with the music. Liz's heart was pounding and she thought she could feel some kind of deep, slow vibration that had nothing to do with the music coming up from the floor. She had no idea what was going on, but she wasn't complaining about it, either. Liz looked into his eyes and saw the same intense expression she'd seen earlier. "Tell me, Ty," Liz was surprised she could find her voice. "Why did you do it?"

"Do what?"

Liz smiled back. "Pay $500 for something I'd have made for you just for asking. Why did you do it, Ty?"

Ty smiled mysteriously. "I have my reasons. One of them being that you didn't expect anyone to pay much for it, did you?"

"No," Liz admitted. "It's not much compared to getaway weekends and baseball tickets."

"Well, I'll bet you anything that 85% of the people in this room are talking about it and watching us right now. Next year, it'll go for over $100 with or without me. Besides, the money went to a good cause, it's tax deductible and I get more of your tiramisu," he concluded. Liz felt Ty's hand slide up from her waist to the bare skin of her back and back down again. Liz almost stumbled from her knees going weak.

"Easy, there," he admonished. "Remember, keep your eyes on me."

"By the way,' he said casually, "I hear you had a nasty confrontation in the ladies room." She felt his hand tighten on hers. "Are you okay?" His eyes searched her face.

"Yeah, it was nothing, really," Liz said. "Some angry words and…"

"She shoved you." He finished.

"Yes."

"You didn't fight back." It wasn't a question.

"I'm not a cat fighter," she said. "I didn't want to cause a scene." She tried to sound dismissive.

Ty pulled her closer. "You don't have to be afraid. I sent her home."

Annoyed, Liz pulled out of his arms and looked at Ty. "Thank you, but I don't need protection." She turned to leave and heard him say, "Maybe I want to protect you."

For the next couple of hours, Liz danced with various partners, most of them men she knew, including Frank McCafferty, and socialized with her friends, admiring Millie's ring and joining the gang in toast after toast. The ball was finally winding down when Liz felt the hand on her shoulder. The hand belonged to Ty. He hastily downed the drink he'd been holding and disposed of the glass. "Last dance, Counselor," he said as he led her out to the floor. "You might even be ready for a dip."

Liz noted that where the dance floor had been fairly crowded earlier, it was nearly empty at this late hour. Ty swept her into his arms and the band struck up "At Last." He saw the question in her eyes and said, "No, I didn't arrange it. They just happen to be playing it."

Ty pulled Liz even closer than he had earlier. They looked into each other's eyes as they danced.

Liz marveled, "I've never been very good at slow dancing and you've got me moving like Ginger Rogers."

Ty smiled and squeezed her hand. "It helps to have the right partner," he said quietly.

They had made their way to a darker, more private area of the dance floor when Ty looked up. Liz followed his gaze and saw a sizable kissing ball liberally spiked with mistletoe hanging just above them. Ty looked into Liz's eyes. She could see the warmth and anticipation in them. "Guess I'll have to do this right then, won't I?" he whispered. And before Liz knew it, Ty was kissing her.

He started off softly, gently until Liz parted her lips under his. Her head was spinning and she put her arms around his neck to steady herself. Ty tightened his hold on her. She felt his tongue slowly ease into her mouth and touch hers, gradually deepening into something that made her sway. Liz put one gloved hand to his face and felt one of his hands slide up from her waist to brush, then cup her breast.

She tentatively slid her tongue into his mouth, tasting the Scotch he had been drinking. She didn't care. Ty pulled her even more closely against his body. Liz felt his hand go above the bodice of her dress to touch the soft skin, then try to slide a finger underneath it. He pulled her even closer with his other arm, sliding his hand down to her bottom and pulling her against himself. Liz could feel his erection and stopped breathing.

They were still there…

Jeering faces, bodies against her, semen being shot into her unwilling hand, her voice begging them to stop…

She froze.

Ty broke off the kiss. His breathing was ragged and heavy.

"I have a suite at the hotel tonight, Liz," he finally managed to say. "Come with me, Darling." He began kissing her neck, down her shoulder and lower. "I want you. I want us to be together tonight." He began to push the stiff bodice out of the way of his questing mouth.

"Ty, please, no." Liz tried to push her dress back into place. He raised his head, misinterpreting her panic.

"I'm sorry. You made me lose my head there for a minute." he kissed her forehead and raised her chin to kiss her again, just as softly and warmly as he had started. He raised his head. "Come back to my room with me, Liz and we won't have to stop."

Liz's spine stiffened and she tried to pull out of his arms. Ty looked confused.

"I can't."

He kept his grip and read her face. "High school?"

She nodded, barely moving her head. Her heart was still pounding as she forced the horror out of her head.

He kissed her forehead. "There." He kissed it again. "They're leaving." Liz found he was right.

"Let me help you put that ugliness behind you. Come with me and we'll have a beautiful night making love." He stroked her face. "Trust me."

Liz realized that she did trust him. And more.

She loved him. She'd fought against it and lost. Elizabeth Gardner had fallen in love with Tyrone Hadley. And he was asking her to spend the night with him. He was murmuring something as he was kissing her neck, a caress that made her go limp. "You look like a queen in that dress, Counselor, but I can't wait to get you out of it."

116

Reality hit Liz. He'd see what the cut of her dress was hiding. She opened her eyes. "Ty, I..."

He cut her off with a kiss. "Sssh, Baby. Let's go. I'll have room service bring us champagne and you'll see. I'm not going to hurt you." He kissed her again. "I love you too much to ever hurt you."

Liz froze. She had almost whispered, "I love you, too" until the aroma of Scotch from his breath hit her nostrils. It was the liquor talking, not Ty.

She pulled away from him, reluctantly disentangling herself. Ty's bewilderment showed in his eyes, those eyes she longed to see on the pillow next to hers and wouldn't. He reached for her, but she stepped further away.

"Liz, don't run away from me."

She shook her head. "Please, it's been a beautiful evening. Let's not ruin it. This is wrong. You've been drinking; you don't know what you're doing or saying. I know what I'm doing. Believe me, I know best."

"No." The one word was quiet, firm and held an undercurrent of anger. Ty shoved his hands into his pockets, ignoring what it did to the line of the tuxedo jacket. He was staring at the floor and continued to stare as he spoke, still quiet, still angry.

"No, Liz, I don't think you know what you're doing." He looked up. "I want an explanation." He held up a hand to stop her protest. "Not tonight. The only thing I want to hear from you right now is 'Yes, Ty, I'll come with you' and we know that isn't going to happen. So, you go. But know this, Elizabeth: we're not done." And he abruptly turned and stalked off.

Liz closed her eyes. The pain she had just inflicted on him had hurt her, too, but she reminded herself that she was only protecting herself and her heart before the real damage could be done.

Chapter 6

The good thing about Hyannis in December, reflected Liz as she drove along Route 132, is that you pretty much have the town to yourself and it's not too difficult to get a hotel room at the last minute and get one for a song, at that. Yeah, it was fun in the summertime with all the crowds, but she craved quiet and solitude right now and Hyannis would offer that. Over the years, it had proven itself as a place to hide and heal.

It had been one week since the Barrister's Ball and Liz couldn't keep her mind off Ty's kiss. Just thinking about it, she could feel it all again, Ty's lips on hers, the warm, sensual probing of his tongue, his arms around her, his hands on her bare skin and how she had so eagerly responded. Part of her wondered if she should have gone back to his room with him.

All hell had broken loose after the ball; the society columnists for the local papers kept calling. Women Liz had never heard of either called the office or dropped by to "go grab a bite." Corey informed Liz all of them had been previously been linked to Ty Hadley. Liz saw none of them, having Corey issue a polite refusal (he had trouble with the polite part). According to Millie and Joe, hiring partners from some of the other firms in town had begun to "sniff around," calling contacts within the Hoffman, Lovell and Dennis to find out more about her. Dan was not pleased and he took his irritation out on Liz by dumping work on her. The Monday after the ball, one dozen sterling silver roses were waiting for her at the reception desk with a note indicating that these were the first of fifty-two weekly bouquets she'd be receiving, per the instructions of Tyrone Hadley, Esq. who'd bought them at auction. Liz was unable to eat, substituting iced coffee for anything more substantial. With the nervous tension added to the caffeine, she had been unable to relax. More than once, Liz had bitten Corey's head off for no good reason. Even Millie was puzzled that Liz refused to confide in her when she was clearly upset and confused. Beanie would chase his toys around in front of Liz, energetically batting and running, then sitting back on his haunches, tail wagging and awaiting praise. When it didn't come, he'd philosophically stretch and curl up in Liz's lap, purring while she mechanically stroked his coat, her mind on a man with a devastating touch.

And there were the phone messages. A small stack of pink paper squares with "Ty Hadley – please call" noted on them. And voice messages both at work and at home. As soon as she heard his voice, Liz erased them without listening.

The kicker had been an email from a society photographer who had been at the Ball. He'd attached pictures of Ty and Liz dancing together and kissing. Liz had been shaken that even this most intimate moment had not been private. She'd gone into Dan's office, told him she was using some of her accumulated vacation time and doing so immediately. When he started to deny her, Liz gave her two weeks' notice. Back at her desk, Liz had made three phone calls: one to Judge McCafferty to accept his offer, one to book a room in Hyannis and one to Vincenzo's.

Once she'd arrived on the Cape, Liz turned into the parking lot of her hotel, patting her car on the dashboard. "Good boy. Just get us back to Salem in a couple of days and I'll buy you a tune-up, I promise," she said. Liz found that a certain amount of begging and bribery kept her ancient VW Rabbit running. It wasn't exactly an image car for a lawyer, but it was paid for, passed inspection, still got fairly good gas mileage and ran.

As Liz waited for the clerk to complete the check-in, her mind went back to her last conversation with Millie and Corey before she left. Millie had just looked at the circles under Liz's eyes and nodded. She knew about the chaos, but suspected there was something more and it had to do with Ty. When Liz told her she was going to Hyannis for a few days, Millie had finally broken down and asked what the hell was going on. Liz replied "Please, Mill. I just want to be left alone for a couple of days. We'll talk when I get back, I promise. Right now, Boston's just too insane."

Millie had nodded and hugged her friend with a silent prayer that Liz would find the answers she sought. Corey had remained silent except for a request that Liz bring back a snow globe for his collection.

After dropping her bags in her room, Liz headed back out into the chilly air of Hyannis. Fortunately, her destination was close and she quickly made her way into Cucina Vincenzo.

A handsome man in his late sixties was seated at the bar reading a newspaper and drinking coffee under a picture of the Rat Pack with a much younger version of himself. He looked up at the tinkling of the bells on the front door and got up to greet Liz.

"Here's our girl!" Vincent DiNardo wrapped Liz in a bear hug. "Lizabetta!"

Vinnie held her out at arms' length and searched her face. "What's wrong? Are you in trouble? I'll kill him." Vinnie hugged her again and Liz returned it, feeling better than she had all week.

"No, I'm not in trouble," she said, still holding Vinnie, "Everything's fine."

"Bullshit," Vinnie answered pleasantly.

"Vincenzo!" A sharp yell from the kitchen.

Vinnie turned his head towards the voice, "Angie, I'm old enough to curse if I want to. Save it for the boys, Darling," he said sweetly. He turned back to Liz. "As I was saying, in my own way, I don't believe you for a minute everything's fine. Look at your face. Belle of the Ball and you look like you lost your best friend."

"The bookstore is holding an order for me and I want to check out some more properties for investment. I thought I'd do some work here, too." And hide, she added silently.

Vinnie released her. "I still don't believe you. The bookstore could have shipped your order and you don't need to personally inspect your rental properties," he pointed his index finger at her, "You, my girl, do not drive for hours with a snowstorm following you just to come visit. I won't pry, but I'll bet it's some man."

Liz shrugged and managed a bright smile. "Hey, we both know Angie got the last good man. I'm just waiting for her to kick you to the curb so I can make my move. You, me and a bottle of Viagra. Whaddya say?"

"Hey!" Vinnie playfully slapped her wrist. "Nice girls don't talk like that!" He put a hand to her cheek. "It's no good you being alone, Liz. You need a good man. We worry about you."

She opened her mouth, but Vinnie cut her off. "You need love. You need to be loved and you need to give love. End of discussion."

Papa Vinnie had spoken. He put both hands on her face and

frowned in concern.

"Your face is so cold! Where did you walk from, Alaska? Angela! Get out here!" Vinnie yelled the last in the direction of the kitchen.

Angela DiNardo emerged from the swinging doors leading to the kitchen, wiping her hands on her apron. "Vinnie! Could you be any louder?" She spotted Liz and held out her arms. "My girl! Lizabetta! Vinnie! Why didn't you say so?" This, thought Liz, was exactly what she needed. Mama Angie gave hugs that could cure just about anything. It wasn't just the firm embrace and Angie's softness that made them special. Somehow, some of the warmth from her big, generous heart would find its way through Angie's arms and into Liz's soul.

Angie held Liz out at arms' length as Vinnie had done. Liz looked back into a face that had grown more beautiful with time. Angie had been a knockout in her twenties, but now, despite some wrinkles, added weight and gray hairs, age had only softened her beauty, made it mortal. Vinnie said it was the beauty of Angie's heart that showed on her face.

Right now, Angie's brown eyes examined Liz closely. "What's wrong? Why are you really here?" Angie's eyes narrowed as she studied Liz's face. "You're in love. Why do you look so miserable?"

Score one for Angie, thought Liz. "Who says I'm in love?" she asked. "For all you know, I could just be getting over the flu." Angie lightly smacked Liz's head. "Don't lie. You're in love. I can see it in your face and it's making you crazy." Angie felt Liz's face. "My God, you're cold! Come. Working will warm you right up. And you need soup." Angie put her arm around Liz and led her into the kitchen.

Liz sniffed deeply while removing her coat. Garlic, fresh bread, onions, something sweet and spicy she couldn't identify. All of those individual aromas combined to work their calming magic on Liz's brain. She was feeling better by the minute. She spotted mascarpone cheese, egg yolks and lady fingers on the center counter next to a bottle of brandy and a pot of steaming coffee. Liz grinned. "Angie, you're making tiramisu?" she asked innocently.

Angie smiled. She knew Liz so well. "No. You are. Someone paid five hundred bucks for yours at auction; we're gonna raise our price. Five hundred bucks. Huh! Nobody ever paid me that kind of money and I taught you how to make it. You get an apron and get busy. Earn your keep." Angie turned back to her enormous soup pot. "I made sausage and spinach soup." Angie waved a spoon at Liz. "You do well enough with the sweet and I may let you have some."

Liz laughed while she tied on an apron. "You made it for me and you know it."

"Maybe I did, but you still have to earn it."

Liz tested the heat of the espresso and put it back on a burner to warm. "Ever thought about putting out a cookbook, Angie? God knows you get enough requests for recipes."

Angie shrugged as she examined a bowl of rising bread dough. "When your first book gets published, Darling, we'll talk about it. Stop worrying so much about making everyone else happy. It's not your job."

As Liz stirred the espresso mix, Angie began questioning.

"So, Joe tells me you've finally fallen in love. I'm glad. Where is he? When do we meet this man?"

Liz shrugged as she added brandy. "You probably don't, Angie. I have no idea where he is right now and he's probably there with someone else, anyway." She tasted the mix. "Angie, could you ask Vinnie for amaretto?"

Angie smiled triumphantly, "Ha! I have the great secret at last!" She yelled to the front, "Vinnie! A bottle of amaretto, if you please!" She turned back to Liz. "You're not changing the subject, you know." She stirred her soup for a moment.

"This man of yours.."

"He's not mine, Angie."

"...is he married?" Angie was looking hard at Liz.

"No, Angie." Just surrounded by more beautiful women. Younger women.

"He's not gay, is he?"

"No, Angie, he's not married, not gay and not interested in anything serious." Liz shrugged again. "We've met a couple of times. He hasn't shown any interest."

"Look at me." Angie's tone tolerated no disobedience. Liz looked at her. She could feel Angie's eyes looking into her soul. "You haven't slept with him." It was a statement.

"No, Angie. I haven't slept with him."

Again, the eyes. "He kissed you?"

"Yes, Angie." And I kissed him right back and I'd shave thirty years off my life to do it again.

"You felt something big, didn't you?" Liz nodded. "Something like a big, slow pulse coming up from the center of the earth, yes?"

Again, Liz nodded.

"You got that feeling in your stomach, too, didn't you? That shiny gold knot?"

Liz couldn't speak. She couldn't look at Angie, either. She just kept her eyes on her espresso mix and nodded again.

"And it's still there." Another statement. Another question. "Lizabetta, don't you know what that feeling is, that pulse? That's two soul mates recognizing each other. I got it when I met Vinnie and so did he. I still have that knot in my stomach forty-five years later." She was about to add something else, but the swinging doors opened to admit Vinnie with the amaretto. He brought the bottle to Liz and kissed her cheek. "Sorry to take so long, Sweetheart, but a man came in looking for a phone book. You should have been out there, Liz. He looked like your type. Almost handsome enough to be a younger version of me." They all laughed. "Here's your amaretto, Sweetheart."

Liz added amaretto and tasted again. Perfect. Vinnie watched her dip lady fingers into the mix and line an enormous loaf pan with them.

"You know, Lizabetta, you add some kind of magic to that." Liz looked at him curiously. Vinnie continued, "It's some kind of love potion. Tell her, Angie" and he headed through the doors again.

"It's true. You make tiramisu for us, people eat it and fall in love. We've seen it happen again and again." Angie smiled. "Quit working for that asshole..."

"Angela! Watch your language!" Vinnie yelled from the other side of the door.

Angie ignored him, "... and work down here full-time. More fun than being a lawyer."

"I quit yesterday morning." Liz felt herself brace for outrage and anger. Something that would have come from her long-dead parents. Instead, Angie paused as she turned her bread dough onto

123

a floured slab.

"Good for you. Go to someone who knows your worth."

"Anthony!" Angie yelled for her younger son. "Tony'll bring your soup out front for you." Angie gently nudged Liz out of the way. "I can assemble this. You go eat. We'll have customers, I promise. Bad weather needs good pasta."

Liz started to take off her apron. She was thoughtful as she dried her hands on a towel.

Liz's cell phone rang. She didn't want to answer it. "Damn it! Tony!"

A handsome young face popped through the door. "Hey, it's Liz! Great to see you!"

Liz cut him off, "Tony, be a doll, would you go grab my phone?"

Liz didn't have to ask twice. While she was quickly cleaning her hands, she heard Tony say, "Hello?" and then, "He hung up." Liz was drying her hands. "Who hung up?"

Tony shrugged. "Don't know. Some guy. Just said, 'Sorry, I think I have the wrong number' and hung up." He handed the phone to Liz.

"Thanks, anyway, Tone." Liz gathered her belongings and headed for her table at the back of the restaurant, directly under a Tiffany-shaded lamp. Liz sat facing the wall to minimize distractions, not that there would be a flood of customers mid-afternoon during the off-season with an imminent snowstorm, but she didn't want to be staring out the window. Tony followed behind her with soup, a bottle of Pellegrino and crusty fresh bread.

"Here, Ma says you have to eat every bite of soup because she's gonna have you making gnocchi." He put the steaming bowl in front of Liz. "Hey, Liz, Joey says you got a big ass shiner playing softball. Some guy knocked you ass over tits. That true?"

"Anthony! Language!" Angie's voice came muffled but strong through the doors.

"How does she know? I swear Ma has bionic hearing," Tony muttered, then yelled, "Sorry, Ma!"

Liz chuckled. It felt so good to be in the middle of this family.

"Mama Angie knows all, hears all and sees all, especially if you're doing something she doesn't like." She sipped her Pellegrino. "The shiner is old news, Joey and Rocco worked him over without asking and if Joey wasn't married, I'd tell him to open a beauty parlor. Christ, he's a bigger gossip than twelve old ladies in a circle. I'm surprised he can maintain client confidentiality."

From the kitchen, "Lizabetta! No blasphemy!"

"Sorry, Angie." Liz looked at Tony. "Look, I'd rather not talk about it. Just keep the Pellegrino coming, get Francis Albert on the jukebox and leave me the hell alone for a while or I'll tell your Mama about the last time you came up to Boston and how much you spent on the strippers."

"You got it." Tony leaned over and kissed Liz on the cheek. With a grin, he pointed to a sprig of mistletoe over her head, then retreated as fast as he could.

Liz stared at the mistletoe, her mind going back to another kiss under mistletoe. Tony's had been sweet, but...she shook off the thought. Her reason for being in Hyannis was to give herself time and space to get over her obsession with Ty Hadley and get on with her quiet, undisturbed life. Let the Cape work its healing magic and recharge her batteries. Before settling in to write, Liz uttered a quick prayer.

"Please, God, either make him a real part of my life or get him out of my head." With that and Frank Sinatra singing "Night and Day" in the background, Liz focused on her notepad and set to writing. Turning events in her life into short stories or essays had helped her make sense of them and she hoped to hell it would work this time.

The afternoon wore on. Tony periodically replaced her Pellegrino, making comments or kissing Liz's cheek and dodging swats. She was so intent on her work that she barely noticed time passing. The jingle of the front door registered only on the fringes of her consciousness.

Her phone rang. Curses be unto those who interrupt in mid-thought. Liz groped for her phone.

"Millie, what part of 'leave me alone' didn't you understand? I don't want to talk right now, okay?" she snapped.

"No, 'leave me alone' is pretty clear, but you never said it to me," replied Ty's voice, with some amusement. "Since you haven't been able to return my calls, I thought I'd stop by your office and take you to lunch so that we could talk, but you weren't in your office. Where are you, Liz?"

Think fast, Liz. "Springfield. Dan sent me out here very suddenly. I didn't even know I was coming until last night."

"Gee, that's too bad. I'm heading down to Hyannis myself. I thought you might like to join me. Excuse me, Liz." She heard him speak to someone. She couldn't make out the words, but it sounded like he was giving orders.

Liz dropped her pen and buried her face in her free hand.

"Don't see how I can. Have a good time." Tony put a glass of red wine in front of her. He had an odd expression and didn't try kissing her. "Just a minute, Ty." Hand over mouthpiece. "Tony, what's going on?"

"Pop thought you'd like a glass. I gotta go. I've got a customer." Very un-Tony.

Ty's voice again. "You were saying?" Liz sighed. "I was saying, I hope you have a good time in Hyannis and I'm very sorry, but I'm in Springfield and I have to stay here. Snowstorm, you know."

Ty laughed softly. "You know, I think you're running from me and I told you we were going to talk. Going all the way to Springfield, though. That's desperate. Can you recommend any good restaurants in Hyannis? I'm in the mood for Italian." Liz smiled in spite of her rising panic. She was going to have to hide in her hotel room. She began to rub the back of her neck.

"Sorry, I don't know the area that well. Know any good massage therapists in Springfield? My neck and back are incredibly tense."

"No, but then, you're not in Springfield." Only this time, she didn't hear Ty on the phone. She heard him. He was speaking inches away from her right ear. She turned her head slowly and looked into his smiling eyes.

"You can hang up now, Liz." She obeyed as he pulled up a chair next to hers. Liz noticed he wasn't dressed for the office, but had on a sport jacket and turtleneck under his expensive overcoat. After shedding the outer layers, Ty sat down and hitched his chair even closer to Liz's. This undermined her careful self-control to a dangerous degree. So much for the weekend to clear her mind. "What's this?" Ty reached over to Liz's notebook. "You were pretty engrossed when I came in." He pulled the book closer.

"I told you I wanted to be a writer when I grew up," she said. "I'm writing."

Ty glanced over the pages. "I'd like you to read it to me later. If your creative writing is as good as your legal writing, this ought to be a real pleasure. Here," he handed Liz the untouched glass of wine. "You look like you could use some of this."

Liz sipped some wine, willing her nerves to calm. She had tried to ignore the thrill as Ty's fingers touched hers when he passed her the glass. She could feel the deep, slow vibration she had felt on the dance floor and the knot in her stomach. And the fear.

Ty took the glass back from her and sipped some wine himself, his eyes never left her face. "You're hiding from me," he stated. She nodded.

Ty reached over and touched the nape of her neck. His fingers stroked downward, probing the tension Liz was carrying there. He began to knead her shoulder, massaging the tight muscles. His eyes were still on hers, looking for the answer to some question she was afraid to acknowledge.

Liz could feel herself begin to shake and tried desperately to will herself to stop.

"What brings you to Hyannis, Ty?" Her voice was unintentionally husky.

"You." He said it softly, his voice caressing the word.

The single word devastated Liz's self-control. Without really being aware of what she was doing, Liz reached up and covered Ty's hand with her. She knew he could feel the shaking.

"Feel that?" He nodded. "It happens every time I'm near you. Kissing me the other night made it worse. I don't want to eat, I can't sleep and I can't get you off my mind." She gently removed his hand from her shoulder. "I came here to find peace. If you're just looking to get laid, Ty, then leave me alone. Please." She released his hand.

Ty sat back in his chair. For a moment or two, he said nothing. When he did speak, his voice was low and angry.

"Is that what you think? Listen, Baby. You're not the only one not sleeping, not eating. If all I wanted was sex, I could have stayed in Boston. I'm here for you, Liz. I want you. I told you that the other night."

"You were pretty drunk. I'm surprised you remember."

Ty looked as if she'd slapped him. "That was cold, Counselor. I remember saying it because it was true then and it's still true now." Liz looked squarely into those beguiling eyes. "You sure it's not just because I didn't want to sleep with you? Wounded ego? We know you don't like to lose. You don't know what you're getting into. Or into bed with, for that matter."

"I don't care. I want you. I want to be with you."

"Yeah, right. The man who's been seen with models and socialites wants the middle-aged, pudgy nobody."

"You know I don't see you like that. Why would you say such a thing?" Ty practically snapped at her. "Christ, won't you even give me a chance?"

"Because every time I give someone the chance, it blows up in my face. I don't want to be hurt again."

"I promise you, I will never hurt you. I love you."

This was too much. Liz stood up and grabbed his hand. "Come with me."

"Why?"

"Show and tell." She led Ty into the only place where she knew they'd have privacy: the ladies' room. Liz locked the door. "Right." She pulled up the hem of her sweater and pushed down the waistband of her jeans to expose the flesh on her hip. "See these?" She was pointing to faint, jagged white lines running vertically and diagonally on her skin. "Touch them."

Ty put his fingers on the lines. Liz tried to ignore the thrill.

"Those, Mr. Hadley, are faded stretch marks." Ty looked at Liz's face sharply. "No, I was never pregnant. But if you gain a lot of weight, regardless of gender, you get stretch marks. They fade when you lose weight. At my peak, I weighed over 220." She pulled the pants back. "As it is, I can't wear designer clothes and nobody's going to put me on the cover of Vogue. However, that's not the star of the show."

Liz unbuttoned her cardigan to expose her bra. "Now, look." She couldn't believe she was doing this, but better to get it over with now. Liz pushed the lace covering her left breast aside, showing a puckered, wrinkled scar. Liz looked away. It had been 3 years and she still hated what she saw.

It disappeared into the rest of the lace and Lycra covering her breast. Ty was staring hard at the spot. His expression was unreadable.

"I'm sorry, Counselor, but I can't see a man like you wanting to wake up next a body like this."

Liz rebuttoned her sweater, keeping her face down. "Show's over."

"I don't understand." She darted a glance at his face and saw puzzlement.

Liz could feel tears in her eyes. "Guys like you aren't supposed to happen to women like me, okay? Over a certain age, if single, we're either supposed to settle for some pudgy, balding middle-aged insurance salesman because he's 'nice' and 'will be a good husband' or we're supposed to finish the journey alone. Being in love doesn't enter the picture. You, on the other hand, are the handsome prince. And you can have any woman you want. I've got at least 15 years and as many pounds on the women you date. I'm not arm candy, I know this."

"Angie says I'm in love and she's right, God is she ever right. I have never felt like this for anyone, Ty and if you don't want what I want, it'll kill me. You have the power to utterly destroy me, whether you mean to or not and I'm scared to death. Let me get over it and get on with my life. Please."

Ty pulled Liz into his arms. He held her close and kissed her forehead. Liz put her arms around him and leaned into his body. She could feel the energy flowing between them, both reassuring and exciting. She closed her eyes and just felt. This could be as close as she ever got.

Ty spoke quietly, "I will kill the first insurance salesman who comes near you. And the second. And the third. And any other man who tries to take what's mine. I said I loved you and I goddamn meant it."

Ty tilted Liz's chin up and looked into her eyes. "I'm not just playing, Liz. The woman I want is right here in my arms." And his mouth came down on hers.

The Barrister's Ball kiss hadn't been a fluke. Liz found her knees going weak as they had at the Ball and she tightened her grip on Ty. He held her even closer.

There was a knock at the door. "Lizabetta?" Liz reluctantly broke off the kiss. "I'm okay, Angie. Be out in a minute." She shifted her hands and gently pushed Ty away. With a smile, he kissed her quickly before turning to flush the toilet.

Liz unlocked the door and peeked into the dining room.

"All clear." She took Ty's hand and led him back to their table. Since he nearly hit his head on it, Ty noticed the mistletoe and pulled Liz in for another kiss. She didn't stop him.

"Ahem."

Liz and Ty both looked up to see Angie. She stood with feet planted, hands on hips and a baleful expression on her face, mostly directed at Ty. Vinnie and Tony stood behind her looking equally displeased.

"Who are you and what are you doing with our girl?" Angie demanded.

Ty hastily released Liz, who, still unsteady on her feet, fell into her chair. "Uh, my name is Tyrone Hadley, Ma'am, and I was talking to Elizabeth." He sounded just like any sixteen-year-old boy facing a girl's father after getting caught necking on the porch swing.

Angie snorted. "In my day, we called that kissing. I just got a call from my Joseph. He told me all about you and said if you upset Elizabeth any more, I should tell him so he and Rocco could take care of it."

Angie looked at Liz. "Lucky for you, Young Man, she doesn't look upset. In fact," Angie peered at Liz's face, "she looks a lot better than she did when she came in here. Vincenzo, get our girl another glass of wine and one for the Kissing Bandit here," she pointed at Ty. "You, Mr. Lips, come with me."

Angie turned on her heel and marched towards the kitchen, Ty following closely, protesting, "But she kissed me first!"

Tony yelled after her, "Ma, what should I do?"

"Stay out of trouble."

Tony muttered, "Shit."

"Anthony!" from behind the door.

"Sorry, Ma."

Vinnie replaced Liz's wineglass with a fresh one and one for Ty. He looked towards the kitchen door thoughtfully.

"That's a determined man, you've got there, Liz. I bet he's been in every restaurant and hotel in town looking for you. He showed up right after you got here, wanting the phone book." Vinnie smiled at Liz. "You know, when he came back, he just sat at the bar and watched you. I was wondering how long he'd do that until he saw you take a swing at Tony for kissing you. He kind of smiled, asked me to send some Merlot to you, got on his phone and told Tony that if he didn't knock it off, he was going to stuff him into a manicotti shell ass first." Tony nodded.

No one emerged from the kitchen. "Angie must be giving him hell. Think she's showing him the big knife?" Liz asked.

Vinnie and Tony both nodded. "Oh, yeah," they said.

Vinnie patted Liz's shoulder. "Every man needs to meet his girl's family." He kissed the top of Liz's head. "It's clear you two are in love with each other. He'd better be good enough for you."

Finally, the kitchen doors swung open and a shaken Ty emerged. He took Liz's hand as he seated himself. She looked at him, imagining the conversation. "And?"

Ty swallowed, "Counselor, if I disappear, don't order anything that comes with just two meatballs."

"Oh, Honey, if you think that was bad, you should have been here the night someone asked for ketchup to put on Angie's risotto. Vinnie had to hide the scaloppini mallet."

Ty picked up the hand he was holding and kissed the fingertips, the palm and the inside of the wrist. Liz could hardly breathe. They just looked at each other for a moment.

"Wait a minute. How did you find me?" Liz asked suspiciously. "And I never gave you my cell number."

Ty just smiled. "I have my sources."

"Uh huh." An idea occurred to Liz. With her free hand, she picked up her phone and dialed Millie's office. She laced her fingers through Ty's, who kissed her hand. Liz was not about to let go.

"Attorney Wentworth."

"Millie, it's Liz." Ty looked at her curiously.

"Liz, are you okay?" Millie sounded anxious.

"Yeah, I'm with Vinnie and Angie. Listen, put me on speaker and get Corey in there, please." She heard the change in the phone to speaker, heard Millie summon Corey and heard them return.

"Hi, Liz," Corey sounded a little too chipper.

"Hi, Corey. Millie, I want you to look into Corey's eyes. Corey, Tyrone Hadley has been prowling Hyannis today. He's even been in Vincenzo's to look for me. Any idea how he'd know where to look?"

"No," Corey's voice was careful. "Maybe Joe told him…"

"Wrong. Try again. Who gave me up?"

Ty nodded. Liz mouthed "thought so."

"Nobody, Liz, I swear." Corey said stoutly.

"Millie?"

"Look me in the eyes, Corey." A slight pause. "He can't look me in the eyes, Liz."

"Corey, you told Ty where to find me, didn't you?" Liz's voice took on the tone of a mother who has just caught her child in a lie.

"Maybe."

"Corey, how much?" Liz looked at Ty who mouthed, "One hundred."

Liz mouthed back, "Are you nuts?" Ty nodded and kissed her cheek.

Liz could hear the panic as Corey said, "I don't understand the question."

Millie jumped in, "Bullshit, Corey. How much did he pay you?"

"Twenty bucks." Liz had to bite back a laugh. "That's all? Man, you're cheap. Ty says he'd have gone to two hundred, no sweat."

Dead silence from the other end. While waiting for a reaction, Liz looked at Ty with arched eyebrows and smiled.

Corey's voice finally came through weakly. "He's there?"

"Well, hell, Corey, did you think he'd pay you a hundred bucks if he wasn't going to use the information?"

Liz could hear Millie's, "OHMIGOD!" in the background. Liz also heard Millie smack Corey, who whined, "Ouch."

Corey protested, "She just hit me."

"Hit him again." Liz heard another smack. "Millie, since I'm not there and Attorney Dennis has found himself understaffed, I'd say that it would only be in the spirit of the Christmas season to lend our assistant to Dan."

"You wouldn't," from Corey.

Millie fell right in, "Why, Attorney Gardner, that's an excellent idea. And I believe Attorney Dennis is between assistants right now, isn't he? He'd be so grateful…," Here Liz heard a muffled scream from Corey, "for the help with his handwritten notes and dictation."

Liz heard a rhythmic thumping over the phone. "What's that?"

"Corey pounding his head on the desk."

"Tell him knocking himself unconscious won't get him out of it. Go, Corey. Millie, I'll catch you later." Liz hung up. Ty was chuckling.

Liz smiled at him, "Rule Number One: never betray my trust."

"I won't, Love, I promise," Ty squeezed her hand. They looked into each other's eyes for a long moment, not speaking or touching except for their clasped hands. Screwing up her courage, Liz leaned forward and kissed Ty, gently taking his bottom lip between hers and stroking her tongue along its surface. When she leaned back, his eyes were dancing with anticipation and he was breathing hard. Liz thought it was one of the sweetest sounds she'd ever heard. Ty picked up his wineglass and motioned for Liz to do the same. "To us." They drank.

Ty set down his wineglass and smiled. "You know, Liz, I have a confession. Ever since that crazy softball game when you kissed me," here his eyes glinted at her, "I've wanted you. I wanted to comfort you and make love to you the night it rained. I want those legs of yours wrapped around me. I've had dreams about us being together," his voice got soft and husky, "and they were wonderful. I want the reality tonight."

Liz could only nod, her eyes locked with his. Ty leaned in and kissed her. "I can't wait," he whispered. "That night in October..."

"Yes?"

"I stood outside the door to your room for a while after we'd said goodnight. I wanted you very, very badly that night."

Liz reached over to touch Ty's face and gently guide it to hers. She kissed him softly, running her fingers through his hair as she did. His eyes were closed as she pulled back. "If you're going to do that, we'd better have dinner." He leaned forward to kiss her as softly. "God knows when we'll eat again." He pressed a quick kiss on her. "Do you think it's safe for me to eat here or is Angie going to put saltpeter in my scaloppini?" They both laughed and Liz wrapped her arms around Ty and kissed his cheek. He pulled her close and held her. When she looked up, Tony was standing awkwardly a few feet away, menus in hand.

"Ma says the two of you have to eat and you'll do it here,"

Tony eyed Ty with some fear as he handed him a menu. "Liz, you want chicken saltimbocca? You know Ma's gonna make you eat broccoli one way or another."

"That's great, Tony." She turned to Ty. "Angie serves her saltimbocca with broccoli sautéed in garlic instead of pasta."

"And for you, Sir?" Tony was very nervous.

Ty smiled at him. "Call me Ty. Saltimbocca sounds pretty good to me, too." He offered his hand to Tony, who shook it with relief.

"Okay, great, sure, Ty," Tony almost stuttered. "Let me get your salads." He turned and fled.

The jukebox was playing Nat King Cole and "The Christmas Song." Ty stood up and offered his hand to Liz. "Care to dance? We didn't get to the dip last time."

They swayed together, bodies pressed against each other, Liz's head on Ty's shoulder and his head against hers. It felt even better and more right than she had hoped.

Ty asked, "Why is Angie force feeding you broccoli?"

"Oh, that. Angie read somewhere that it has anti-cancer properties, so she makes me eat it every chance she gets." Liz answered. "Has been ever since I left the hospital. Lucky for me, she knows how to make it edible."

Ty's hand moved up to her shoulder, gently squeezing. "Still tense? I can fix it for you." His thumb rubbed up the back of her neck. "I know a great method for relieving stress, but we can't do it right here. It might shock Angie."

Liz smiled into his shoulder. "Now that you mention it, I'm feeling much more relaxed. But you can keep doing that." She tilted up her face to kiss him.

The music changed to "At Last" by Etta James. Ty and Liz started laughing. "Just can't get away from that song, can we?" Liz said with a smile.

"I'm not complaining," said Ty. He pulled her closer again. "Maybe it's meant to be our song" and he kissed Liz again. "Damn, that's fun," he said huskily.

"Ahem." Angie interrupted their dance. "Eat. Already, Vinnie's getting phone calls wanting to know if we're open. I'll need you two working. And you," she glared at Ty. "Will NOT be distracting Lizabetta while she's working. Can you wait tables without breaking all my dishes?" He nodded as he led Liz to their table.

They ate quickly without rushing. Ty would sneak a kiss when Angie wasn't looking. When the tiramisu was served, Liz dug a spoonful and fed it to him, relishing the sudden heat she saw in his eyes. "Vinnie told me this is a love potion," she whispered. "I'm not taking any chances with you." She followed up the dessert with a kiss.

Gradually, the restaurant began to fill with the voices of hungry locals, coming in out of the snow. Angie and Liz bustled around the kitchen preparing orders, Ty helping with serving.

When the doors finally closed and Angie shooed them out, Ty and Liz strolled back to the hotel under the fast falling snowflakes. Ty's big Mercedes sat next to Liz's battered VW in the hotel lot. His luggage sat in the hallway next to the correct door for her room. As he took the key from Liz's hand, he said, "See? You can run, but you can't hide from me." As the door swung open, he added softly, "I will never let you get away from me." With that, he swept Liz off her feet and carried her over the threshold.

Chapter 7

Liz opened her eyes. The light in the room had the ashen look of pre-dawn. She tried to orient herself in the unfamiliar surroundings. She was still in Hyannis. There was a strange weight across her legs and another across her ribs, something warm and solid against her back and someone's face in the back of her neck.

Ty's face. Ty's face was in the back of her neck because they were in bed together and he was holding her as he slept.

Liz tried to move and was thwarted when the arm around her sleepily tightened its grip and Ty's leg moved even further over hers. Liz surrendered and contented herself with remembering last night.

They had taken their time. The shaking had come back as soon as Ty had pushed Liz onto the bed. He'd lowered himself next to her and pulled her body against his, just holding her close and stroking her hair until she'd stopped shaking. No, this man did not want to hurt or humiliate her.

In the weak morning light, Liz remembered how, after he had removed her sweater, she had instinctively tried to shield her breasts from his sight. Instead of cajoling or trying to remove Liz's hands, Ty had just smiled and slid one bra strap off her shoulder. He had bent his head and left a lingering kiss where the elastic had been. His kisses followed a trail down to her hands and he had whispered, "They're beautiful because they're yours," before gently sliding her hands out of the way. He had kissed the scarred area of her left breast, his tongue and lips caressing every inch, slowly working his way down to the nipple. The gesture was so loving that Liz had wanted to cry.

As she lay there, listening to Ty's deep breathing, Liz knew that her previous sexual experience had been just that – sex and nothing more. Her pleasure had been as important to Ty as his own and the pleasure had been deep, powerful and mutual. Last night, for the first time in her life, Elizabeth Gardner had actually made love.

Ty rolled onto his back and Liz slipped out from under his arm and leg. She wandered to the window, anxious to see the sunrise. Instead of sun over ocean, Liz found herself looking at a snow storm. Liz watched the flakes falling, swirling and rising according to the shifts in the wind. Her mind was like the snow still in mid-flight, now here, now there, not settled onto the ground. The one thought dominated.

What happens next?

One part of her mind said, "It's okay. It'll be fine. He's the one" while another questioned, "Maybe so, but am I the one for him? Is he going to disappear now that he got what he wanted?" She stood and stared, not seeing.

"Liz? Honey?"

Liz had been so lost in thought she hadn't heard Ty get out of bed. He came up behind her, wrapping them both in a blanket. As he pulled Liz's body close against his, one of Ty's hands slid across her midriff and up to her breasts, cupping and stroking. He kissed her neck and asked, "Everything okay, Babe? You'll get cold standing here."

Ty looked out the window. "Good thing we're not going anywhere, huh? C'mon." He tried to draw her back with him, but Liz resisted. She could feel his body tense as hers did. Liz knew she was testing his patience, but she really needed to sort out things in her mind. Liz heard Ty exhale slowly before he caressed her belly again, pulling her body back against his. She leaned into him, loving the feel of his chest against her back, his arms around her. Her hand slid along his arm to his hand and she laced her fingers through his.

"Want to tell me what's wrong, Liz?" Ty's voice was soft and gentle as he kissed her ear. "Please, Honey, let me help you."

Liz shrugged. "Nothing, really. Just being neurotic, I guess. No big deal."

She felt him nuzzle her neck, trailing kisses up to her face. He paused when he got back to her ear and softly whispered, "Bullshit," before kissing her ear.

Startled, Liz turned her head. Ty said, quietly and firmly, "If something's bothering you enough to get you out of bed, naked, to watch snow fall, it's not 'no big deal.' Now, tell me. What's wrong?"

Liz leaned into him again. "I just want to know what happens next."

Ty considered the question while he leaned his cheek against her hair. "I don't know, Liz."

Liz wasn't satisfied with the answer. Ty turned her around to face him. Almost automatically, their arms encircled each other. They looked into each other's eyes, Liz's questioning, Ty's full of love and reassurance.

"Liz, Darling, I don't have a detailed plan for us. Hell, if you'd told me 24 hours ago that I'd be spending the day combing Hyannis, I'd have suggested, politely, that you were crazy. If you'd then said I'd be spending the night in Elizabeth Gardner's arms, I'd have said, 'It's a lovely thought, but I doubt it.' Yet, here I am and here we are." His voice caressed the word "we." Ty smiled at Liz.

"I don't know what's going to happen next week or even this afternoon. We could go back to Vincenzo's for dinner or the roof could collapse on us while we're making love. You're just going to have to trust me." Ty kissed Liz. Under the blanket, his hand slid down her body, fingertips skating across smooth skin, lightly brushing across her vulva. She caught her breath. He pulled her closer, his erection rubbing against her belly.

"Right now, Liz, I want to go back to sleep." Liz arched her eyebrows as she stroked him under the blanket. Ty sucked in his breath. "Okay, well, back to bed right now. Sleep later." They both laughed softly. Ty looked into Liz's face and kissed her forehead. Her eyes were glowing as she looked back into his.

"One thing I've been dying to do," he whispered, "Besides make love to you, was to wake up next to you. I almost couldn't sleep. It was like being a kid on Christmas Eve again." Ty brought up one hand to cup her face. "By sneaking out of bed, you denied me that pleasure. I think you owe it to me, Love."

Ty leaned in again and kissed her again, deep, slow, erotic as hell. When he spoke, his voice was husky and rough.

"I want to wake up next to the love of my life, Elizabeth Gardner and you're not going to stop me. We're going back to bed and do it right this time." Ty scooped up Liz and carried her back to bed.

When she woke again, Liz found herself facing Ty, her head

pillowed on his shoulder, their limbs in a lover's tangle. His eyes were closed and she couldn't tell if he was awake or asleep. Liz lay still, not wanting to disturb him. She heard a chuckle and saw his eyes open.

"I know you're awake."

Liz smiled as she studied his face. "How do you know that?" This time, he laughed. "The snoring stopped."

Oh, God. Liz tried to burrow under the covers, but Ty stopped her. "Get back up here."

He pulled her back so that they faced each other again. Ty pushed some stray hair out of her eyes and said, "I was right. I want to wake up seeing you like this every day for the rest of my life. This is not a one-night stand."

Despite snoring, he was still there. Liz smiled at the thought and tangled her fingers in Ty's hair.

"Well, it's true you're still here, but there's a snowstorm outside. You couldn't go very far if you wanted to, Big Boy."

He leaned forward and pressed a deep, soft kiss on her. "But I'm exactly where I want to be and that's with you," he said at last. Ty traced Liz's face with his fingertips, just smiling. She continued to stroke his hair, loving the vital, springy feel of it.

The mood was broken abruptly when Ty farted. Liz looked at him, "So much for magic."

She rolled onto her other side, her back to Ty now, giggling. Not exactly Prince Charming.

"Turn back over. I don't want to look at the back of your head," Ty said, laughing. Liz complied. He propped himself up on one elbow so that Liz was looking up at him.

"Gonna ditch me now, Liz?" Ty said teasingly. "Got your T Pass ready to go?"

Liz touched his face and he turned to catch her fingers with his teeth. He caressed her back, fingertips lightly sliding down to her hip then up to her breast. She slid one leg along his in response, stroking his toes with hers. "No. If you're still here after listening to me snore, I think I can deal with the gas." He laughed as he was nibbling her fingertips.

"What were you thinking before I, ah, interrupted?" Ty asked, still holding her hand to his lips.

"You'll think I'm ridiculous."

"Please. I told you to trust me. What were you thinking?" Ty took her hand and put it around his neck, then positioned himself so that he was directly over Liz.

Liz bit her lip, partly from hesitancy and partly from the erotic effect of their position.

"I was trying to remember some poetry."

"Poetry. I see. Yours?"

"Good Lord, no," Liz said.

Ty asked, "Okay, whose poetry? Please don't say John Milton. I hate that bastard."

"Oh yeah. Paradise Lost, very romantic," Liz replied sarcastically. "No, I was trying to remember something by John Donne."

Ty looked thoughtful. "'No man is an island' and 'for whom the bell tolls.'" He shifted his weight so that his legs were holding one of Liz's legs between them, working his thigh in tight.

"He also wrote some beautiful love poems," said Liz. "I was trying to remember 'The Sun Rising.' It's the one where he says something about his love like 'she is all princes and I, all states' and nothing exists outside of their bedroom." Liz pulled Ty down and kissed him with all the passion she felt for him, her hand sliding down his neck, down his chest and lower to caress him. He rolled slightly and pushed himself against her hand. When she spoke again, she could barely speak above a whisper.

"I know how he feels."

* * *

Liz was semi-conscious when she heard the bedroom phone ring. Before she could locate it and shut up the infernal ringing, Ty had it. Liz thought, as she looked at him, even with his hair rumpled, sleepy eyes and unshaven, Ty made it worthwhile for a girl to open her eyes.

"Hello? Yes, Angie, it's the Kissing Bandit." Ty was smiling. Liz groaned and buried her face in the pillow. "No, Ma'am, I don't think your girl is some kind of puttana." To Liz, he whispered, "What's a puttana?"

"It's Italian for 'whore.'" Oh, shit. Liz squeezed her eyes shut.

"Definitely, not, Angie," Ty reiterated. "I love her." Liz smiled

140

into the pillow. "My intentions? Well, Ma'am, we're going to stay in our room a while longer. It's snowing outside, so... What? No! Angie, I swear to God I wasn't being fresh." Ty was pinching the bridge of his nose.

Liz heard a "Tyrone! No blasphemy!" from Angie's end.

"Sorry, Angie." Ty handed the phone to Liz. "Save me."

Liz sat up, clutching the sheet to her breast. "Angie? Good," Liz checked the clock. "morning." Barely.

"Lizabetta? Are you all right?" Angie was worried.

"Angie, I'm fine. Really." Ty was trying to tug the sheet out of Liz's hand. "Stop it, Ty," she hissed. He just grinned and kept tugging.

"Tell Tyrone to turn off the hormones for 5 minutes or else." The voice of authority. "I don't know what to think of him, taking a girl to bed on the first date..."

Liz interrupted, "Actually, Angie, it's our third..."

"Fourth," Ty corrected.

"Fourth," Liz stated, "and, well, we're not teenagers and these days..."

"I don't care!" snapped Angie, "It's not proper. Stop for 5 minutes already."

Liz turned to Ty, "Cool it. Angie says."

Ty obeyed. "Yes, Ma'am," he muttered. He contented himself with pulling Liz close to him and kissing her shoulder.

Liz collected herself. "I'm listening, Angie."

"Listen, whatever the two of you do the rest of the afternoon, I don't want to know. But, you are here for dinner tonight, capice? The snow is supposed to pick up and I need you in the kitchen again. The Kissing Bandit can bus tables or peel potatoes. I'll find some use for him."

"Yes, Mama Angie." Liz didn't mind.

"Okay. You kiss that man for me and Honey," Angie's voice suddenly got serious. "I'm praying he's good enough for you. I don't want to see you with someone who's gonna end up hurting you. You've waited too long and been through too much."

"Angie, this is why I love you. See you later." Liz passed the phone to Ty for him to hang up, trying to ignore Angie's concerns. "Here," she kissed Ty. "That's from Angie."

"Really," Ty was grinning. "I'll return it later."

Liz shook her head. "Don't even joke. You do not mess with Vinnie DiNardo's woman. Angie's not the only one in that family willing to use the big knife." She kissed Ty and pulled out of his arms. Liz slid to the edge of the bed, safely out of his reach, gathering a blanket around herself as she did. Ty watched her tuck it in, sarong style. He leaned over, grabbed the corner of the blanket and tugged.

"You don't need that," he said.

"It's time to get up," she said. "Snow or no, I have things to do in the outside world. It seems a good idea to be presentable. Therefore, a bath is in order." She tried to pull her cover out of his grasp, but his grip was firm.

"Fine. Why are you covering up?" Ty asked. His tone was even, but Liz could hear the steel behind it. She gave one hard tug and he released the blanket.

Liz said nothing and looked away. She tucked the blanket more securely around her. She heard Ty move behind her and felt his hand on her waist. He made a move towards untucking the blanket, but Liz held it tightly. Ty turned her to face him, his eyes locking with hers.

"You have nothing to be ashamed of," he said quietly, "and nothing to hide from me." His fingers trailed from the side of her face and downwards.

"It was dark. You didn't see anything," Liz finally said. He hadn't seen her body in full daylight.

"Maybe not with my eyes," Ty agreed, "but I know you have a mole on the back of your left thigh. Your skin is as creamy and smooth as it looks, your body feels wonderful against mine and I do not give a damn about your scars." He touched her face again. "C'mon. You don't need the blanket." He tugged at it. "I'll show you where the goat bit me."

Liz smiled, but held firm. "Right buttock, near the Great Divide," she said as she evaded his grasp. Liz rummaged in her suitcase and produced a bottle of bubble bath. She hesitated a moment before turning back to Ty. "I'm sorry. Did you want to get into the bathroom?"

Ty rolled onto his stomach and gave her an unfathomable look. "You know, I hear the latest thing is for couples to bathe together. What the hell, let's find out what the big deal is." He started to get out of bed.

Liz shook her head. "No. Please. Daylight's not very kind and I'm not ready for you to see everything at once."

Ty smiled, "Okay, I can wait."

Liz made her way to the bathroom, nearly tripping over the blanket. As she filled the tub for a bath, Liz told herself that she was right in not letting Ty see her. Not yet, she thought. Let me lose some weight. Let me look better for him. She washed her hair while waiting for the tub to fill. Liz turned off the taps and eased herself into the fragrant water. She closed her eyes and leaned back.

"Move over."

Water sloshed as Liz jumped. Ty was already stepping into the tub and Liz looked away from him. He settled himself into the water and sniffed appreciatively.

"Mmm. Smells like that perfume you wear. I like it." He rested his arms on the edge of the tub and grinned at Liz. A series of bubbles broke the water's surface midway down the tub. Liz stared at him, crossed arms shielding her breasts.

"You said you were going to wait," she accused.

"True," he pulled her close, "I just didn't say how long." He kissed her as he gently pulled her arms away from her body, putting them around himself. They washed each other from head to foot, frequently exchanging kisses or just lying in each others' arms in the warm, soapy water.

Liz was still drying her hair when Ty excused himself with another kiss, towel around his waist, to get dressed. She remembered how much she had wanted to share the shower with him in October and had denied herself the pleasure that time. She smiled dreamily at her reflection in the foggy mirror. It had been worth the wait.

Wrapped in another towel, Liz followed Ty into the bedroom, looking around. She frowned. No suitcase.

"Ty, where are my clothes?"

"Safe and sound," he answered casually. He was dressed and sitting in a chair. Liz could see mischief in his eyes. She clutched her towel closer.

Liz hated being naked or nearly so. It made her too vulnerable. Ty was looking at her and smiling. All of a sudden, the towel was far too small for her comfort.

"Ty, may I please have my clothes?" she asked sweetly.

"You don't need them," he replied. Gesturing at the towel, Ty added, "You can even get rid of that."

"No, I can't." Liz answered.

Ty reached over and tugged at the towel. Liz tightened her grip. "I said you had nothing to hide from me. Give me the towel."

"No. Please give me my clothes." Liz tried to maintain her temper. "Ty, Sweetheart, it's December in Massachusetts. I can't leave the room without risking hypothermia. May I have my clothes?"

"You want your clothes?" She could tell by his tone that something was definitely up. He released his grip on the towel. "Yes, Darling. May I please have my clothes before I find it necessary to kill you to get them?"

Ty grinned, "Here's the deal: See, you're trying to hide behind that skimpy little towel. This tells me that, despite everything, you don't trust me completely yet. Therefore, if you want your clothes, you're going to have to learn to trust me with everything. And I do mean everything. I could pull that towel off your body, but I want you to trust me enough to do it yourself."

Liz clutched the towel tight for a moment, then took a deep breath and let the towel drop.

"Much better." Ty leaned back, now grinning broadly.

Liz hugged herself, shivering a little, partly from nerves and partly from the cooler air in the room.

"How long do I have to stand here like this?" Liz looked at the bed. He had stripped it of linens. Maybe the curtains, she thought.

"You'll get your clothes back when you realize that scars and stretch marks and the things you're hung up on don't matter to me." His tone softened. "You are more than a body to me, Liz. If you don't believe that, then how can you believe in my love for you?"

Liz bit her lip and said nothing. Ty continued. "Actually, there is one more thing you can do to get your clothes back." Liz saw the glint in his eyes. She tried unsuccessfully to bite back a smile.

"I'm almost afraid to ask."

Ty chuckled. "I want you to read me one of your stories."

"No." The answer came so fast, she was surprised.

Ty got serious, "Fine, then. No reading, no clothing."

Liz felt panic building. "Be reasonable."

"No."

"Let me have my underwear, at least," Liz bargained.

"No."

Liz sighed, "Why can't I have my clothes?"

Ty leaned back and put his hands behind his head. "Because for once in your life, you are going to have to drop all that emotional armor. It's crap," He cut her off as she started to protest, "I mean it, this crap that you believe about yourself. My God, Liz, you have armored yourself so well I can almost see it. Because I want you open to me, in body and in mind. You are glorious and I want to bask in it."

Liz ducked her head. Nobody, not even former lovers, had ever called her "glorious" or complimented her body. It would take some getting used to. "Okay, you win, but please, may I have something to wrap up in? I'm getting cold."

Ty looked pointedly at her breasts. "I see that." He handed the towel back to her and she wrapped herself as before. "Thanks. You win."

"You'll see. No losers in this one." Ty pulled Liz into his lap. "I like what you do for that towel. Here," he handed Liz her notebook with a kiss. "Read."

"Don't expect Andre Dubus or O. Henry," Liz opened her book. Which story? Turning towards the back of the book, Liz began to read what she'd been writing when he found her. They relived the Barrister's Ball through her words, felt the magic again.

"...and under the mistletoe, in the quiet corner, his kiss set her heart free." She closed the book.

Ty put his hand to her face. He kissed her cheek, "What are you doing practicing law? You should be writing and publishing." Liz turned her head to kiss the palm of his hand, "Well, Ty, right now, law is paying the bills and creative writing is not. I have the rejection letters to prove it."

"How can it pay the bills if you quit your job?" He asked. Liz stared at him. "That's right, I heard." He chuckled. "Dan gave me an earful pretty much as soon as you left his office. Seems to think I stole you away." He kissed her face. "I just might at that."

"Sorry, Sweetheart. Judge McCafferty offered me a clerkship and I accepted." Liz kissed him back, but Ty was frowning.

"That's kind of a step back, isn't it, Liz?"

"Not from my perspective," Liz said.

Ty frowned. "Let me set you up at my firm. This clerkship doesn't seem like a good idea to me."

Liz sat up, "Maybe not to you, Ty, but you thrive on the law firm experience. I hate billable hours, I hate going into court, I hate the gotta-make-partner-before-5-years mentality. Those kinds of pressures are going to have me back to compulsive eating. Plus, I can just hear the whispers about you hiring your girlfriend. No. I like the research, I like the writing and I really like Frank McCafferty. So, it seems like a very good idea to me. Now," she kissed him and put her forehead to his, "may I have my clothes?"

Ty laid his head against her shoulder and Liz closed her eyes. Just touching him made her heartbeat race. She felt his hand slide along her leg and under the towel.

"Not just yet on the clothes," Ty murmured as he started to rise from the chair. He had nearly succeeded when there was an ominous creak and a section of the ceiling crashed onto their bed, collapsing it to the floor.

Astonished, Ty set Liz on her feet, holding her close. She wrapped her arms around him. After a few moments, Liz said, "Well, maybe it was for the best."

Ty looked at her, puzzled. "Why do you say that?"

Liz grinned, "We were never going to get out of that bed otherwise. Now may I have my clothes?"

Chapter 8

"Step aside, please, Ma'am. Thank you," the mover said to Liz. She stepped aside as requested as he and his colleague moved her breakfront onto the waiting truck.

"'Step aside, Ma'am?'" Millie asked. "You're going to let him call you 'Ma'am?'"

"Hey, it beats the hell out of the usual 'Move your ass, Gardner' that I get from you," Liz responded.

"You know," said Millie as she watched the proceedings with Liz, "This beats moving all your shit ourselves in the cold, having to bribe the guys to help us, buying beer and pizza and then hurting for three days afterwards."

"I agree," said Liz in a distracted tone of voice. Millie gently poked her arm.

"You know, for someone going to live with the man of her dreams, you don't seem very excited or enthusiastic," Millie remarked.

"Mill, not all of us know how to dance the Funky Chicken," Liz said, still watching the movers, "You gave the neighbors quite a show that day."

The men came back in from the truck, blowing on their hands from the January cold and headed back to the living room for more furniture.Liz was still kind of dazed from the speed with which Ty moved after their weekend in Hyannis. It had been little over a month and here she was, leaving her house and moving into his.

Almost immediately, Ty had begun to chafe at the distance between his home in Wellesley and Liz's house in Salem. He had wanted Liz to come home with him after their weekend, but she'd refused, reminding him that she had Beanie to care for.

Christmas had been an experience, both wonderful and stressful. The wonder had come in being with Ty for the holiday, making love the night before, waking in his arms only to be showered with gifts that took away Liz's breath, including a new

147

car. Liz had noticed that Ty gave her old VW a bad look whenever he saw it, declining to ride or drive in it. One day, the car had refused to start altogether. She was at Ty's house in Wellesley, preparing to leave when he had asked her for the keys. Liz gave him a quizzical look as she handed him the keys.

"I just thought it would be nice if I started the engine for you and let it warm up a bit, so you don't get cold," Ty explained. He'd taken the keys from Liz with a kiss and she thought she could see something devious in his expression.

Ten minutes later, Liz was beginning to worry since he hadn't returned. Just as she was about to head out the door to see what was going on, Ty returned, threw the keys onto a table and announced, "The Rabbit died" on his way out of the room. He had taken Liz home to Salem and stayed with her for a few days.

Indeed, Liz's mechanic did pronounce the car dead, beyond even his considerable skills. The man looked upset and Liz put her arm around him and said, "Hey, you probably kept him going longer than he would have otherwise. He had a long, good life because you took care of him." He nodded, although Liz thought she saw him well up slightly.

As Liz began looking through the used-car ads in the Sunday Globe, she had a sneaking suspicion that the Rabbit hadn't died so much as been assassinated. Ty had motives: he'd never liked the car and it was an effective way of keeping Liz closer to him. She had surreptitiously looked at him while pretending to study the Volkswagen column in the automotive classifieds, but he just kept working on the crossword puzzle and ignored her look, even though Liz thought she detected a slight smirk when she mentioned her conversation with the mechanic.

On Christmas Day, after getting several pieces of expensive jewelry and a full ounce of her favorite perfume, Ty had handed Liz an envelope and told her, "Come with me."

He had taken her out to the garage where something sat under a tarp next his Mercedes. Something big. "Okay, open the envelope," he'd instructed as he picked up a corner of the tarp. Liz found a registration, title and insurance in her name for a brand-new Mercedes coupe. Looking up, she saw Ty standing proudly next to the car described in the paperwork. Liz had dropped the envelope.

"My God, Ty! You shouldn't have!" Liz had gasped as she stepped forward to look at it. "This is too much. I can't accept this."

"Yes, you can," he had insisted, "You need a car and it is my pleasure to fulfill your needs," playfully squeezing her ass, he'd added, "all of them."

Liz had wrapped her arms around Ty and kissed him, her tongue darting around his, teasing and luring until he'd taken control, pulling her against himself.

Liz had broken off the kiss long enough to give him a sassy look. "Wanna break in the back seat, Counselor?" she'd asked. Ty gave her a look of pretend shock. "You shameless hussy! There is no back seat!" He had kissed her, saying, "Anyway, my bed's much more comfortable."

Before the office Christmas party, Ty had handed Liz several credit cards over lunch one day. "Here, these are yours. I took the liberty of looking through your closet and you're going to need to do some shopping."

Liz looked at the cards. They were all either platinum or gold cards for the usual credit card companies or VIP cards for upscale department stores like Neiman-Marcus. And they had her name on them.

"Shopping for what, Babe?" Liz asked in confusion.

"We'll be going to more black-tie functions and as much as I love that blue velvet dress of yours," he had said, "you can't wear it to all of them. Take the cards, take Millie and have fun. Shop 'til you drop. Buy whatever you want. I love you. Gotta run." And he had kissed her before leaving for a client meeting, 5 minutes after his meal had arrived and 25 minutes after he had sat down with Liz. Her first use of the cards had been to pay for the meal and Beanie had gotten leftover grilled salmon for dinner.

The stress had come from the scrutiny of Ty's colleagues and their wives at his firm's Christmas party. Sarah Washburn had somehow managed to separate Liz from Ty at the Christmas party, nominally to introduce her to some of the other women, but also to put Liz in front of them for interrogation. The small group of women had asked mundane, polite questions with nasty edges to their voices and even nastier smiles on their faces. Rachel Dunn had given Liz a withering look before remarking in a careless way,

"So, you're Tyrone's latest. I guess bigger IS better." And she had then taken a big swallow of her vodka martini. Even Sarah Washburn had bitten back a gasp.

Liz had smiled a saccharin smile back at her, remembering Corey mentioning that Rachel had pursued Ty to no avail. "You're right, he is very well-equipped. No complaints here." Rachel had almost choked on her drink and Liz excused herself, in search of Ty.

She hadn't gotten very far when a familiar sneer stopped her. "You know," said Cheryl the Silicone Queen sullenly, "I put a lot of time in on that man and then you come along and steal him. You think you won, but I can take him away from you any time I want, Bitch. And don't you forget it. "

Liz turned to face the younger woman, who was clearly drunk. She was clutching a margarita and had spilled some on her dress, but didn't seem to be aware of it. The usual sex kitten air was gone, drowned in the tequila, no doubt and replaced by bitterness. Liz noted that the woman was alone, none of the usual male hopefuls to be seen. Her eye makeup had spread out, creating a raccoon effect and her hair looked like a haystack. She was glaring at Liz as usual.

"I said, 'I can take him away from you any time I want to'," she repeated with a bitter edge. She swallowed more liquor. "Whaddya think of that, you fat bitch?"

Liz looked at her evenly, feeling some pity, "I heard you the first time and you know what?"

"What?"

"There will probably be days when I'd let you. This isn't one of them. Merry Christmas." And she'd walked away. Hearing a crash behind her, Liz turned. The Silicone Queen had flung her glass at Liz and missed, both in distance and accuracy.

The background murmur of a party in full swing had come to a dead stop at the sound and people stared at the two women.

Liz bit back the impulse to crack a one-liner and instead repeated, "Merry Christmas" before returning to her search for Ty. "YOU FUCKING BITCH!" She heard screamed behind her. "YOU FUCKING THIEVING BITCH! I'LL KILL YOU!"

Liz kept moving forward, although now she could feel her heart hammering and her throat closing. Knowing that eyes were on her, Liz kept her head high and her pace deliberate.

"Liz? Honey? What was that about?" Ty found Liz before she found him. He slipped an arm around her waist. Liz noted the cocktail glass in his other hand.

She smiled at him and kissed him on the cheek as she slipped her arm around his waist. What Liz wanted to do was throw herself on him and sob hysterically into his shoulder, beg him to take her home now. She made light of the encounter. "Someone's had too much to drink," she said casually. "It wouldn't be an office party otherwise. Just have to wait for someone to find a copier and sit on it. You know, if I ran a printing/copying shop, I'd decorate copiers in Christmas colors and rent them out for parties. That way, you get the traditional butt copies without damage to the office equipment."

Ty chuckled, but his eyes probed her face and he squeezed her. "You want another drink?" he asked.

"Actually," said Liz, "I think I'm going to find the powder room and freshen up a bit." She kissed Ty slowly and deeply, mostly because of the pleasure of it, but also for the benefit of the onlookers.

Liz found her way to the powder room of the Park Plaza Hotel and sat in front of the vanity. She rested her elbows on the counter and pressing her palms together, leaned forward, closed her eyes and rested her face against her hands. Without her gang around her and Ty busy networking, Liz thought, this was going to be a long, miserable night. Luckily, the powder room made for a comfortable hiding place.

"Praying for deliverance?" asked a warm voice behind her. Liz jumped and looked at the speaker. She recognized Nancy Brooks, wife of one of Ty's partners. With a smile, Nancy seated herself next to Liz, who braced herself for another round of catty conversation.Nancy saw this and waved a hand. "Oh, don't worry about it. I'm not in league with that tramp, Rachel Dunn."

Liz smiled. "I feel like the red-headed bastard at a family reunion."

"So you're hiding?" the question was gentle. Nancy laid a hand on her arm. "Don't let them win."

"I prefer to think of it as a strategic retreat to regroup. It's not often I have drinks and invective hurled at me simultaneously.

151

Usually it's just one or the other. I was unprepared to get both."

Nancy laughed. "You're funny. If that had been me, I'd have turned around and slapped the little bitch."

Liz smiled ruefully, "Apparently, in her eyes, I'm a thief."

"Don't worry about her," said Nancy, "That woman's gone down on more men than the Titanic and she's already moved on to one of the junior associates. She's even gone after my husband, but Bill didn't bite. I saw you at the Barrister's Ball. Ty couldn't keep his eyes off you. That pissed her off no end. I don't know what you did to him that night, but Bill says he was unapproachable for the next week, in a pitch-black mood and that isn't Ty. He was terrorizing everyone who came near him."

I know exactly what he was going through, thought Liz.

"And now?" she asked. "He's his usual self, according to Bill," said Nancy. "Works hard, makes a ton of money for the firm and himself. He's a good man, Elizabeth, and I'm glad to see him with someone worthy, not Silicone Sally the Super Slut."

Liz laughed. This wasn't like the viciously funny debriefing she would have done with Millie and Corey, but it was an immense relief to have a conversation with this kindly soul. She held out her hand to Nancy Brooks. "Call me Liz."

Nancy shook it. "Good. Now, Liz, you come with me and we'll talk to some people who aren't looking to stick a knife in your back. I'm sure you'll enjoy the party much more after that."

And she had. In the course of her conversations, Liz discovered that Ty had been telling stories about her to anyone who would listen. More than once, someone would smile and say, "I feel like I already know you." Or, "Ty says you write. Have you published anything?"

Ty had booked a suite at the hotel for that weekend and they had made the most of their time in town, returning to the Top of the Hub for dinner, going to a blues club and making love until daylight both nights.

Liz had been astonished the first time she saw Ty's house. It was a graceful modern interpretation of a cape-style house. Five bedrooms, four and a half bathrooms, including a Jacuzzi in the master suite plus a swimming pool and substantial lawn.

"Wow," Liz had remarked. "All this for just you?" she had asked.

"Well, I do entertain here," Ty had said. "I just saw the place and really wanted it. It came on the market about the same time I won my first class-action suit and I paid cash out of my fee." There had been a look of pride in his accomplishment on Ty's face.

The interior was as elegant as the exterior, beautifully decorated and maintained in pristine condition. Ty's housekeeper took care of the place as if it were her own, even doing laundry and arranging for dry-cleaning pickup and delivery. Liz loved the kitchen, especially. It was big, equipped with the best appliances and had counter space enough even to satisfy Liz. What I couldn't do in there, she had thought.

They had dined out that night and most of the nights Liz stayed in Wellesley. And on the last night of an extraordinary year, Liz couldn't stop looking at the house as she removed her bags from her car. It had been decorated for the season with white lights, fresh greenery and red velvet ribbons. A huge wreath hung on the front door. All very tasteful and understated.

Ty had given Liz a key to let herself in, explaining that he was undoubtedly going to be running late, but he'd come fetch her for the party and, by the way, they had a suite at the Ritz Carlton for the night, so pack accordingly. Liz had reflected that it was lucky that Beanie was not only a forgiving animal, but his baby-sitters enjoyed looking after him.

Juggling her bags, Liz opened the front door and half-walked, half-fell inside. "Hello?" she called out.

"Yes? Who's there?" a female voice called back. Liz heard footsteps and Ty's housekeeper strode into view. "Oh, Miss Gardner, it's you. Happy New Year."

"And the same to you, Mrs. Wyman. Has Mr. Hadley called?" Liz asked as she closed the door.

"Yes, Ma'am, he just called to say he'll be here by 8:00 at the latest and you should make yourself at home."

Liz looked at her wristwatch. It was 6:00 PM. "Okay, that gives me 2 hours of unchallenged access to the bathroom and I'm gonna take full advantage of it. Ty doesn't know it, but I'm really after him for his tub."

Mrs. Wyman laughed. "You do that, Miss Gardner. Mr. Hadley instructed me to make sure you had wine and hors d'ouevres available."

"Sounds good, thank you. Do you have big plans for tonight, Mrs. Wyman?" Liz asked.

"Oh, I'll be leaving here in a half-hour and going to my son's house in Dedham. He always brings together his family and friends on New Year's. We'll have a buffet dinner and watch some movies, then we toast the New Year and have breakfast around 2 in the morning, then everybody sleeps until the football starts," she said with a smile. "It's a nice tradition." She turned to get wine and hors d'ouevres for Liz.

"Sounds great," said Liz. Sounded like Joey's party, something she hadn't missed in years. It wouldn't be the same, ringing in a new year without them, but sometimes you have to let go of things, no matter how much you love them, to make room for something better. "I'll just head upstairs and get started." Liz huffed her way upstairs with her bags, dropping them in Ty's master bedroom. As with the rest of the house, it had been decorated with understated elegance in shades of blue. The end result was something out of Architectural Digest. Actually, remembered Liz, the house had been in Architectural Digest a few years before. A specially bound copy lay on the coffee table in the den downstairs.

Liz carefully unpacked her dress for the occasion, full length, one shoulder, black with silver beading. It had cost a small fortune in a snotty Newbury Street boutique, but Millie (and Corey) had argued that she couldn't leave it behind. She located the shoes and other accessories to go with it.

"Here you go," said Mrs. Wyman with a smile. She had a tray with a Waterford wine glass, a small crystal decanter of Merlot and canapés that she set down on the bureau. "Now, you enjoy your bath and Happy New Year again, Miss Gardner. You know, I don't think I've ever seen Mr. Hadley so happy as he has been with you. You two have a good time at your party. I'll be thinking of you, all dressed up like Cinderella."

Liz laughed and hugged her. "Thank you and a very good New Year to you, Mrs. Wyman. You have a blast." Mrs. Wyman left.

Liz shampooed before drawing the bath for herself. The tub was deep and designed for extended soaking and she wanted to take full advantage of it. Liz found her bubble bath next to the tub, the same scent as her perfume and purchased for her by Ty to be used only here. She dumped a generous amount into the tub and poured herself a glass of wine while she waited for the tub to fill.

So, here she sat in the home of her love. Alone. She had been waited on upon her arrival, but no Ty. She was alone in his house.

New Year's Eve had also been her last day at Lovell, Hoffman and Dennis. They'd thrown a party for her, including parting gifts such as a new briefcase and desk nameplate. Millie had cried a little and Corey had cried a lot, mostly because he feared being reassigned to Dan. Joey and Rocco had hugged her and vowed that they weren't afraid of roughing up judges if necessary. Win Lovell and David Hoffman had come by. Dan was playing golf in Palm Beach. They told her that her work and herself would be missed at the place. "You mean my cooking, don't you, Sir?" Liz had asked of Win. He had laughed and patted his stomach. "My wife seems to think I'll lose weight if you're not here. Now, you go knock F.L. McCafferty's socks off and remember," he became serious, "if you change your mind, you always have a place here." They both knew she wouldn't.

Ty and Liz had debated whether to attend his firm's party or to go to Joey DiNardo's annual bash. Liz had been unable to persuade Ty to even consider just stopping in at Joe and Jenna's, agreeing that, yes, as a named partner, he had certain obligations outside of office hours and as his girlfriend, it was her place to be with him. It had been a wrench to tell the DiNardos that, no, she and Ty wouldn't be joining the celebration as they'd thought. Maybe next year.

Joey had looked hard into Liz's eyes. "Liz, you sure you know what you're doing?"

"Working for McCafferty? It'll be a blast," she had answered.

"No. I mean Hadley. I know you love him and I know he loves you, but...," Joey's jaw had set and his eyes had taken on a steely glint. "He'd better treat you right, Sister Lizabetta or he'll regret it."

Liz had hugged Joey. "Brother Giuseppe, how many Hail Marys do you think Angie's going to make you say for that?"

Taking her wine, Liz turned off the tap, slipped under the bubbles and closed her eyes. The scent was a blend of roses, orange blossoms and jasmine with, according to the ads, "a dash of liquid starlight." Perfume ads were almost as ridiculous as wine reviews.

Liz allowed herself to drift and dream. She saw herself in Ty's arms as they lay in bed, smiling into his face. She saw the love in his eyes, felt his hands knowingly stroke her body, how quickly he had learned the ways to pleasure her as she had him. Ty brought out an eagerness and passion in Liz that she hadn't known she had; the intensity was almost frightening. Ty encouraged her. They seldom went to sleep before the small hours of the morning, Ty reading John Donne's love poems to her from a copy they'd found in a Hyannis bookstore on that magic weekend. She'd wake as she had in Hyannis, Ty holding her close as he slept. Liz didn't sleep very well on the nights they were apart. Within a couple of weeks, she'd become accustomed to sharing her bed with him. Without him, the loneliness that had been her life seemed even greater and made their time together that much sweeter.

"Ty, I love you so much," she murmured out loud. "I just wish I could have more of you."

"You can have me right now, Counselor," the real thing murmured in her ear.

Liz sat up with a splash. "TY! DON'T DO THAT!"

He was laughing too hard to respond, so Liz splashed bath water at him, soaking the front of his suit. His response was to set down his glass of Scotch, laugh even harder and strip.

"Room for one more, Counselor?" he asked.

"You're going to smell like a perfume counter, you know," she said as she made room for him. "No cannonballs."

He slipped into the tub next to Liz and pulled her close as he sank in. "Mmmm, I needed this."

"Bad day, Counselor?" Liz asked as she snuggled close.

"Oh yeah. The usual year-end nonsense. I finally said, 'Why am I here when Liz is waiting for me at home? Fuck it.' So I left." He kissed her, "That was one helluva a smile you were wearing, Sweetheart. What were you thinking about?"

"You." Liz saw the weariness on his face and stroked his cheek with a soapy hand. "Are you sure you want to go to this party tonight, Love? You look beat."

Ty smiled as he caught her hand and kissed it. "I'll be fine and we can sleep tomorrow. I just need to catch my second wind and this helps." He reached for the Scotch and drained it, then handed the glass to Liz, who set it down again. "How was your day?" he asked, stroking Liz's thigh under the water. His hand moved inward and upward, fingers making little circles.

"Actually, pretty good. They threw a going-away party for me and Win Lovell said I could come back if I wanted to." She had a hard time sounding normal with the currents racing through her body at his touch. Ty knew it, too and slipped his hand to the cleft between her thighs, fingers slowly probing. Liz inhaled sharply and arched her back. Involuntarily, she dug her fingernails into him, spurring him on. A throaty gasp escaped her. Ty maneuvered himself into position and entered her under the water. Minutes later, still throbbing, Liz looked over the side of the tub. The floor of the bathroom resembled a small lake.

She half-laughed, half-groaned. "Time to swab the decks," she said. Ty pulled her closer.

"So, Counselor, you want more of me, huh?" he asked. "I can arrange it." He kissed her deeply. "Move in here with me," he said.

Liz's eyes opened wide. "Are you serious?" she asked.

Ty regarded her lazily. "That I am. I want you here, with me. I want to know that this is your home, too. How can I wake up next to the love of my life if I'm here and she's over 30 miles away? I don't like being that far away from you and having to jump through hoops to see you. I mean it, Liz. I want you to move in with me and do it soon. Next weekend."

"Oh, God, Ty. I can't organize a move that quickly. I know the crew has plans, like Millie and John are going to see his parents. Plus, I start with McCafferty next week and I'll need to settle in there."

Ty wasn't put off. "Two weeks, then."

"I can't sort through and pack up my house in that time," Liz said.

"Rent it furnished. Am I sensing reluctance on your part?" he asked. Ty sat up. "Liz, I want to be with you so badly I can taste it. I thought you felt the same."

"I do," Liz answered honestly.

"So what's the problem?" he asked gently.

"Honey, this is an awfully big step," Liz said. "We're still just getting to know each other. I've...I've never done this before. I don't know. I really need to think about this."

Ty reached forward and touched Liz's cheek. "You don't need

to think about it. I do know. I promised that you could trust me and I meant it. Hell, if I'd had my way, you and your cat would have been installed here the night we got back from Hyannis. We're not teenagers, Liz, we don't have the luxury of time. This feels right. This is right. You're the one for me." There was a warm light in his eyes that reassured Liz. "We're great together, you know that. We'll be together every day and," He pulled her close and kissed her again, "every night."

Liz wrapped her arms around his neck. She didn't know what to say.

"Ever since I met you, I've wanted to take care of you, spoil you and protect you. I need you next to me, need to wake up to your face," Ty said softly, stroking his fingers down her throat. "You're mine and it's frustrating not to be able to reach out in the night and touch you, to know you're still with me." He traced the scar on her breast. "You've been hurt and sick and on your own before and that makes me angry. That's not going to happen again. I want to be right there when you need me. This is the only way I know how." He kissed her again. "What do you say, Liz? 'Come live with me and be my love...'"

" 'And we'll some new pleasure prove,'" finished Liz, smiling.

Ty kissed her forehead. "Buying that copy of Donne's poetry was a great investment," he murmured. "We won't have to keep schlepping it between your house and mine if we're together all the time." He kissed her again.

"You know, Counselor," said Liz, "you can be irresistible when you choose."

"Where you're concerned," he answered, "It's my ace in the hole. Is that a yes?"

"It is," she whispered. She ruthlessly quelled her misgivings.

At the New Year's Eve party, Liz hadn't felt the same wall of hostility that she'd gotten walking in on Ty's arm at the Christmas party. Liz had noticed that the Silicone Queen was not there to ring in the new year.

Everything was top-shelf. The champagne was expensive, the food was catered by a five-star restaurant, everyone was dressed in designer labels. Yet while she was enjoying conversation with Ty's colleagues, Liz was missing the casual-dress gathering at Joe's, the arguments over which movies they'd watch, the board games,

Angie yelling at "her" children, the warmth that came from being within the group. Here, the people were friendly, but it was a distant, detached friendliness born of career advancement.

No sooner had they removed their coats but a couple of the junior associates pounced on Ty to talk about some pending cases. He had shrugged helplessly, kissed Liz and excused himself. Finding herself alone among virtual strangers, Liz squared her shoulders, held her head high and determined to charm and impress anyone she met, but the back of her mind was replaying Ty's proposition. God, if she was still alive, thought Liz, my mother would have a fit. "Obviously, you're not good enough to marry," or something like that. Liz pushed the thought down. Not tonight. She didn't need to run those old tapes tonight.

As time closed on midnight, Liz looked around for Ty. He had finished business with the junior members of the firm and was talking with one of the named partners. Liz approached the men and slipped her hand into Ty's. Without missing a beat of the conversation, he squeezed her hand, but that was the only acknowledgment of her presence Liz got for a couple of minutes. At five minutes to midnight, a waiter came by with champagne and Ty finally broke off the discussion.

"C'mon," he said as he led Liz towards the crowd waiting for the countdown. He and Liz slipped arms around each other and joined the countdown.

"Three, two, one, HAPPY NEW YEAR!"

Instead of rowdy cheering and everyone singing "Auld Lang Syne" in his or her own key, here there were polite murmurs of "Happy New Year" and hand-shaking. Ty took Liz in his arms and kissed her as he had at the Barrister's Ball.

"May we be together at this time next year," he murmured.

And, two weekends later, Liz and Millie were watching professional movers empty her house onto a truck. Liz had managed to find a tenant for her place, students starting the second semester at Salem State who were happy to take the place semi-furnished. However, it seemed to Liz that a lot of stuff was headed for storage with no definite date for getting it out again.

"You know, this is your life going onto that truck, Liz," Millie remarked. "Ty wouldn't allow any of it and you just smiled and said 'Fine'?" she asked incredulously. "Doesn't sound like the stubborn bitch I know."

"You've seen the house, Mill. It's gorgeous. None of this would go with it. It's not that Ty didn't allow me to bring my furniture, it just wasn't needed," Liz replied.

"Uh huh," said Millie, "and where is Prince Charming today?"

Liz shot her a sharp look, "Working. Millie, am I going to have a problem between you and Ty?"

Millie shrugged. "Probably not. I'm just pissed because I'm not going to see you at work anymore, you're moving to Wellesley and it just feels like he's taking you away from us."

Liz didn't say anything, but she'd had the same thoughts. "Well, I see your point. But, Judge McCafferty allows me a lot of freedom to do my job, just as long as it gets done on time. We can get together for lunch in the city and we can still do things together. Besides, I know you're going to start bitching soon enough that we're getting on each other's nerves as we put this wedding of yours together. Let's face it, Mill, you've already taken steps to more or less dump me for a man. I'm just returning the favor."

Millie laughed and punched her arm. "Fine. Be that way. I will say, though, the two of you are hot together. It's clear you guys are in love with each other."

"That's the last of it, Ma'am," a mover interrupted. "Sorry to interrupt you ladies, but it's wicked cold. Where are we going?"

With a smile, Liz gave him an address on Route 62 for a self-storage facility. She and Millie put on their coats, took a last look around and stepped outside, closing and locking the front door. They followed the truck to storage and observed the unloading. Once the movers rumbled off, Liz turned to Millie.

"Come on down this afternoon. We'll have a moving-in party."

Millie shook her head. "I'm sorry, I can't. John and I have an appointment at the Danversport Yacht Club about the reception and the menu." She hugged Liz. "I'm sorry, but we can do brunch tomorrow." She looked at Liz's face. "It's scary, I know. But you'll be fine." And she left.

Liz got into her car and turned over the engine. From force of habit, she uttered a quick prayer, "Please Lord, let it start," but unlike the old Rabbit, the Mercedes never gave her a problem. She eased out of the parking lot and headed south to her new home.

Beanie had gone to Wellesley the night before. Fortunately, he had the soul of an explorer and going for a ride in the car didn't require drugging him. Even a trip to the vet clinic was routine and calm. Beanie had sat in his crate, nose and whiskers twitching as he took in the new car smell, occasionally stretching a paw out through the mesh covering the front of the crate. Liz would reach over and gently hold the paw, feeling it flex as Beanie tried to pull her hand back to his face for a lick.

Right now, Liz's car was filled with boxes. Clothing, her most treasured kitchen paraphernalia, her computer and her pictures. Ty was at work. At the time she was heading to Salem to oversee the move, he was heading into Boston for a strategy session. They had each filled travel mugs of coffee and clinked them together in a toast. Liz had started to set hers down, when Ty stopped her.

"It's bad luck to toast and then set down the glass without drinking." She had sipped some coffee. "Liz, I'm sorry I'm not going to be there to help you out," he had started.

She had waved him off. "Don't worry about it. You got me hired muscle and I'm just supervising. I'll be fine and be unpacked by the time you come home." It had felt odd to use that phrase and know that by the end of the day, her definition of where home was would change. And that home wouldn't be solely hers anymore, either. Rather, she was joining another established household. This was going to take some adjusting.

Ty had smiled and lightly kissed her. "After tonight," he said, "no more barriers between us." He took Liz's hand and started to lead her into the den. "I have a surprise for you and for Beanie."

The den was one of Ty's favorite rooms. It was elegantly appointed, but with an eye towards creating a space where people felt free to relax and unwind. The sofas were overstuffed and long enough for a tall man to stretch out comfortably. There was a coffee table topped in green marble that Beanie had already claimed as his domain. A top of the line home theater system had been installed and Ty had an extensive library of movies, stored in an oak cabinet.

The prize, however, was the rug covering the floor. When he had first showed her the room, Ty had moved a sofa out of the way to show the rug to Liz. During his Rhodes scholarship period in England, Ty had befriended a young man from one of the sultanates of the Middle East also studying at Oxford. The boy had been struggling with his classes because of the language difficulty. Ty had tutored him in English. He found out later that his friend's father was a powerful advisor to the sultan when two large men from that country's embassy to Britain had arrived at Ty's dormitory room with the carpet and a letter of gratitude from the father.

The rug was beautiful. Liz had felt the surface, expecting to feel the prickly sensation of wool. Instead it was smooth and soft. "It's silk," Ty had said as he stroked the surface with pride. The colors in the rug did have the shimmer that only silk can lend and those colors were rich and deep. Jewel tones of ruby red mixed with clear blues and forest greens in an intricate geometric pattern.

"You know, Liz, I'm not into possessions. I have stuff and I like to have good stuff, but I don't get off on having it. This, however," and he picked up the corner of the rug, "really means something to me and I love seeing it on the floor in my house." He had carefully laid down the corner of the rug and gently replaced the sofa where it had been.

Next, Ty showed Liz something in the corner of the den. She laughed, "Ty, you are going to spoil that cat." Beanie was already perched at the top of a floor to ceiling kitty jungle gym in front of a window. Its branches were topped with small carpeted platforms in a variety of shapes. Liz could hear him purring from across the room. Ty walked over to the corner and Beanie reached down from his perch to playfully slap Ty on the head. Ty laughed as he darted a hand back to Beanie, who caught it and licked it. Liz watched the two of them play.

"I guess you're officially in if he's already bopping you on the head," she said.

"I found a catnip mouse in my shoe this morning," Ty said. "Does that mean anything?"

"He's made himself at home and he wants to share his toys with you," Liz answered.

Ty withdrew his hand from Beanie and stepped over to where Liz was standing. He encircled her waist in his arms and asked, "Does he consider you one of his toys? You're the only thing I care about him sharing" and he'd pulled her close, kissing the top of her head.

Liz smiled as she remembered the scene. They'd left on their separate missions shortly afterwards, exchanging a long, deep kiss at the door. The one problem had been that Beanie had made a successful dash out the front door and recovery was complicated by the presence of a squirrel. Ignoring Liz's calls, Beanie had taken off after the squirrel, almost getting into the street before Liz caught him. On the way back into the house, Beanie had watched the spot where he'd last seen his prey and struggled to get out of Liz's arms and finish the chase. Liz had barely managed to get him inside.

And now, she had to unpack the car and keep Beanie from escaping. Simple, she thought, I'll just throw him in the den and shut the door. He'll be happy.

Liz pulled into the driveway and pressed the button to open the garage door remotely. After years of parking on the street, Liz appreciated this small luxury no end. She pulled into the second space, noting that Ty's car was already in its space. He was home. Liz turned off the engine and closed the big door.

She began unloading the trunk of her car, kind of surprised that Ty hadn't come out to the garage upon hearing her arrive. Maybe the soundproofing in the house was really good. She opened the door leading from the garage into a small mud room off the kitchen. Beanie dashed by her.

"Ha! Foiled again! The big door's closed!" Liz called after him. She turned to continue moving items into the house.

"Hello?" Liz called out. "Anybody home?"

Silence. She shrugged and went about her business, finally shooing Beanie back into the house after she'd emptied the car. It hadn't taken long.

Liz was in the process of schlepping cartons upstairs when Ty emerged from the den. "Hey, Babe, when did you get here?" he asked. "Let me." He took the boxes from Liz and headed upstairs with them.

"About 20 minutes ago," she said. "You didn't hear me?"

"I was on the phone. I thought I heard something, but I wasn't sure," he answered over his shoulder.

It didn't take long to unpack. The last item to be put into place was Liz's print of Pygmalion and Galatea. With Ty's help, she hung the picture on a hook near his bed. Their bed.

163

Ty leaned back on the bed propped on his elbows and studied the print. Beanie jumped up on the bed and rubbed against him, whacking Ty with his tail.

"It's such a dark background," he remarked. "Every time I see it, I think about how gloomy it looks. And I can't understand how you of all people, would be attracted to a story about a man creating the perfect woman. Doesn't strike me as something that would appeal to you, Liz."

Liz sat next to Ty and put her arm around his shoulder. "Well, that's one interpretation. I got the chance to talk to a sculptor at a thing at the Museum of Fine Arts and I asked him how he chose what he would sculpt. The guy said that he'd look at a piece of stone and see something in it, then carve until he freed it. It was after that conversation that I found this picture and it occurred to me that Pygmalion hadn't created Galatea; he had seen her trapped in the marble. Chiseling away the stone was how he could free her. It's dark because nothing else matters but freeing her. And I think, maybe, in that way, she changed him, brought out qualities he didn't know he had until he began the work of chiseling her out."

Ty leaned his head against Liz. "I see," he said slowly. He brought one arm around and gently pulled Liz down to the bed beside him. "So, are you the statue or the sculptor?" he asked.

Liz thought for a minute, studying the picture. "I'd say I'm the statue," she said. "I was locked in that marble until you found me." she said softly.

Ty kissed the side of her face. "I think you're the sculptor," he murmured, "Since I met you, I've felt more alive than I ever have." He kissed her again.

He leaned back, stroking Liz's face. "Wow," he said.

"What's wow, Ty?" Liz asked.

"I can't believe you're here," Ty whispered. "You're here and you're going to stay here and I get to wake up next to you every day and come home to you every night." He pulled her closer.

Liz pulled herself even closer to Ty. "I should have known that when you clobbered me at home plate that it was the start of something." She kissed Ty's forehead. "Maybe that's why I kissed you."

Ty chuckled. "You caught me by surprise with that one." He moved so that he was on top of Liz. "All we need is the ball. Hit

164

me with your best shot." And Liz kissed him like she did the first time, except that this time, Ty definitely kissed her back. Liz's hands grasped the back of his shirt and began tugging it out of his pants. Ty responded by unbuttoning Liz's sweater and kissing the flesh he exposed. In moments, they were naked and entwined. Within minutes, Liz was gasping from a powerful climax as Ty spent himself into her.

When she had caught her breath, Liz finally asked him, "So what do you want for our first dinner as bunkies? I'll fix you anything but sushi."

Ty smiled and kissed her hand, "From now on, Elizabeth, as the mistress of this house, you don't have to lift a finger. We'll go out to this little Italian place in Chestnut Hill. It's not Vincenzo's but it's very good."

"I'd be delighted to cook for you," said Liz, "Maybe we could go to that place tomorrow. Millie wants to get together for brunch."

Ty winced. "Babe, you'll have to go without me. I have to go back into the office for a while tomorrow. I'm sorry." He kissed her again. "I'll make it up to you, I promise."

After dinner, they'd come back to the house and made love for hours. Liz could feel Ty spooned up behind her, his arm around her as he slept, his breath stirring her hair; he radiated contentment. She was sated with lovemaking and tired from moving, but still unable to fall asleep. Something at the back of her mind was nagging at her but didn't want to fully disclose itself.

Liz gave up and tried to fall asleep. For some reason, she kept remembering Ty saying the word, "mistress."

Chapter 9

"Millicent Wentworth, I do believe you're the biggest sadist I've ever met who wasn't a licensed dentist," Liz winced. "I don't think there's a part of me that doesn't ache except maybe for my hair." Liz gingerly reached up and touched her scalp. "Nope. That hurts, too."

Millie laughed. "Hey, you SAID you wanted to go hiking. You SAID you wanted the exercise. You SAID you wanted something challenging. You SAID you wanted something that would keep you occupied. You SAID you trusted me." Millie put up one hand. The other was on the steering wheel. "You're unhappy now because I did as you said. Talk to the hand. You got what you wanted."

Liz leaned back in the passenger seat cautiously. "You know I've said and done a lot of damned fool things in my life. As my best friend, you're supposed to stop me, not pack a lunch and go along for the trip." Liz winced again. "That's it. You're fired. I'm getting a new best friend. Wonder if Corey wants the job?"

They had spent the early May weekend in the White Mountain National Forest day-hiking. Millie had been going almost since she was in utero and considered the area her backyard. What Millie considered "a good workout" had the potential to drop an entire platoon of Marines. Liz, unfortunately, had forgotten that.

Millie laughed. "I still can't believe you. The Border Guard asks us if we have anything to declare and you say, 'Only my undying love for Andy Garcia.' He wasn't amused, Liz."

"First requirement for such a job, Millie, is no sense of humor." Liz laughed.

"I thought he was gonna bust us or take apart the car. Instead, he just gets annoyed and tells us to get the hell out of there."

They both laughed, Millie more heartily than Liz.

"Hey, how come you didn't pick up any booze at Duty Free?" Millie asked with genuine puzzlement. "How often do we get up there to get Brador?"

"Guess I've kind of lost my taste for it." Liz said offhandedly. "I got perfume, though, so while you're smelling like a brewery, belching and singing 'Friends In Low Places' in some key no one's ever heard, I'll be smelling like a rose. Or rather, a blend of roses and starlight. Nyah."

Millie continued laughing. "Good thing, too. You need it right now, my friend." She pretended to wave away unbearable odors. Liz made a face at her and they laughed some more. She was glad Millie hadn't questioned her further about the beer.

Millie leaned back in her seat. "I can't wait to see John," she smiled a secret little smile. "I think I'll let him clean the Great North Woods off me." Millie glanced at Liz. "Of course, you've got Ty waiting for you. Good thing we're almost there. He's probably pacing and watching the door. Gotta get you home pronto."

Liz just stared at the dashboard. "You don't have to rush." She said it very softly.

Millie glanced at her, frowning. "Now that I think about it, you were pretty quiet when you weren't cracking jokes like that Andy Garcia one. I know you, Elizabeth. Your sense of humor is your defense mechanism and your armor. You've got it on so thick right now, I can almost hear clanking. What happened with you and Ty? I thought you couldn't keep your hands off each other."

Liz shrugged. "Must have just been a phase, like having acne all the time when you're a teenager. You grow out of phases."

"What happened?"

"Nothing, really," Liz was pensive. "I've been falling asleep by myself a few nights lately."

"Bullshit. You wouldn't be that depressed if it was just an occasional thing."

"He's been getting buried at work. Success attracts success and he's extremely successful. He works hard."

Millie's eyebrows were as high as she could raise them. "Tyrone is too busy to have sex with you?"

"I didn't say that. Can we change the subject, please?"

"No, this is the kind of stuff girlfriends are supposed to talk about and obsess over. What's happening, Liz?"

Liz felt her chest tighten, "Nothing much."

167

"As in," Millie intoned delicately, "nothing much?"

Liz stared at her knees. "If he's there, which doesn't happen as often as it used to, he's not there." You should have been more careful what you wished for, Girl, thought Liz, because, by God, you got him.

"Meaning?" Millie prompted.

Liz snapped, "He's either too tired, preoccupied or drunk and when he is interested," Liz hated this conversation, "there's not much left for me, if you catch my drift."

"Oh, Liz. What happened?"

"His team lost a big class-action suit because someone missed a filing date," Liz answered. "And the judge dismissed it. He was so angry for a few days that I was afraid of him. As soon as he came home, he'd start pouring the Scotch and get on the phone. I caught a look from him a couple of times like he blamed me."

"How could it be your fault?" Millie was aghast, "You don't work for him!"

"I distracted him," said Liz.

"Did he say that?" asked Millie.

"No," said Liz, "but he's spent more time with me than he has with any other woman and I overheard one of the associates make a remark about it. If he'd maintained his focus, the error wouldn't have happened. When they restarted the case, he threw himself into it."

Liz stared out the window and continued, more or less to herself, but out loud, "He breaks plans and then buys me jewelry to make up for it and for not coming home. When we do go out, and that doesn't happen much, he's on the phone non-stop; he doesn't eat much of what he orders and it's one drink after another until I have to drive us home. At least, he's smart enough to let me do that. I mentioned to him that I thought maybe he should cut back and he said, 'Nah, don't worry. I can stop. Once this case is done. I'll stop, I promise.' And he's been on the road for this case, most of the time in Houston. I'll call him and it sounds like a huge party in the background. He sounds drunk most of the time when I talk to him. When he's home, his mind is in the office. Millie, I swear some days I could go down on him and he wouldn't notice."

"Ouch."

Liz was fighting her tears. "In the beginning, yeah, we couldn't

168

get enough of each other. We almost didn't want to fall asleep and when we did, he'd be spooned up behind me, sound asleep and if I tried to get out of bed, his arm would tighten around me. I'd kiss him in his sleep and he'd smile or make a little 'mmmm' sound. If I put my arms around him, I could feel him relax and snuggle closer." Liz smiled at the memories. "Before we'd fall asleep, he'd read to me. Oh, Mill, that voice and John Donne's poetry..."

"He'd kiss my face and whisper something like "Goodnight, Love" as I was falling asleep and I'd feel him pulling me close as he fell asleep. In the morning, we'd look into each other's eyes for a couple of minutes before saying or doing anything, then he'd tease me about snoring and I'd give him grief about farting in his sleep."

Millie asked quietly, "And now?"

"The poetry book has stayed in the drawer. He stays on his side of the bed, doesn't touch me. I still see those wonderful eyes across the pillow, but they're bloodshot now. If I try to put my arms around him, he pushes me off and rolls away. The night before I left on this trip," this really hurt, "I kissed him in his sleep and he slapped at me like I was a mosquito biting him." Liz unconsciously touched her cheek where Ty had hit her. He'd been too drunk to wake up even after that.

"Did you yell at him, at least?" Millie was getting indignant and angry.

"What's the point? He didn't know what he was doing. When I first moved in, he would have given me a huge argument about leaving him alone for a weekend. When I asked if he minded that I'd go up to New Hampshire, he didn't care. I've tried to talk to him about it, but all he'd say was, "Liz, Baby, I'm sorry, but can we do this later? I'm running late for a meeting with Jimmy.' and head out the door, but come back with something to show me how sorry he was. But," Liz had to pause, "he wasn't sorry enough to make time."

"Who's Jimmy?" Millie asked.

"Jimmy Carlisle, Esquire," Liz practically spat the name, "is the up-and-coming litigator busted for cocaine possession last summer. Remember the hecklers at the auction? Well, that was Jimmy and friends. Anyway, Brooks, Washburn made a deal with the DA to keep him working and to avoid the bad publicity.

"Well, part of the deal was that he'd be closely supervised and they assigned him to work with Ty, figuring a mentor would straighten him out. So, they've been working together and more than one night, Jimmy's been crashed in one of the spare rooms at our house. He'll keep Ty up, talking and drinking until 4 AM. The housekeeper was on the verge of quitting two weeks ago."

"Why?"

"Well, Jimmy switched from coke to vodka, 'cuz vodka's legal, Lizzie. Don't you worry.' Millie, the man is a binge drinker and he goes until he vomits. Usually all over the bed or the bathroom." Millie made a disgusted sound.

Liz leaned her head against the window. "He graduated top of his class from a first-tier school, but you've gotta wonder how. I've heard him choke on some basic law questions that even I can answer, but then, Jimmy is the king of cutting corners."

Liz sighed, "Instead of Ty being a good influence on him, Jimmy's dragging Ty down to his level. Ty was a really sharp, hard-nosed litigator, you know. Really thorough preparation and a huge presence in a courtroom. He fought hard, but clean. I don't know anyone who didn't respect him, including the guys who lost to him."

"Things have changed. Jimmy walks just a hair on the wrong side of ethics, pushing and pushing and pushing at the line. He relies on borderline misrepresentation, questionable billing and deliberately losing documents. He's doing this on cases he's working with Ty and word is getting around. That's not all; every chance he gets, the bastard's trying to grope me or rub against me. It's gotten so I don't want to be home if he's in the house."

"Oh, my God," exclaimed Millie, "Have you told Ty? He'll kill him."

"No, Mill, I haven't. When I get to see Ty, he's in no state to deal with it." Liz looked at Millie, "Our first date, he mentioned how much he used to enjoy rowing, that he hadn't done it in ages and that he missed it."

"Yeah."

"I got him a new racing shell. It was delivered last week." Liz had smoothed the hull with her hand, admiring the deep, glossy green of the surface, hoping the gift would reconnect Ty to better times and lead him out of his downward spiral.

"Must have cost you a fortune," said Millie. "What did he say?"

"If it does what I hope it will, it's worth it," Liz answered. "And no, he hasn't seen it. He hasn't come home before 11 PM for the last month. And he hasn't been alone or sober. The time hasn't been right." Liz sighed.

"You tried to tell me, Mill. The night of the Barrister's Ball, you tried to tell me he had a drinking problem, but I didn't listen." Liz was silent for a couple of minutes.

"You know, Millie, I've been wishing and praying that this would pass; all I'd have to do is wait it out." Liz bit her lip. "Now I'm not so sure. I don't know how much further down he can sink and I can't stop it. I know he hates me seeing him like this. I'm thinking this relationship was a huge mistake and it may be time to undo it."

She continued almost unconsciously, "It's been at least two weeks since I've been able to make him smile or laugh. I lost him, Millie, if I even really had him in the first place."

Millie opened her mouth to say something, then snapped it shut and slammed the brakes.

"Liz, don't look." Millie scrambled out of the car.

Liz knew. She dove out of her side and bolted for the pathetic little bundle of white and black fur in the road just ahead of the car.

"Oh, Beanie."

He was still alive, but there was a trickle of blood from his nose. Blood was slowly leaking from a long laceration on his side. At least one of his legs was obviously broken and his eyes were glazed. Liz whipped off her sweatshirt while Millie yanked a floor mat out of the car.

"Easy, easy, easy," cautioned Liz as they slid him as gently as possible onto the floor mat. Beanie tried to meow but couldn't make the sound. Horns began to honk behind Millie's Saab. One guy yelled something and Millie fired back with, "Fuck you! This is an emergency!" as they lifted Beanie. The harassment ended when the drivers saw what they were doing. Millie helped Liz ease Beanie and herself into the back seat. Liz glanced out the window and spotted the carcass of a squirrel in the lane across from where they'd found Beanie.

"Hang in there, Kitty," Liz whispered. "We're gonna get some

171

help." Beanie's black tail twitched slightly.

"Vet clinic?" Millie asked as she jumped into the driver's seat.

"Next left, 5 blocks, no lights and step on it." Millie gunned it and they were on their way. Two guys were outside smoking when the car screeched to a halt. Millie jumped out, yelling, "We need help!" The assistants recognized Beanie, one of the favorite patients of the clinic. One guy got Beanie out of the back seat and directly into an examining room while the other fetched the vet. Liz and Millie were hot on their heels.

"What the hell was he doing away from home?" Millie asked.

"No. The right question is 'what the hell was my indoor cat doing outside in the first place?'" snapped Liz. "He doesn't go outside. Ever. Ty knows that."

The vet examined Beanie gently. "Internal bleeding, leg fracture, possibly more than one, broken ribs," he looked at his assistant. "X-rays. Now." Beanie was wheeled down to the X-ray room. Liz's throat tightened and she began to hug herself. Millie had her arm around Liz. Neither woman said a word.

When the vet returned, his face was grim and sad. Liz knew it was the worst. She felt the tears stinging the back of her eyes.

"Ms. Gardner, it doesn't look good. In addition to the fractures, his spleen is ruptured, probably damage to his liver and other major organs." He paused, "We can operate if we can stabilize him, but I can't promise you it'll do any good." There was a brief pause.

"Put him down." Liz said the words almost mechanically. The veterinarian nodded and signaled the assistant to get together the necessary items. "Do you want to be with him?"

Liz could only nod. She and Millie followed the doctor back to Beanie. He looked so little and helpless on the X-ray table. Two legs were splinted and an IV had been inserted to try to stabilize him if Liz had opted for surgery.

Liz felt like she was betraying her best friend. He had asked so little, but given so much and she was ending his life. She stroked his head and he tried to wag his tail and purr. The vet inserted a syringe, pushed the plunger and Beanie's breathing stopped.

"Take her out front. Now."

Millie firmly guided Liz back to the lobby, Liz sagging against her friend. Something splashed against Liz's face. Millie was quietly crying.

"Phone." Millie handed Liz her wireless. Liz took a deep breath, slowly exhaled and dialed the house.

"'Lo?" Ty's voice was thick, indistinct.

"It's me, Babe," Liz was surprised she sounded normal. "Miss me?"

"Course I do," Ty answered, "When you comin' home?" His normally clear speech was slurred. She'd never heard him sound this bad.

"How's Beanie? You remember to feed the kitty?" Liz held her breath against the answer. The desk assistant at the clinic was typing up the bill.

"Emergency visit, X-rays, intravenous," she recited as she typed. The girl squinted at the last word. "What's that word?"

Liz put her hand over the phone. "Euthanasia. 12 pounds." She felt a stabbing pain near her heart as she said it.

Unaware, the girl said, "Thanks" and continued typing.

"Whadja say, Liz?" Ty wanted to know. She could hear Jimmy yelling "Ty One On!" in the background.

"I said, 'How's Beanie?' Liz answered.

"I think you love him more'n you love me," Ty grumbled, "You didn't ask how I am. Anyway, he's fine. Lyin' here so I'll scratch his belly for him, purrin' his head off." Ty was nonchalant.

"That'll be $255.48, please," said the desk clerk. "Oh, here." She handed Liz Beanie's red collar. "Do you want the body?"

"I guess we've got a bad connection, Ty." Liz turned over the collar in her hand and shook her head at the clerk to indicate she didn't want Beanie's remains.

"When you gettin' home? We gotta celebrate," Ty tried to put a sexy edge on the word and failed. "Big case settled for big bucks. Yer man done good, Woman."

"Sounds like the party's already started. I've got one or two stops but I'll be there as soon as I can. Bye, bye." Ty hung up without saying goodbye.

Liz hung up and stared at the phone. No one interrupted her thoughts. In a few minutes, she turned to Millie. "My wallet and purse are out in the car. Would you get them for me?" Millie nodded and headed for the car. Liz pulled her sweatshirt back on, pausing to look at the smears of Beanie's blood staining the front.

173

She turned to the desk clerk.

"May I use your phone book?" The girl rummaged under the counter and produced it. Liz turned to the name of a truck rental company nearby. Millie returned with Liz's purse as she connected to the rental agency.

"Hi. What do you have available right now?" As she talked to the dispatcher, Liz fished out her wallet and handed a credit card to the desk clerk. One of hers, not Ty's.

"Let's see, I have mostly clothing, some kitchen ware and a couple of pictures and a fairly small amount of furniture." A pause. "That sounds good. I'll need boxes, too." The desk clerk slid the credit card slip across the desk for Liz's signature. As Liz signed, she concluded negotiations for the truck. "Elizabeth Gardner. We'll be there in 10-15 minutes." She hung up and handed the phone to Millie. "Millie, he lied to me." Liz said the words quietly, tonelessly.

"He told me he was scratching Beanie's stomach while I was paying to put him to sleep. That's it. We're over."

Millie punched up a number on speed dial. "Hi, Sweetheart, it's me. Listen, can you drop whatever you're doing and meet us at Ty's house?" Millie's choice of words was not lost on Liz. "Great, see you in about a half hour."

They headed for the car in silence and drove to the truck rental agency in silence. Their only conversation there was a discussion of the size and number of boxes needed.

On leaving, Liz lead in the truck, Millie followed and they met John coming into the driveway, followed by Joey DiDonato's car. Liz parked the truck and swung down from the cab. Joey saw the question on her face.

"Millie called me. Let's go. Let's get this done."

Liz looked at her friends, "Look, this is between Ty and me so resist the urge to give him a piece of your mind.

"Guys, please get my computer and books. Millie, you know my kitchen stuff, including the cookbooks. I'll start with the bathroom." Liz's throat tightened. "Don't forget Beanie's things." They entered the house. Millie and John headed off to their assignments, Joey headed down the hall towards the den, where a TV blared. Before heading for the den herself, Liz had a quick look at Beanie's feeding area. His food dish was completely empty, not even crumbs around it and the water dish was bone dry. No wonder he'd been out hunting. She steeled herself and headed down the hallway towards the den. Joey met her in the hall and stopped her.

"Liz, I took a quick look. It looks like a crack den in there. Brace yourself." He gave her a quick hug. "We'll get you through this." He headed upstairs and Liz entered the den. She was appalled by what she found.

The room reeked of stale beer, cigarette smoke and body odor. Bottles in a variety of shapes and sizes littered the room, all of them had contained types of alcohol at some point. The coffee table held an assortment of Chinese food cartons, some had tipped over and spilled over onto the beautiful green marble of the coffee table then dripped into stains on Ty's treasured rug. The rug's beauty was also spoiled by cigarette burns, ashes and used butts. Someone had taken the framed enlarged picture of Ty and Liz from their first date and set it up on the coffee table, along with a photo of Liz holding Beanie and smiling. Hidden behind the photos was the antique mirror from the hallway. There were lines of white powder neatly chopped out on the mirror, a razor blade, a straw and a crumpled piece of paper. There was an overflowing ashtray hiding the mirror as well. Jimmy had apparently just done a line because he was sniffing hard and surreptitiously watching Ty to see if he had noticed.

"There, see? I set up her pictures in front of you so you won't miss ol' Lizzie so much there, Ty," Jimmy said with a phony smile on his face.

Liz could hardly keep from throttling him. Liz watched him dip two fingers into a glass on the table and inhale the droplets, all the time watching an old college football game on cable. The hand not stuck up his nose held a cigarette with a dangerously long ash. As she watched, Jimmy picked up the glass from the table and took a big swallow. She wondered idly if he'd still been doing coke the whole time he was supposed to be clean.

Liz looked around. Ty was sprawled on the other sofa, a large glass of Scotch in hand. The glass was on the verge of spilling onto the carpet. Liz looked at him from the door. He was wearing the same clothes he'd had on when he'd gone to work two days ago. His hair looked greasy and matted. Ty had a dark stubble across his face; Liz doubted if he had shaved in the last 48 hours. Or slept. Or really eaten. He turned his head to say something to Jimmy and Liz saw the puffiness under his eyes. In turning, the Scotch finally spilled onto the rug. Ty sat up, cursing. As he reached for the Scotch bottle to refill his glass, he noticed Liz leaning against the doorway.

"Lizabeth! My Love! C'mere!" He waved her over unsteadily. She came closer, but stayed out of his reach. This seemed to penetrate Ty's alcoholic fog because he looked at her as intently as he could.

"Victory party," he said.

"I see. Pickup or delivery?" Liz asked, motioning to the cartons. Well, now she knew how Beanie had escaped.

Jimmy answered, "Livery. We're in no shape to drive." Both men found this hilarious.

"The new Emperor of China there, ol' Ty Wan On," Jimmy was delighted with his own wit.

"Where's Beanie? He didn't greet me at the door."

"I haven't seen that damn cat since the Chinese food came," said Jimmy. He swallowed some more vodka. "I think that furry little shit hates me."

Ty swallowed some Scotch. "He's prob'ly asleep upstairs." He tried to look meaningfully at Liz. "We should be there, too."

Liz pretended to look shocked. "Beanie? Asleep? With an unguarded box of spare ribs in the house? He must be dead to the world. Are you sure he didn't get out when the delivery came?"

Ty paused in the act of drinking again. He stared at the table. "You're right." He set down the glass instead of drinking.

Liz looked into Ty's bloodshot eyes. She could see awareness dawning. Liz walked to the table and picked up the Scotch bottle. Grabbing the neck, Liz swung down onto the marble table, shattering the bottle.

"Fuck, Man!" from Jimmy.

"Here," she forced the neck of the bottle into Ty's hand, the jagged edges still dripping Scotch. "You want to kill yourself with a bottle, Hadley, I suggest you slit your wrists with it. It's far more efficient than the way you're going about it. Just wait 'til I leave, okay? I've already cleaned up one of your messes today." Liz turned and left. She could hear Jimmy in the background.

176

"Crazy, fuckin' bitch."

Liz ran for the stairs, bolting for the bedroom. She could feel her heart breaking.

Liz grabbed suitcases and flung the contents of her closet into them. She was doing the same with the bureau drawers when a pair of hands grabbed her and flung her onto the bed. Liz tried to scramble back up only to find herself pinned under Jimmy.

"All right," he said, "Now we're gonna see what's what. I figure you gotta be really somethin' between the sheets if ol' Ty wants you." He tried to kiss her. Liz twisted her face away and tried to gouge his face with her fingernails. Jimmy pinned her arms down and laughed.

"Ooooh, rough stuff. Hey, works for me." He released one of her arms to grab her hair and force her head still for a slobbery kiss. Liz twisted again, ignoring the intense pain from her scalp and screamed, "TY! Where are you?"

Jimmy slapped her across the face with all his strength. Liz tasted blood from a cut on her lip.

Jimmy laughed, "He ain't comin,' Lizzie Baby. So why don't you relax and go with it." He straddled her, letting go of her right hand to grab at her sweatshirt. "Hell, you might even like me better than ol' Tai Wan On."

"NO!"

Jimmy pulled his arm back to hit her again and Liz seized the opportunity. She smashed the heel of her right hand into his nose, years of suppressed rage driving her arm so hard, his head snapped back and Liz heard bone crunch. As he grabbed his broken nose, Liz pushed him off of her and scrambled to safety.

"FUCKING BITCH!!! YOU'RE GONNA PAY FOR THAT!" Jimmy made a move towards her, only to be hauled off his feet by Joey and thrown into the hallway. Jimmy made an attempt to get back to Liz, finding his way blocked by John and Joey's big bodies.

"Get out," snarled Joe. "Get out or I'll throw you out the goddamn window."

John added, "Then I'll drag your sorry ass back up here to do it again."

Jimmy tried again to get back at Liz, but Joey grabbed his arm and yanked a bag of cocaine out of Jimmy's pocket and tossed it to

177

John.

"Gimme that!" Jimmy screamed.

"Leave now and we'll flush it," said Joey evenly, "Don't leave and John, the Assistant DA there will have you on possession with intent as well as an attempted rape charge. You can see if your cell mate likes it rough."

Jimmy looked for a minute like he was going to challenge the other men, but changed his mind. Blood was flowing freely from his nose. John took a step forward and he changed his mind.

As Jimmy stumbled downstairs, he collided with Ty who tried to pin him to the wall. Jimmy easily broke his grasp and shoved Ty out of his way.

"Your fucking girlfriend broke my fucking nose!"

As Ty entered the bedroom, sounds of a gunning engine and squealing tires reached the group upstairs. Ty slumped against the doorway and took in the scene.

Joey was holding a sobbing, bloodstained Liz while John and Millie were filling boxes with the items of hers that they recognized. Ty stumbled forward, trying to push Joey away from Liz. Joey pushed him back and Ty's face darkened with drunken rage.

"I knew it! You were with him all weekend, weren't you? My ass, he's like your brother. Now you're runnin' off with him. Christ, Elizabeth, I thought I could trust you. God damn it!"

Joey started to move towards Ty, but Liz stopped him. "That's not true and you know it!"

"So, why you leavin'?" Ty was still angry and confused.

"Because I can't live like this anymore, Ty," Liz could feel more tears rising.

Ty looked around and snorted, "Yeah, you've got it real bad, Baby. Big house, new car, anything you want. Shit, you're just like my mother running off."

"Yeah, well you're just like your father, Tyrone. Success demands sacrifice and I guess it was our relationship that had to go," snapped Liz, "that and Beanie." She almost broke down again.

Ty blinked at her. "What? What are you talking about? What happened to Beanie?" He looked at her sweatshirt and really saw the bloodstains for the first time.

Liz rummaged in her purse and thrust Beanie's collar and the vet clinic invoice into his hand. "You were so busy getting plastered with your pal that you let Beanie escape. I found him dying in the street."

She saw the anger take control. Ty turned and smashed his right fist into the wall, punching a hole through the sheet rock. Liz caught her breath at the violence.

"Was that supposed to be my face, Ty?" she asked.

Ty pulled his hand out of the wall and sagged against the door frame. He stared at her through bloodshot eyes, comprehension slowly rising. "What have I done?" he said hoarsely.

"Shown me why I'm right," said Liz, "you can either have me or your Scotch: not both."

John and Millie looked at her. Liz jerked her head towards the door. Joe followed, pausing just long enough to ask, "Liz, you gonna be okay?"

"I'll be downstairs in a few, Joey, just as soon as I finish this," she said.

Joey looked at Ty and shook his head. "You need help, Man," he said. He pulled a card out of his wallet and stuck it into Ty's shirt pocket. "If you're as smart as I think you are, you'll call this number tonight." He took a step forward and pointed a finger in Ty's face. "And if you come near Liz again, I'll fucking finish you. I don't care how much she loves you." He left.

Liz looked at Ty. She was still shaking from the encounter with Jimmy, in shock over Beanie's death and ready to collapse. But she couldn't fold. Not yet. She took a deep breath.

"Don't leave me, Liz," Ty pleaded, "I need you. Please don't leave."

"We're done. I can't fight a bottle. And I can't watch you drink yourself to death, either." Ty made a move towards her, but Liz held up her hand and he stopped.

"I can't do this anymore. You said I could have anything I want. Well, I want the man I fell in love with. I want the man who followed me all the way down to the Cape because my love was that important to him. I want the man who made me feel beautiful and desired and loved for the first time in my life. But he's not here anymore. So there's no reason for me to stay, either."

Liz picked up her purse and started to pass by Ty. She paused, went to kiss his cheek and stopped. No, she couldn't do it. Her eyes met his briefly, both brimming with pain. She turned away, then walked out of the house and away from Ty.

Chapter 10

The doorbell rang. Liz paused to catch her breath. Damn it. The bell rang again and she headed for the door, viciously stripping off her rubber gloves and throwing them into the kitchen sink. She was in a foul mood. Another round of nightmares had awakened Liz before dawn, leaving her sitting up in bed, gasping and crying. It had been two months and part of her still expected Ty to pull her into his arms to hold her and kiss away the tears. And she'd cry even more.

Liz still blocked the front door as she came and went, only to remember that Beanie wouldn't try to escape ever again. She needed him now, needed his playfulness and affection to ease her heartache. His absence was part of her heartache and a part that made it even more painful.

She couldn't remember the last time she'd eaten a square meal. Since she'd left Wellesley, Liz had existed in a gray twilight of anxiety and depression. She went in early to the office, stayed late, politely declined to join the other clerks for Friday afternoon drinks or socializing. She sleepwalked through life.

Millie and John's wedding had been beautiful. The only awkward moment had come during the bouquet toss. Liz had been pushed onto the floor by well-meaning friends, intending to just stand there and applaud. Liz had caught the spray of lilies and roses when she'd put up her hands to protect her face. Millie and Liz had exchanged a long look as Liz handed the flowers to Millie's 8 year old niece and excused herself. She'd had to run outside to compose herself. Maybe it was too soon or maybe it ran too deep, but instead of subsiding, the pain and grief increased.

A split second before she opened the door, Liz took a deep breath to gain composure and to mentally utter a curse on whomever was interrupting her work. Big, pleasant smile plastered on her face (she hoped), Liz opened the door. What she saw caused the smile to disappear.

It was Ty.

Liz just stood and stared. Tyrone, her Tyrone, stood on the front step tanned, bearded and holding a kitten.

He had a homemade sign around his neck that read "In Need of a Good Home (Both of Us)."

"Can we come in?" he asked. Liz opened the door, still too stunned for words. At least, as Ty passed her, he didn't try to kiss her, thank God. She couldn't have handled it. Two months since she'd left him and not a word, no phone calls, letters, nothing. Now here he was, casual, relaxed, looking far better than he had the last time she'd seen him and as irresistible as ever.

Liz, as usual, was at a disadvantage: sweaty, no makeup, wild hair, two months of bad sleep showing on her face and she was dressed in her house cleaning uniform of gym shorts and ratty T-shirt. Liz closed the door after Ty and braced herself. She wasn't ready for this confrontation, not by a long shot. She had half-expected never to see him again and had been fighting to put him out of her mind.

"Ty."

That was all she could manage. What do you say to a man you love desperately, but had to leave to save yourself?

"Liz." The tone was casual enough, even mocking hers slightly, but Ty was watching her face closely. Liz knew that look. Keen observation carefully hidden behind a casual exterior. His litigator's face. Apparently, though, some tension in his body was making its way into his hands. The kitten began to squeak and mew at being squeezed.

Liz looked at him. "What's that? The Trojan kitten?"

Ty held the kitten out to Liz. "I'd like you to meet Norton." Liz accepted Norton, who wrapped oversized paws around her hand and began licking her fingers, purring loudly. Just like Beanie. She had to bite back her angry tears.

"He's beautiful, Ty, but I don't want…"

"Fine. I have a huge scratching post that needs a cat." Still the close examination. Liz couldn't meet his gaze. She knew she'd throw herself into his arms and sob hysterically if he made one wrong move. Like smiling again. Or touching her.

"Look, why don't we let him go play while we talk?" Ty carefully took Norton from Liz's hands and put him on the floor.

Norton scampered upstairs to explore. Once he disappeared from sight, the uncomfortable silence returned.

"You look good, Ty." An understatement. Liz could feel the knot forming in her stomach. It was half dread and half an emotion she'd been trying to purge herself of over the past months. Control was going to be hard to maintain. "How've you been?"

"Is that all you have to say?" he asked.

Liz felt her temper begin to slip. "Look, I didn't expect to see you today and I don't have time to waste here, so why don't you tell me what you want me to say, I'll say it, you'll leave and I'll continue getting over you." Liz surprised herself at the sharpness of her tone.

"Okay," Ty kept a casual tone. "I don't remember everything that happened the last time we saw each other."

"Lucky you," she retorted. "I've been reliving it. Where should I start? Beanie's last hour of life or a blow by blow description of Jimmy trying to rape me? I still have screaming nightmares."

That remark really got to him. She saw the pain cross his face.

"My God, you're determined not to give me an inch, aren't you?" he asked.

"I told you, you had the power to destroy me. And you did. I trusted you, I put my fears behind me because you promised you'd never hurt me, you'd always take care of me and protect me. If that was your idea of loving and caring, then I'm better off on my own. I have nothing to say to you. So if you don't mind," she started to lead him back to the door, "please gather up your kitten and go."

Ty stood his ground. He grabbed Liz's arm and pulled her to stand close in front of him. His grip was steely, long fingers digging into her upper arm. Ty's free hand went under Liz's chin and forced it up so that she was looking into his eyes.

"I do mind," he said, softly, with an edge. "I'm not leaving until we've had this out. You've got plenty to say, I can see it in your eyes. And you're going to hear me out. So let's cut the bullshit and start talking."

"Okay, fine, sure, I'll play," She took on a sarcastically bright tone. "Ty! What a pleasant surprise! How nice of you to come by! How's the hand you smashed into the wall? Oh, by the way, Ty, where the hell have you been for two months?"

"Drying out."

The answer was quiet, matter of fact. The steely edge to his voice was gone. "I found a place that took me right after you left."

Liz knew Ty well enough to know the truth. She felt her rage subside somewhat, but...

"You've got one hell of a tan. Where were you, Betty Ford at Club Med?"

Ty's gaze remained steadily on her face, still watching closely, but slightly relieved at provoking her. "I was in the Caribbean. Good place, not likely to run into a lot of people I knew and they had a bed available right away. It seemed like a good idea to put some distance between us for a while."

The words ripped into Liz's heart. "You'd already done that by the time I moved out, Ty. We didn't have a relationship anymore. Let's just admit we made a huge mistake, apologize and end it."

"No."

Ty grasped Liz's wrist gently, but firmly. He started towards the nearest chair from the dining room, but Liz resisted being pulled. Without a word, Ty scooped her up and continued for the chair. In the process of seating himself, his grip loosened and Liz managed to get free and stand up. Again, silently, he grasped her wrist and successfully pulled her into his lap, facing him. Liz found herself straddling Ty, her bare legs dangling over his, his hands resting in the small of her back. She knew better than to try to break free again. Something in the back of her mind noted that he was still wearing the "In Need of a Good Home" sign around his neck.

Moving one hand to the back of her neck, Ty gently but firmly bent Liz's head closer to his and softly, slowly kissed her forehead, lingering over it, murmuring, "My God, I've missed this." She closed her eyes, reveling once again in the warmth of him, the sensual pleasure of his lips on her skin, the joy his kisses always brought, the unfamiliar sensation of his beard against her skin and the love she had for this man, no matter what. Ty fished in his shirt pocket and handed something to Liz. "Here."

Liz looked at the plastic disk in her hand. "What is it?"

"It's an Alcoholics Anonymous first day disk." Ty cupped her face, stroking her cheek with his thumb. "I got it the day after you left. That card that Joe gave me was the Bar Association Crisis Hotline. I got on the phone and they got me into rehab. You said I was killing myself and you were right."

Liz turned over the disk in her hand, looking at the printing. "So you came to apologize? Okay, you've apologized. I forgive you. Please leave." She tried to get out of Ty's lap again, but he tightened his grip.

"I'll leave, Elizabeth, if you can look me in the eyes and tell me you don't want me anymore. If you can do that, I'll go and never bother you again," he spoke softly. "Can you do it? Can you honestly say you don't want me?"

Liz looked him in the eye. "I can't," she whispered.

"I may not remember much from the last time I saw you," he said, "but I do remember you telling me you wanted something. Well, I brought it to you today."

"What's that?" she whispered.

"The man who loves you," he said, emotion beginning to choke him, "and who desperately wants you to love him again." He began to shake as he said it. "You called me the handsome prince once, but I'm the one in distress. You are my rescuer and I don't want the story to end without winning you back."

Elizabeth Gardner, for the first time in two months, wrapped her arms around the love of her life, Tyrone Hadley. She was shaking, too. Liz buried her face in Ty's shoulder, feeling the texture of his shirt and the muscles underneath as they moved his arms to hold her close. She could smell the fabric softener he'd used. Ty's skin had the aroma of soap clinging to it from a recent shower, the sexiest fragrance on Earth. Liz inhaled and clung even tighter.

"Are you really here?" Liz dreaded the answer. If this was a dream, she couldn't stand the disappointment.

Ty's arms tightened to the point where Liz had trouble breathing. He moved his lips closer to her ear. "Swear to God, Babe. It's really me. I've missed you so." He buried his face in her neck again. Liz could feel the sensation all the way down her spine. His words were muffled against her shirt.

"I wanted you badly, but my sponsor told me to wait; I wasn't ready and you probably weren't, either. It was like a knife in my gut. I don't know how many times I picked up the phone to call anyway, but I was so afraid you didn't want me anymore, I just chickened out. I'm still afraid." Ty lifted his head and Liz could see the fear, something she'd never seen in his eyes.

His voice was a hoarse whisper. "I only want you to be happy, Liz and I know I should only want you to be with the right man, but Liz," here, his voice dropped so low, she almost couldn't hear him. "I'd give half my life to be that man. I'll do whatever it takes to make you love and trust me again. I don't want to go on without you. Please don't throw me out, Darling."

He put his lips to Liz's and said," Please."

Liz couldn't hold out any longer. She returned the stealthy kiss with all the love she felt. And then, she began to really cry. Ty gently guided her head back to his shoulder, stroking her hair as he would a child.

Ty kissed her cheek again and Liz could feel tears on his face. She tightened her arms around him to comfort him and they held each other as if the intertwined circle of their arms could banish the bad memories and the pain they brought.

At length, Ty kissed Liz again, gently, softly, sweetly with a promise of greater things to come. His fingers found the spot on the nape of her neck that could send shivers all the way down to her toes and he deepened the kiss until Liz clung tighter to him because her senses were too overloaded for her to sit up by herself. Ty stopped kissing her long enough to speak. He was breathing hard and his eyes were soft and dark as they looked into Liz's.

"Liz, Honey, may I take you to bed?" He stroked her ear. "I need you, need to feel your warm, soft body under mine. Please?"

Liz wanted exactly that but it was too fast. Her face was still wet with tears and some of them were from anger. There was something magic in his touch, but it wasn't enough to erase all the pain with one kiss.

Liz lifted the hem of her shirt to brush the tears from Ty's face. Ty's body tensed up as his eyes searched her face. She gently removed the sign from his neck and smiled at it. Holding the sign with one hand, Liz touched his beard with her free hand. "Furry face and a hard luck story."

Ty nodded, smiling, but he watched her closely.

"You were paying attention," she said as she put the sign on the table behind them.

"I always did," he answered.

"No," she said quietly, "that's not completely true. The past few months, we weren't even on the same planet. I couldn't take it."

Liz could feel the tension returning to his hands. How well he knew her. She looked into his eyes and gently laid her hands on his shoulders.

"I love you, Ty. But, Darling, I'm not ready to go back to where we were. We were two fools who rushed in where angels feared to tread and it cost us."

Here, she felt Ty pulling her close again, trying to comfort her. Against the wishes of her body, she resisted.

Liz smiled sadly, "I know you're the one man I could spend the rest of my life with. And you know it, too. But you took me for granted. We didn't share a home. I occupied space in your house and bed. I deserve better." Ty opened his mouth to protest and Liz gently closed it with her fingertips. "I felt like my presence was more for your convenience than for closeness. I wanted to be there to love you, to help you through good and bad, but you pulled away from me and hid yourself in your office or in a bottle of Scotch. Beanie's death was the last straw. I can't go back to living like that. Especially with you. I want to be more important to you than that."

Ty kept one arm around Liz and covered her hand with his. Closing his eyes, Ty began kissing Liz's hand, starting with her fingertips and lingering over her palm. Liz hardly breathed. He finished with a long, lingering kiss on her inner wrist. Guiding her arm around his neck, Ty gently pulled Liz close, molding her body to his. This time, she didn't resist. He nestled his cheek against her hair and began to stroke her back. Liz could feel herself relax. They sat like this for a minute or two, then Ty spoke.

"I'm sorry. I didn't know what I was doing. I knew I wanted you in my life, but I forgot to make room for you. You're right. You were right when you said I thought you'd melt when you saw me this morning. You were right when you said I took your love for granted," here she could feel him laugh a little, "even after I'd had to work so hard to get it." Liz felt him rub his cheek against her forehead. "Hell, you were even right to leave me when you did."

Ty sat Liz back up and held her by the shoulders. Again, his eyes locked with hers as he spoke softly, but firmly, "But I get to be right, too. Coming here today was the right thing for me to do and you know it. We belong together, Liz. I know this without question. Do you remember when I told you that we'd have no idea what was coming, that you'd have to trust me?"

Liz nodded. Ty kissed her forehead. "Okay. Anytime things get sticky for you, Liz, you run. When it's fight or flight, Liz chooses flight. And I keep running after you. You know why?" Liz didn't answer. Ty stroked a finger across her lips, "This," he said very softly, "The two of us is worth fighting for." He lightly kissed her lips and whispered, "I don't care who I have to take on. You got away but that was temporary. I'm back in the game. I've had two months of missing you and that was more than enough. I've found the love of my life and she's not getting away from me again. I'll get on my knees and beg, if you want, Liz. I love you that much." Ty's voice dropped into a deep, dark whisper, "You said you still love me. Enough to try again?"

Liz didn't say anything. Ty tried another tack. "Look, I'm on a serious losing streak with you. Softball game, court case, contempt charge; if word gets out, I'm gonna start losing clients. Throw me a bone, Liz, let me win once in a while. It's a guy thing."

Despite herself, Liz giggled for the first time in months.

Ty kissed her forehead again. "All hope is not lost if I can make you laugh. Will you take me back?" He leaned his forehead against hers. "Name your terms, Counselor."

Liz leaned forward and kissed Ty, slowly reacquainting herself with that particular pleasure. Ty let her take charge of the moment. Liz leaned back and said huskily, "I guess you still want me."

With a wicked grin, Ty grabbed her backside and pulled her as tightly as he could against himself. She could feel his erection. "What do you think?"

Liz was blushing softly. She leaned into his embrace, savoring the sensual warmth of him and his arms tightening around her, feeling more at home and relaxed than she had since she'd last seen him.

She felt and heard Ty sniffing her neck. "Mmmm. Who'd have thought Lysol could be such a turn-on?" she heard him murmur.

Lysol. "As much as I want to make love to you right now, Ty, my love, I have to finish cleaning the house since I no longer have a housekeeper." Liz tried to sit up and remove herself from his lap.

He held her in place.

"It's spotless. I bet you've been up since about 5 this morning cleaning it. Am I right?" Liz nodded. Ty continued, "In that case, I think you'd better get back to bed for a while and," he paused to kiss her again, "I'm coming with you." He emphasized the "coming."

Liz raised her eyebrows. "Are you inviting yourself into my bed?"

"Into your bed, your house, your arms, your heart, your dreams, anywhere I can be with you," Ty replied. "Told you I wasn't letting you go again."

"I haven't said I'm taking you back," Liz said teasingly. "Yes, you are," he countered, "or you would have slammed the door in my face."

Liz bent her head and kissed him lightly. "Answer one question for me and then..."

He returned the kiss. "What?"

"How much did Corey overcharge you for Norton?"

Ty looked innocent. "I don't know what you're talking about."

"Oh yeah? He's a purebred Maine Coon Cat and Corey's the only local breeder." Liz turned her head and called, "Here, kitty, kitty."

In a minute, two very similar kittens bounced down the stairs and into view.

Ty stared at them, a bewildered scowl on his face. "I'm sober."

"Uh huh." Liz kissed his temple.

"I'm not seeing double."

Liz kissed him again. "Don't think so, Babe."

"Why am I seeing two kittens? I only brought one with me."

"Right. You only brought one."

As he thought about it, Ty rested his face against Liz's breasts again. "Your shirt needs a V neck. I brought one kitten and you already had one here."

"Not bad for a Rhodes scholar. Ouch!" as he pinched her bottom.

Ty rubbed the spot he had pinched by way of apology. "They look so much alike because they're from the same litter. And Corey's Alexis produced the litter the same day Beanie died." One hand began to creep under the back of Liz's shirt, heading for the band of her bra. She didn't stop him.

"That's Norton's brother, Dodger, as in Brooklyn. I got him from Corey a few days ago. He and Norton were chewing on each other and Norton was very distraught that I took his buddy away from him." Liz rubbed her cheek on Ty's head. "I was going to go back for him tomorrow. Thanks for saving me the trip." She tried to kiss his cheek, but Ty turned his head and Liz found herself kissing him on the mouth again. A moment later, he had her bra unhooked and his hand was sliding forward to cup her breast. Ty broke off the kiss long enough to say, "That's it. Upstairs. Now."

"Ty's way or the highway?" Liz asked. "What if…"

She didn't get any further because Ty abruptly set her on her feet with, "My way now, debate later."

They made their way to Liz's bedroom hand in hand. As Liz tugged off Ty's shirt, she noticed new definition in his chest and abdomen, bigger shoulders and arms. Ty didn't object as she ran her hand down his torso, feeling the ripple and play of his muscles. She slid her hands upward and felt the stronger, more defined body underneath his tanned skin.

"Counselor, you've been working out," Liz purred, "I like it." She wrapped her arms around him and began kissing his chest, working her way up to his neck and mouth. "Such strong arms you have."

His breathing was ragged as he said, "The better to hold you with, my dear. I found a rowing shell in the garage one day." Liz felt him slide his hand under her shirt and noticed the change. Where there had been softness, now there were calluses on his hand.

Ty kissed her, tasting deeply from her lips. "I've started rowing again. It's the best gift anyone's ever given me." He hastily removed his pants and they twined their naked bodies together. He kissed her again and whispered, "You've given me myself back, Darling."

Liz kissed him and murmured, "And you've brought back the man I love."

Chapter 11

Liz opened her eyes and raised her head from the pillow. Had she been dreaming or…

"Ty?"

"I'm here, Baby." She heard the deep, soft voice and felt the bed give as he sat next to her.

"I was afraid I was dreaming again," she whispered.

"No, Darling, you're awake. Want me to prove it?" He leaned over and gently nipped her earlobe.

"Feel that?"

"Uh huh." It felt divine.

"You're not asleep, then." He stroked her hair. "What do you mean 'dreaming again'?"

Liz squeezed her eyes shut. "It was bad. I either had nightmares of Jimmy coming after me again or dreams that we were together and making love like we did in the beginning. I'd wake up crying. It got so I didn't want to sleep."

Ty gathered her in his arms. "My poor Liz." He kissed the side of her face.

As they leaned back from each other, Liz noticed Ty wasn't under the covers, no longer had a beard and was clothed. A sneaking suspicion entered her mind.

Liz leaned back and folded her arms. "You shaved."

"It itched." He rubbed his jaw. "And it had served its purpose."

"Uh huh. Just how long have I been asleep?"

"About two hours." She could see mischief in his eyes.

"And how long have you been awake?"

Ty checked his watch. "Actually, I didn't really fall asleep." The suspicion got stronger.

"Why didn't you stay in bed with me, Mr. I-Want-to-Wake-Up-Next-to-My-Love?"

He was smiling. "I had things to do and I was next to my love as she slept. She just didn't wake up at the same time I did."

Liz sat up. The closet door was open, revealing......empty hangers.She closed her eyes. "I suppose my bureau is empty, too."

"Probably. I may have missed a sock or two."

Liz opened her eyes and looked severely at a grinning Ty. "Where are my clothes, Ty?"

"Safe and sound."

"We've done this before. You've already seen me naked today..."

"Still one of my favorite sights," Ty interjected.

"Thank you, may I have my clothes, please?"

"You don't need them." He was suppressing a big laugh.

Liz sighed. "Fine. You know what, I'll just sleep until you get tired of this." She started to settle herself back into bed.

"The sheets'll be gone and I've removed everything but a face cloth from the bathroom," Ty stated matter-of-factly.

Liz frowned. "Why didn't I hear you doing all this?"

"I doubt you'd have heard a mariachi band in the hallway. Judging from the snoring, you were sleeping pretty soundly." Ty added quietly, "Obviously something you haven't really done for a while." His grin was replaced by loving concern as he gently pushed hair from Liz's face and smoothed out the frown lines with his fingertips.

"Why did you steal my clothes, Ty? I'm not going anywhere. This is my house." As delightful as the caresses were, Liz tried to stay focused on the issue of clothing and why she didn't have any. It was tough with the distraction.

"I have my reasons. We're starting over. You need to learn to trust me again. This worked before," Ty continued to stroke her hair as she lay there. "Besides, I like the thought of your beautiful body just underneath that sheet waiting for me."

Liz gave him a skeptical look. "You are so full of it, Tyrone, your eyes ought to be brown." She pretended to peer closely at them. "Oh, wait! They are brown!" They both laughed.

The playfulness was returning and it felt wonderful.

"Liz, Liz, Liz, Liz, Liz. When will you learn that you are beautiful?" Ty looked deep into her eyes as he said, "And you always will be." Liz ducked her head. It amazed her that such a simple statement could have such a powerful effect. Ty kissed the

192

top of her head.

"What's this?" Ty held a bundle of sealed envelopes in his hand.

"That was in a drawer in my night stand." Liz held out her hand. "So?" Ty kept the packet out of her reach.

"What were you doing in my drawers?" As soon as the words were out of her mouth, Liz could have bitten off her tongue and not missed it. Ty roared, laughing so hard he almost choked. Liz sat, face buried in hands, shoulders shaking while she laughed. When he could talk again, Ty answered her, still laughing. "I was looking for something."

"What?" Liz could barely talk herself.

"Our copy of John Donne." The mood suddenly went somber.

"It's in Wellesley." Liz was quiet, serious. The pain of having left him was still too near the surface.

Ty got serious, too, picking up on Liz's mood. "Okay, we'll find it later. But right now," Ty held up the packet again. "What are these?"

"Letters. I wrote them over the last two months." No sense being evasive or defensive. This was Ty.

"I see my name on the top envelope. Are they all for me?" Ty was watching her face. Liz nodded. "You never mailed them."

"No." Barely a whisper. "I just wrote them and threw them into the drawer."

Ty moved closer to Liz and put one arm around her. She shivered at the feeling of his hand on the bare skin over her spine. Almost absently, he pulled her tightly to him and began to stroke her back. "Why didn't you send them?" From the gentle tone, Liz knew he already knew the answer. But he wanted her to say it.

"I was afraid you didn't want me anymore. That I'd hurt you too badly by leaving you and you didn't want to hear from me." She let it all out. Liz could feel her chest tighten again. "Leaving you was the hardest thing I've ever done and until today, I didn't know if I'd done the right thing."

Ty rubbed his cheek on Liz's head as he said, "I have never stopped loving you and I will never stop. I've been angry at you and at myself, but I've loved you all along." Ty looked into Liz's eyes. "Never, and I mean never, doubt my love for you ever again." He kissed her. "Now, will you read one to me?"

"No." Liz's refusal was quiet and firm.

"Why not?" The question was gentle.

Liz put her arms around him. "Because I'll start crying again and I've done nothing but cry for the past two months. I don't want to cry anymore, Ty. Not for a long, long time."

"Okay." Ty's answer was soft. "Do I get to read them?" He kissed the top of her head. "I won't if you say 'No.'"

As much as she wanted to say "no" and take back the letters to burn them, Liz knew what was at stake. Ty would allow her to withhold the letters because he loved her. Liz knew she had to trust him and here was the first step. With a kiss, she said, "They're yours. Take them."

Ty returned the kiss, tenderly, skillfully. They held each other for a few minutes.

At length, Ty asked, "Still want your clothes?"

"Well, I can't stay like this for the rest of my life," she said. "What do I need to do to get my clothes back?"

Ty's face grew serious. "Come home with me. Now."

"No." It was barely a whisper.

Ty was surprised at the answer. "Why not?"

"I can't go back there. I wasn't safe. I wasn't happy. The bad memories are too bad and I'll be reliving them every day if I go back. I lost Beanie there. I lost you in that house," Liz's face and tone were deadly serious. "I don't want to be there even for another day."

Ty looked puzzled. "But Liz, I've had it thoroughly cleaned."

"No."

"I had the den repainted. The furniture's been replaced and I had someone clean and repair my rug."

"No."

Ty was exasperated. "Do you want me to have an exorcist come in?"

Liz shook her head. "No."

"Well, do you expect me to move in here?" He didn't sound pleased with the idea.

"No."

"Okay, I give. What's your idea?"

Liz pulled him close and kissed the top of his head. "Can't we find a new place together? Something that hasn't been exclusively yours or mine."

Caught off guard, Ty froze, his lips close enough that Liz inhaled his breath. "What just happened?" His tone was a mixture of confusion and passion.

Liz tried to wriggle out from under him. "On second thought, I do need clothes. And a towel. Now. Move." She pushed at Ty, who obligingly rolled out of the way. Liz kissed him quickly as she slid out of bed and ran for the bathroom.

While she was lathering up, Liz heard Ty enter the bathroom. He stuck his arm into the shower, towel in hand. "I hear and obey. Now, what's going on and do you want me to scrub your back for you?"

"Tempting, but no thank you," she replied. "In fact, you may want to leave. Now."

Liz jumped as the shower curtain was suddenly shoved aside and she found herself face to face with an angry Ty.

"What the hell, Liz? One minute you're seducing me and the next you're throwing me out. I want to know what's going on!"

Liz reached a soapy hand towards Ty's face. "I'm sorry, but I forgot that I have company coming," she glanced at his watch. "Almost any time now."

"So who's coming?" Ty was thoroughly confused now.

Liz turned off the water and stepped out of the shower, taking the towel from Ty. "As far as you're concerned, it's a lynch mob."

Ty understood immediately. "Millie, John, Joey..."

"Jenna, Angie and Vinnie." Liz finished. "Sure you want to stay?"

She was amused to watch Ty's internal debate. Of course, being Ty, it didn't last long. He looked up and smiled.

"Just two questions. Am I dressed right and does Angie know where you keep your big knife?"

Liz stopped combing her hair long enough to smile and nod. "You're dressed fine. As for Angie, you're almost certainly screwed, Big Boy." She pushed Ty out the door. "Be with you in a minute."

When she got to her bedroom, Liz noticed that although most of her clothes were still missing, Ty had returned the dress she'd worn on their one and only date.

She stared, then blinked to keep from crying. He loved her.

195

Still.

Liz shed her towel, slipped into underwear and with a tiny pause, pulled on the dress.

"Here. Zippers are my duty." Ty spoke quietly as he zipped up her dress, just like the first time. Liz hadn't heard him come up behind her. When he finished, Ty turned Liz to face him. She twined her arms around his neck and looked into his eyes.

"Really going back to the beginning, huh?" Liz asked.

"Why not? In my mind's eye, I always see you in this dress, unzipped and barefoot chasing Beanie down the street. Not a bad mental picture." Ty smiled down into her face, eyes warm and dancing. Liz noted how the life was back in them and silently gave thanks.

Ty kissed her forehead. "Any interest in hanging out with a dry drunk? Just for the next 40 or 50 years."

Liz looked at him, almost afraid that she'd put the wrong spin on his words. Ty returned her gaze.

"Marry me, Liz."

"I will." The words came automatically.

Liz had thought highly of Ty's kissing skills, but this time, he outdid himself. They weren't aware of anything around them until…

"Ahem."

They broke off their kiss to discover Angela DiNardo glaring at them, arms crossed, back straight. Angie was as angry as Liz had ever seen her.

"Angie, Hi!" Liz's voice sounded breathy and distracted. She and Ty were still clinched. "I didn't hear you come in."

Ty made a quick recovery. "Angie! I'm glad to see you."

Angie was angry. "Well, I can't say the same, Tyrone." She turned towards the stairs. "Vincenzo! I need a big knife!"

Ty looked sharply at Liz. "She's kidding, right?"

"No, she's not."

"Vinnie!" Angie yelled again. "Where's that knife?"

Liz hastily separated herself from Ty. "No, Angie. You don't understand! Vinnie!" Liz yelled. "Forget the knife!"

Angie was not amused. She pointed her finger at Ty. "You! I warned you about breaking our girl's heart and you didn't listen. Two months we've been worried sick, wondering if she'd ever get over you. Two months praying and lighting candles…"

"I guess I'm an answer to a prayer, then." Ty interrupted.

"Don't be a smartass!" Angie snapped. "Two months! Where have you been all this time while my Lizabetta is crying her heart out over you and making herself sick? And you have the nerve to stand here and paw her like she's some kind of slut? You've got a lot to answer for and you'll do it right now. I want the big knife."

Liz stepped in between Angie and Ty. Unconsciously, she spread her arms out. "Look, Angie, you don't know the whole story…"

"I don't care." Angie bit off the words. "Get out of my way."

"No." The firmness in Liz's refusal surprised even her. "I left him, remember? You want to get to him, you've got to go through me." Liz straightened up. "And I'm not letting you through. Mama Angie, I love you and I respect you, but I love Ty. If you hurt him, you hurt me. Is that what you want?"

Angie was astonished. "Lizabetta! You've never talked to me like this."

"I've never felt like this about anyone," Liz said with all the passion she felt. Ty put his arms around her waist and squeeze slightly. "Not even Joey. You still want the big knife? Fine. You'll have to use it on me first."

Angie looked at Ty. "Did you hear that?"

"Yes, Ma'am. Couldn't help it."

The finger came up. "Don't be flippant with me, Tyrone. I'll smack you upside the head."

"Sorry, Angie." Ty was contrite, but Liz could hear the underlying amusement.

"Elizabeth, your guests are here. Vinnie's unpacking an antipasto. You go help." Angela DiNardo was somewhat calmer, but she wasn't done yet. "The Kissing Bandit and I are gonna have a little chat. Go."

Liz opened her mouth to protest, but Angie cut her off with, "Don't you sass me or I'll smack your head." Liz obeyed and heard her bedroom door slam shut behind her. Oy vey, thought Liz.

She found Vinnie and Joey in the kitchen unpacking not only antipasto, but melon with prosciutto and several other dishes.

"Vinnie, I said a salad. A salad. Singular," Liz kissed Vinnie on the cheek. "Joey, why didn't you stop him?"

"Ma smacked me and Jenna told me not to be disrespectful to my parents." Liz got a bear hug from Joey. "What's going on, Liz? Why is Ma so upset? Where is she?"

Before Liz could answer, Vinnie paused in his labors and peered at Liz's face. Frowning, he took her face between his hands and looked more closely. "You're glowing," he said. Vinnie kissed her. "Much better than last time, eh, Joe?"

Joey stopped to look at Liz's face. "Pop's right. You look like you've just been thoroughly..." Liz saw Joey figure it out and heard him swear under his breath. "That fucking bastard! I'll kill him."

"No, you're not." Liz blocked Joey's path out of the kitchen. "If either you or Rocco raise a hand to him, I'll kick both of your sorry asses from here to Key West. Capice?"

Joey still looked like he wanted to push past Liz and head upstairs, but he stayed in the kitchen. Liz continued.

"Joey, he came for me. Ty is here for me, asking me to give him a second chance. If you needed one, wouldn't you want Jenna to give you a second chance? Think of how you feel about your wife, Joe. I feel the same about Ty." Liz paused, watching Joey's face. "Joe, things are different, okay? You told him to get help and he did. He's not the same man he was two months ago. It's okay, Joey." She hugged him and kissed his cheek. Joey hugged her back. Liz looked at Vinnie and smiled. Vinnie was smiling, too.

"All right. Let me see if I can stave off any assassinations from the living room gang. That is, if there's anything left of Ty by the time Angie gets done with him." With that, Liz headed out towards the living room. Two furry blurs bolted by Liz and fled in terror for the safety of upstairs. In pursuit was a determined toddler. Liz intercepted Vincent Joseph DiNardo and scooped him up.

He looked at Liz, a huge smile on his face. "Kitties!" announced Little Vinnie.

"Yup. Those were kitties and you've probably seen the last of them for today." Liz said. "Where's Mumma?"

Little Vinnie pointed towards the living room and Liz carried him in that direction where Jenna, John and Millie sat in the middle of what looked like a toy factory explosion. She shook her head at the sight.

"Guess I don't need to tell you to make yourselves at home.

Mrs. DiNardo," Liz took on a mock severe tone. "Haven't we warned you about Salem's leash laws? Next time, he goes to the pound." Liz handed Little Vinnie to his mother.

Millie was looking hard at Liz, suspicion all over her face. "You didn't open the door. I had to let everyone in."

Liz looked back at her. "I was getting dressed."

Millie arched an eyebrow. "Nice dress. Kind of fancy for a backyard barbecue, isn't it, Liz?"

Liz folded her arms and shrugged. "I didn't have anything else."

"Where'd the second kitten come from, Liz? Last time I checked, you only had Dodger."

"Got a do-it-yourself cloning kit from an infomercial. It was a lot cheaper than buying another kitten from Corey. All you need is a little kitten spit and you're in business. His name's Norton, by the way."

Millie ignored the humor. "There's a car just like Ty's parked out front and it appears to be full of clothes just like yours."

Liz remained cool. "And now you know why I only had this to wear. Someone broke in while I was in the shower. I guess the thief didn't like periwinkle blue."

Millie was still undeterred. "For someone who's been suffering badly from a broken heart, you look pretty chipper right now."

John chimed in, "She looks like she just got extremely well..."

"Not in front of the baby, John!" Jenna yelped.

Liz shrugged again. "In the words of Abraham Lincoln, folks are about as happy as they make up their minds to be."

Millie said nothing, but Liz could see the mental wheels turning. Jenna held up the "In Need of Good Home" sign, keeping it away from her destructive son. "Liz, what's this?"

"It's a joke to go with Norton. Furry face and a hard luck story."

"So Ty has a beard now?" Millie asked innocently.

"He did, but he shaved, AW DAMMIT!" Liz had walked right into Millie's trap.

"Lizabetta! Language!" from the kitchen.

"Sorry, Angie!" Liz threw up her hands. "Yeah. Ty showed up this morning. We talked..."

Millie snickered. "Looking at your face, I'll bet that's not all

199

you did."

Liz ignored her. "Anyway, the bottom line is that we're getting back together."

The three adults regarded her silently. Their emotions ranged from disbelief and bewilderment to frustration and anger at Liz's apparent folly.

Millie asked quietly, trying to keep control, "Why?"

"Because we love each other too much to be apart," Ty answered, stealing up behind Liz and encircling her waist with his arms. He kissed the side of Liz's face. "Two months of misery was about all either of us could take."

Ty smiled at Millie, but it didn't quite reach his eyes. Liz prayed that she wasn't going to have to choose between her love and her friend.

"I'm sorry I missed your wedding, Millie and John. Congratulations. We'd be disappointed if you missed ours," Ty very casually dropped the bomb.

Millie shot a startled look at Liz. "You're getting married?"

Liz nodded. She felt Ty's grip tighten, lending her support. "It's a shotgun wedding. Ty says he's pregnant."

It took a minute, but people started to laugh. Millie hugged Ty, whispering something Liz couldn't hear, but it made him relax and return the embrace. "Wait a minute." Angie spoke and the room fell silent. "Where's the ring?" She looked at Ty. "I don't see a ring on that girl's finger and let me tell you, Tyrone, you'd better give her a good one."

Liz held up her hands. "So, we'll take care of that later."

Angie was adamant. "I refuse to believe the Kissing Bandit here is serious until I see a ring." The others nodded their agreement.

"C'mon you guys. This is supposed to be a private, intimate moment between my fiancé," Liz savored the phrase, "and me. We don't need an audience."

"Wrong!" Millie contradicted. "My engagement was public. It's payback time, Gardner. I want to see this happen."

Liz smiled back at her, "Up yours, Mrs. Reynolds."

Ty handed Little Vinnie to his grandmother and reached into his pocket. Liz felt her chest getting tight.

Ty knelt before Liz and with a smile that was almost shy, he

200

deftly thumbed open the box. Taking Liz's left hand, Ty kissed it, then said as he slid a ring onto her finger. "It would give me tremendous honor and lifelong pleasure if you, Elizabeth Duer Gardner, would be my wife."

Liz was dumbfounded. The emerald cut blue diamond ring they had seen on their first date was now on her hand. It sparkled in its platinum setting, the smaller blue-white diamonds adding their own glints.

"I don't know what to say."

Ty was looking in surprise at the ring. "I thought it was going to have to be sized." He looked up into Liz's eyes. "I guess it was meant to be yours."

Ty stood up and lifted Liz's hand to his lips, kissing it again, his eyes never leaving Liz's. No one else in the room made a sound. Nobody wanted the moment to end.

Ty held out her hand. "This is you," he said, pointing to one of the side stones. "This is me," pointing to the other side stone, "And this" he touched the blue of the center stone, "is we." Liz just threw herself into his arms and held onto him as tightly as possible. Ty returned the embrace as fervently. "Don't leave me again, Love," he whispered. "It'll kill me."

"It would kill me, too," she whispered back. "It nearly did this time." And they tightened their grip on each other.

"Shit."

"John! Language!"

"Sorry, Angie." Everyone looked at John. "I told a friend of mine that I knew a nice girl for him. He was planning to drop by to meet Liz." John looked sheepish. Millie pinched him. Hard.

Liz felt Ty's body stiffen. "John, you'd better call your friend off right now or my honeymoon is going to be conjugal visits at the state pen."

John headed for the phone as fast as he could.

Still holding tightly to Liz, Ty called after him, "What does this friend of yours do?"

"He's my insurance agent."

Liz had to tighten her grip on Ty to keep him from charging. "Down, Boy. Don't make me get a tranquilizer gun." she said to him. Ty relaxed, but he still glared in the direction of the kitchen.

Little Vinnie piped up from Angie's arms, "Hungry. Kitties?"

"I hope those were two separate thoughts," said Angie. "Men, you're working the grill. Girls, we're doing everything else. As usual. You two," she pointed at Liz and Ty, "break it up, just for a little while."

They let go of each other reluctantly. "Why is it that men are always in charge of the barbecue?" Ty mused.

"It's one of those Y chromosome things, like the Three Stooges and knowing every sports statistic," answered Liz.

Ty laughed, "What's on the second X chromosome?"

"Shoes and being able to differentiate among 500 shades of beige."

Angie bustled out of the kitchen with a platter piled high with marinated steaks. She handed her burden to Ty. "Here, be a good boy and go cook. I'm taking your girl and we'll be talking wedding."

Ty smiled, "Yes, Angie." He leaned over and kissed Angie on the lips, then kissed Liz one last time before heading out the door. The two women watched him go.

Still watching Ty talking with the other men on the patio, Liz asked Angie, "All's forgiven?" She could see Angie's nod out of the corner of her eye.

"He told you." Angie nodded again. They finally turned to look at each other as Liz continued. "I don't think Vinnie's ever regretted giving you a second chance. And that was what, 18 years ago? You've managed to stay sober and with the love of your life, huh, Angie?"

"I couldn't have done it without him," Angie admitted. "That man gives me strength. I thank God every day for his love."

"I knew you'd understand." As they headed for the kitchen, Angie remarked thoughtfully, "That man of yours is looking pretty good, Lizabetta. If it wasn't for Vinnie,…"

Liz interrupted, "You're not the only one with a big knife, Angela. Stick with Vinnie."

After the meal, the clean-up and the departure of the guests, Liz and Ty stood hand in hand out on the patio looking at a summer night sky, full of stars and the sliver of a waxing moon. They were silent, just enjoying the moment and the joy of being together. Behind the screen door of the house, they could hear the kittens playing together, the sounds of wrestling punctuated with squeaks. Ty spoke. "You know, we could catch a flight to Las Vegas and by this time tomorrow, we'd be married."

Liz just said, "No."

Ty looked at her and smiled as he slipped his arm around her waist. "Long engagement? We're not teenagers, Liz."

She leaned her head against him. "I know, but we have all the time we need. I will marry you if it's tomorrow or ten years from now." He pulled her in closer.

"I don't want a big wedding, but I don't want to elope, either. I want our friends to share the moment with us and most of all," Liz tilted her face up to kiss Ty, "I want to see your face as I come down the aisle."

They kissed for a moment or two, then Ty broke it off. "I forgot. I need to make a phone call." Liz started to protest, but Ty shook his head. "I should have done this earlier today, but I forgot. I have to call my sponsor." Liz shut her mouth. Ty took her hand and led her back into the house.

As Ty made his way to the phone in the kitchen, Liz hung back in order to give him privacy. She sat on the floor next to the kittens, tempting them to pounce on her hand. Dodger seemed particularly attracted to her new ring, batting at it as she wiggled her hand. Norton contented himself with batting at Dodger. They weren't Beanie, reflected Liz, nor would they ever be. He had been unique and she still missed him. But these little guys clearly had charm and character of their own. Norton, after an especially energetic pounce on Dodger, sat back and yawned, showing tiny little teeth. Liz picked him up and settled him in her lap. Norton rolled onto his back and purred loudly as Liz scratched and rubbed his striped little tummy. Dodger settled himself with licking her spare hand, also purring as loudly as he could.

Ty walked up and gently tapped Liz on the shoulder. "You're wanted on the phone, Sweetheart," he said as he scooped Norton out of her lap. "I'll take care of the boys." He helped Liz scramble to her feet.

Liz headed for the kitchen, her curiosity fully aroused. Why would Ty's sponsor want to talk to her? She picked up the phone.

"This is Elizabeth Gardner."

"I just wanted to congratulate the bride," came back Frank McCafferty's voice.

Liz shook her head, "You sneaky, deceitful, poker-faced, black-robed son of a..."

"You leave my mother out of this, Liz," the judge interjected with a chuckle. "Or I'll lay a contempt charge on you."

Liz was bewildered. "Why didn't you say something? You listened to me breaking my heart often enough. Why couldn't you at least tell me he was all right?"

McCafferty became serious. "Now, Liz, I can't break confidentiality with AA members, especially the ones I'm sponsoring. I promised Tyrone I'd keep an eye on you for him if he'd promise not to contact you until he'd been through the program. And give me some credit for being an old man who's been in love himself. The two of you needed this time without each other. It was painful and I had a tough time watching you go through it, but I think your relationship will be better for it. Now, I get to perform the ceremony, right?"

Liz was laughing, "Do I have a choice?"

"Not if you want to keep your job as my star clerk." McCafferty changed his tone. "Seriously, it's been a long day for me sitting by the phone waiting. I expect you at work on Tuesday with a big smile, like you've been very thoroughly..."

"I get the picture, Judge," Liz interrupted. "How can I ever thank you for everything?"

"Just take care of each other. Now, hang up and go back to your man." With that, McCafferty hung up. Liz stood in the kitchen for a few minutes just thinking. Her man. Once again, Ty was her man. She was so lost in thought, she didn't notice him approaching. He leaned on the wall, watching her face. Liz looked at him and smiled.

Ty asked, "Everything okay?" He took her hand.

Liz looked at their clasped hands. "I still want my clothes back. And I'm willing to bet you're planning to spend the night." Ty nodded, watching her face.

Liz looked at him. "Let's go to bed."

Later, when Liz was sure that Ty was sleeping, she reached out and put her arms around him, drawing her body closer to his. She could feel Ty stir slightly, snuggling himself up to her in his sleep. Liz softly kissed his cheek. Ty responded with a deep sigh and a smile, still sound asleep. Liz laid her head on the pillow and let sleep claim her, too.

Yes, everything was okay.

29268410R00117

Made in the USA
Lexington, KY
19 January 2014